INTO THE
BLOODRED
WOODS

ALSO BY MARTHA BROCKENBROUGH

The Game of Love and Death

Devine Intervention

INTO THE
BLOODRED
WOODS

MARTHA BROCKENBROUGH

Scholastic Press / New York

All rights reserved. Published by Scholastic Press, an imprint of Scholastic Inc., *Publishers since 1920.* SCHOLASTIC, SCHOLASTIC PRESS, and associated logos are trademarks and/or registered trademarks of Scholastic Inc.

The publisher does not have any control over and does not assume any responsibility for author or third-party websites or their content.

This book is a work of fiction. Names, characters, places, and incidents are either the product of the author's imagination or are used fictitiously, and any resemblance to actual persons, living or dead, business establishments, events, or locales is entirely coincidental.

Library of Congress Cataloging-in-Publication Data

Names: Brockenbrough, Martha, author.
Title: Into the bloodred woods / Martha Brockenbrough.
Description: First edition. | New York : Scholastic Press, 2021. |
    Audience: Ages 14 and up. | Audience: Grades 10–12. | Summary: On his
    deathbed King Tyran divides his land between his twin children,
    first-born Ursula, a werebear, and Albrecht; but Albrecht wants it all
    and makes war on his sister, killing her people and the werebeasts,
    becoming a tyrant to his own kingdom—but their family history is
    far more complicated and mysterious than he knows, and Ursula has
    powerful allies in the living forest that surrounds their lands,
    including her aunt Esme who has been in hiding for years.
Identifiers: LCCN 2021009190 (print) | LCCN 2021009191 (ebook) |
    ISBN 9781338673876 (hardcover) | ISBN 9781338673890 (ebook)
Subjects: LCSH: Animals, Mythical—Juvenile fiction. | Magic—Juvenile
    fiction. | Twins—Juvenile fiction. | Brothers and sisters—Juvenile
    fiction. | Aunts—Juvenile fiction. | Good and evil—Juvenile fiction. |
    CYAC: Animals, Mythical—Fiction. | Magic—Fiction. | Twins—Fiction. |
    Brothers and sisters—Fiction. | Aunts—Fiction. | Good and
    evil—Fiction. | Fantasy. | LCGFT: Fantasy fiction.
Classification: LCC PZ7.B7825 In 2021 (print) | LCC PZ7.B7825 (ebook) |
    DDC 813.6 [Fic]—dc23

10 9 8 7 6 5 4 3 2 1   21 22 23 24 25

Printed in Italy   183
First edition, November 2021

Book design by Stephanie Yang

TO HEIDI AND JAKE AND EVERYONE
DISCOVERING THEIR DEEPEST TRUTHS

One fine day, an eyeless man with a mutilated face arrives in a village by a pale gray sea.

The white-skinned man unrolls a blanket. He arranges himself on it. He sets a small metal monkey beside him. He winds something in its back, a black iron key topped with a glass eyeball.

The monkey extends an uncanny metal hand. The man sets a coin on the monkey's palm. Its fingers snap closed; its hand moves to its mouth; the coin drops in. It's a show. A nudge. A hint to passersby.

Clink, clink. "Feed the monkey a coin and see what happens."

People always do, and the eyeless man offers them a tale in return. His face might be startling, but his voice is beautiful. People stop when he speaks. They listen. Gasp. They feel as if the skin of the world has been peeled away and they are seeing the truth that lies beneath for the very first time.

He knows this. He uses it.

"Once upon a time, there was a queen who gazed into her enchanted mirror and asked if she was the most beautiful in all the land.

"Every day, the mirror set her heart at ease, until one day, the mirror's answer changed, filling the queen with envy and rage.

"This is because women cannot help but be creatures of vanity. And this vanity is dangerous, for it leads women in power to destroy that which they are bound to protect: their queendoms, their thrones, their own daughters . . ."

Mesmerized, the people pass along the tale, from lips to ears to paper to eyes, across acres of land and oceans of time again and again until eventually the man's tale becomes truth.

I know otherwise. I know what really happened. I was there.

This is the story of a werebear and her brother, one of whom will inherit a kingdom . . .

It's the story of another werebear who wanted to burn it all down . . .

Of a sister who traded everything to spin grass into gold . . .

Of an angry musician who loved a gentle werewolf . . .

Of a girl who loved a singing forest more than life itself . . .

And of a kingdom shattered like a mirror, the pieces of which can be put back together, but only by someone brave enough to look.

PART
ONE

I

The people who lived in the kingdom would tell you differing stories about when the forest started singing.

The woods have always made music.

No, it started as a warning. The princess arrived before her twin brother. This disrupted the order of nature, and ever since, nature has objected.

Neither was true.

The forest started singing when a girl named Esme struck a bargain in exchange for the magic that she needed to save her sister's life. And that was necessary because their father had lied to the king to make himself seem important; he'd claimed that he had a daughter of surpassing beauty who could spin grass into gold.

The Golden Lion, as the king's people called him, hastened to the humble farm to examine the daughters.

"Surely it's not *that* one." He'd pointed at Esme. She was many things: resourceful, loyal, and kind, as well as nimble and strong from her work on their farm. She had a brave and generous heart. But her beauty wasn't the obvious sort.

Their father laughed. "Of course not."

He pushed his younger daughter, Gwyneth—a maiden full of fresh and easy beauty—toward the king, who made a threat: If she fails to spin, she dies. Then he took her to his castle and locked her in the tower.

The threat unhinged Esme. She ran to the woods, where she often went in times of sorrow. She dropped to the earth in front of the trees and made them an offer. A deal to save the sister she loved. Her womb for magic.

She didn't expect a response. But then there was a rustling of leaves. A moaning of branches. All that, in the absence of wind. Taking it as an agreement, Esme removed her own womb and buried it; in return, the trees told her the secret to pulling elements from the soil and turning them into something else. She was the only person they'd ever trusted with this knowledge. And the woods used her womb for a wish of their own: a voice that all could hear.

Still bleeding from her sacrifice, Esme reached the tower, where her sister's shadow filled the highest window. Racked with pain, Esme climbed the stones hand over hand until she reached Gwyneth, alone and weeping before an enormous pile of dry grass. Esme slid inside and spun the gold, more than could ever be used. She'd saved her sister. She had no regrets.

Not yet anyway.

According to the law of the land, the firstborn child was to inherit the throne. But the tradition had always been that a king rule. This created a conundrum for the royal couple.

"Let our daughter rule," Queen Gwyneth said. "She was born first. It is only right."

"It should be our son," King Tyran said. "You are but common born yourself, so you would not understand such things."

"I understand," the queen said, "that your kingdom depends on the gold that I provide."

That would invariably pause the argument. But it would not end it. Despite their unresolved disagreement, the king and queen grew to love each other, and they loved the children they had made.

The king also grew fond of the queen's sister, who'd been permitted to stay in the castle to help care for the children. Over time, her looks became very pleasing to him. He desired her. He had two hands, after all. Why should both not be full?

Embarrassed to have been put into such a position, Esme avoided him and her sister. She doted on her infant niece and nephew instead.

Even so, the king persisted. Esme refused him again. This time she threatened to tell her sister if the king did not leave her be.

The king dared her to. "Let us tell her right now."

Astonished, Esme did, but privately.

The queen slapped Esme so hard across the cheek, her ear rang. "How dare you attract my husband! Did you tell him you make the gold? Is that why he wanted you? Oh, Esme. You have ruined me. You have ruined everything."

Esme burst into tears. "I would never betray you. Not with the gold, not with the king. I love you. You're my sister."

Esme could see that Gwyneth was afraid. Afraid that Esme would betray her, afraid that the king would choose Esme if he knew the truth about the gold.

Even so, Esme was surprised when Gwyneth told Tyran that Esme had gone mad. That she wanted to eat the children and destroy the future of the kingdom.

The king, seeing a path out of trouble, decided to believe his wife. Esme was a witch. A child-eating witch who'd cast a spell upon him. It was not his fault his eyes had strayed.

Having come to an understanding that suited them both, the king and queen agreed that something must be done.

They sent Esme to the dungeon to die.

II

Esme chose not to die in the dungeon. Placing her hands on the dirty stones, she summoned gold to make a key. She escaped through a forgotten tunnel that had once been a hallway in an older castle, long buried.

Then she was in the forest and alone, except for the trees. Only one other family lived there, a woodsman and his wife. She avoided them lest they recognize her. Isolated as she was, she had time to think. In her solitude, an idea struck.

Gold might not be the only thing she could summon. She could also, perhaps, draw out something she wanted far more. On her hands and knees, she put her lips to the soil and begged. *Please. Please let me do this.*

The forest breathed music back on her. Was it permission? A warning?

It didn't matter; her desire would have drowned out either. She wanted a child. She had no womb. But the forest did. This was her only choice, her only chance.

At first, she summoned nothing more than gobbets covered in fur. She had to return them to the soil when they stopped quivering. Eventually she crafted something that felt perfect. Beautiful. Flesh as hairless and smooth as new bark. Beneath the lids were eyes as brown and beautiful as soil itself. Ten tiny fingers. Ten tiny toes. A soft, round belly she could not resist kissing.

This one, she knew, would work. With one hand over the child's heart and the other deep in the earth, she opened herself to the flow and extracted magic to fill the child, to animate her spirit, to give strength and suppleness to her limbs and stars in the darkness of her eyes.

At first, it was pleasant. A trickle of water. Then it shook her bones as the power coursed through her. In the darkness, she saw red.

But then, like a flame blown out, it stopped.

The babe moved and cried, and Esme looked with hope upon the infant she'd wrought.

She went cold.

The child that had been so perfectly formed, so beautifully coated in flesh, was now a raw thing. Sinew and fat, veins and bones. Spilling organs. Slender ribs heaving with sobs. Whatever had animated her had also flayed her. Nothing protected the baby from the world all around, and it was eating her alive.

Esme did the only thing she could. She held the child. She sang to her. She promised that everything would be all right, that it wouldn't always hurt like this.

It took the rest of the night for the baby's spirit to depart. When the searing morning light came, the child breathed her last, and Esme returned her to the soil, deep and dark and safe. She crumpled to the earth and wept. The trees fell silent, made mute by grief. The shame Esme felt was infinite. Indelible. Worse than anything she'd ever experienced. She did not expect to live.

The forest had other ideas.

Day blended into night and became day again, and Esme never stopped punishing herself. She never stopped wishing for a child, though she would never again try to pull one from the earth, and every day, she whispered her apologies to the soil for trying.

One night, three years into her solitude, Esme followed a sound. A mewling cry, heartbreaking and beautiful. The forest had pushed something miraculous through its network of roots. A baby, wrapped in a blanket of lichen and moss, a black-eyed girl with skin the shade of summer-dry soil.

She brushed dirt from the baby's cheeks and brow. The child stopped crying. Her tiny fingers wrapped around Esme's, and the lonely young woman's heart was lost forever.

She brought the baby to the hollow tree she'd turned into her home. She made a tiny bed. Strung acorns and flowers and other pretty objects on a golden thread and hung them overhead so the baby would have delightful things to look at. She gave her a name, Cappella, which meant "accompanied." She meant it as a promise.

"You will never feel alone," she whispered.

Esme tended Cappella gently through the stages of babyhood. Sitting. Standing. Walking. The music of the forest itself was an accompaniment to her as well. By the time Cappella was three, she was already playing music on a golden pipe Esme had made. The little girl loved to sit in a tree and play along with the forest.

She was smart and lively, with straight black hair streaked with a single patch of white, a remnant of the time she'd hit her head on a rock. The streak was a constant reminder of the day she'd bled and cried in Esme's arms. Esme worried not just that her daughter would be injured again, but that she might someday go into the kingdom and never want to leave, that she might someday meet someone she loved more, that somehow Tyran and Gwyneth would discover Cappella and take her away—or worse.

Esme gave the girl two rules: She must never talk to another person, and she must never venture into the kingdom.

Cappella promised she wouldn't.

This was why Cappella avoided the woodsman and his wife. Why she hid from their daughter, a golden-haired girl who sometimes sang along with Cappella's music. Most of all, why she kept distance from their son, a quiet, shaggy-haired boy with soulful gray eyes.

Despite her mother's promise that she'd never be lonely, Cappella yearned for a friend. One day, when she was five, she spied the flick of an ash-gray tail behind an old log rough with moss. She froze as a wolf cub popped up his head. He was the most precious thing Cappella had ever seen, with charcoal fur, gray eyes ringed in black, and a nose like a corner of night sky.

She put her pipe in her pocket, and they watched each other, the girl and the wolf. Finally Cappella approached and the cub put his paws on the log, letting his tongue roll out. Her hand met his nose, and he lowered his head and straightened his front legs.

Let's play, the gesture said.

She darted behind a tree and he followed. The forest floor was soft beneath her bare feet. Cold, but her soles were used to it. They ran hard and fast, always stopping before either caught the other, because that was the point—to chase, not to catch. Despite the chill air, her face and hands were warm, and her body felt the satisfaction of having been properly used. Arms, legs, heart, lungs: spent.

After a while, the girl and her wolf collapsed in a pile of new-fallen leaves, breathing in air rich with the smells of dampness and new soil. The cub panted and it sounded almost like laughter.

Overhead, leaves wearing fall colors made a shushing sound as the wind played them like instruments. She listened. A sound rose from the roots. The trees themselves and the tiny living things in the soil doing the work of being alive. It was also music, this work. Extracting, exchanging, transforming. The making of something beautiful from nothing at all.

It was so quiet she might not have heard it had she not been trying. And yet she knew the song the way she knew her own name. She was alive. So was the wolf. They would not live forever, but they'd be bound for as long as their hearts beat. It was the song's promise.

Cappella rolled to her side. The little wolf had already done the same. She scooted close and put her arm around him. He smelled of bracken and musk and was softer than anything she'd ever touched.

They breathed together.

Just as Cappella was about to drift off into a contented sleep, the wolf snapped to attention. His ears pricked up, hearing a call that she could not. And then he was sitting, and then he was running, running, running, and even though she shouted for him to stay, he didn't.

III

One day when the prince was nine, his limbs plump with muscles, his hair a wild golden mane like his father's, he ventured into the woods with his sister.

He ran ahead to prove he was faster.

They found a tree together and resolved to climb it. Albrecht vowed he could climb higher.

"Watch me," he commanded.

Ursula stopped far below him, weaving a crown of daisies on a lower branch. *That's the only crown she deserves*, he thought.

Satisfied, he leaned against the trunk. Soon, he was lulled by the music. The trees were sleepy too, for it was sunny and they'd feasted on endless beams of light.

The prince dreamed, and in his dream, an enormous beast emerged from its den. The prince had always hoped to hunt a beast in the woods. He lurched awake, fumbled for his bow, and in his groggy state, he slipped.

The fall seemed endless. Time stretched. His limbs pinwheeled; the world blurred. In the midst of his fall, he opened his mouth and screamed through his fine white teeth. The note was high-pitched. It would have cracked something brittle, like a mirror. But forests are made of stuff that bends. The forest music shifted. The trees, who know what it is to fall, sympathized with him then. They would not always.

The prince landed standing up. A leg bone snapped, its sound sharp as a breaking branch. The trees hushed. When he finally took a breath, when he fell and wept and clutched his leg, the music started again and Ursula dropped beside him, unhurt.

His leg was turning colors. His skin felt clammy. The pain made him want to vomit. He hated Ursula seeing him like this, even more than he hated seeing her take her bear form.

None of this was fair. Albrecht should have been firstborn. He should have been a werelion. A flying one. That would be superior in the same way it was better to be a boy.

"Oh, Albrecht," Ursula said. "Your leg."

He clenched his jaw. He hated when she was nice to him. He wasn't a weakling.

"A beast did it."

"I don't smell anything." She looked around. "Are you certain?"

He scoffed. She was always pretending her sense of smell was better than his, that it was a werebear thing. He didn't believe her. It was easy to make things up. It was easy to get people to believe whatever you told them. You could make anyone believe anything if you told them so three times. He did it plenty. It wasn't even magic. People liked believing what they were used to hearing.

"Yes," he said. "A beast. A great big one. Vicious."

She crouched by his leg.

"Don't touch it."

"I'm quite sure you've broken it."

"It wasn't me who broke it. It was the beast."

She glanced up. "I suppose you're lucky this beast didn't bite you, then. We need to get your leg fixed. I can carry you."

"Carry me? No!" Everyone would laugh.

"On my back. I'll go as my bear self."

That was different. He wouldn't be embarrassed to ride a bear. It wasn't as good as a lion, especially a flying one, but it was better than a horse.

"All right."

Ursula undressed. Albrecht hated to watch her shift, but he couldn't look away. The expression on her face as it stretched, the way her skin looked as the fur emerged, the sound her bones made as they bent. It looked as though it hurt, which was the part that riveted him. He usually liked pain. He liked picking his own scabs precisely because it hurt, and seeing someone else in pain felt even better. How much pain could a person take before they broke?

He'd once asked his mother this question and she'd shushed him, saying it was wrong even to think about such things. Now, with his leg throbbing like an exposed heart, he took pride in the quantity of pain he could withstand.

Ursula lowered herself to her belly, and he eased his hurt leg over her back. He settled behind the hump between her shoulders, his hands buried in her golden-brown fur. Then she ran, her paws beating the forest floor in time with the music.

Every step shot an arrow of pain through his leg, but the suffering was worth it. It meant he was strong, that he was his pain's master. What's more, he was riding a bear. To command such a beast, to dominate her, was glorious. The next best thing to being a were himself.

"Take me to Jutta," he said.

As they sped through the cobbled streets, people stared, and Albrecht loved it. Everyone knew who he was. And he supposed everyone knew who the bear was, though he didn't care as much about that.

Jutta would know what to do. She always patched him up. She was the kingdom's blacksmith. Her father had been one, and *his* mother before that, and people used to joke that Jutta hadn't been birthed so much as smelted and pounded into existence. She had pale skin, golden hair like Albrecht's, a long face, and powerful limbs. Her hands were tough too, as tough as hooves, which seemed only right, given that she was a weremare with a white coat and cream mane.

Albrecht loved Jutta. He knew he was her favorite, and he loved being first in someone's heart. He was also fascinated by her. She usually did what he asked, and he always asked for one more thing than he wanted, to see if he'd get it. He often did.

He also loved the heat and smell of the smithy. He thrilled at the clang of hammer against metal, the only sound he knew that was louder than the music of the forest. He tracked such things. The first. The loudest. The biggest. The fiercest. The best.

Everything Jutta made was strong and shiny: His father's throne and crown, both golden. Swords and knives made of steel. Even the cages that werefolk had to sleep in. Albrecht thought that a clever law. Should any were change in the nighttime, when they'd be a danger to sleeping humans, they'd be stuck inside the cage because paws and talons and hooves cannot undo locks. Even Ursula had to sleep in one, although she didn't have to live on Cage Row with the rest of the weres.

When Jutta saw Albrecht, she set down her hammer and wiped her palms on her apron. "What have we here?"

Albrecht fought tears. He'd been fine until Jutta gave him a pitying look with her ugly old face. He dug his fingernails into his palms to give himself fresh pain to focus on instead. His voice cracked when he told Jutta that a beast had chased him.

"A beast." Jutta crouched and gently examined Albrecht's leg. "Well, now. That's a broken leg."

"Are you going to have to cut it off?" Albrecht sometimes had nightmares about his body being cut up. About losing some part of himself.

"Cut it off? 'Course not. You've broken it, and I'll set it quick as a rabbit hops, and you'll heal perfectly fine. Up you go." Jutta took a bottle from a shelf, pulled the cork out with her teeth, and offered Albrecht a swig. Whatever was in there tasted like his finger after he'd stuck it in his ear, but it made him feel warmer and softer inside. He was glad his leg hurt less, but he hated that soft, warm feeling. He'd choose pain every time.

Jutta took a sip herself and then turned to Ursula. "Off with you now. I can't have a bear in my shop. You'll knock things over and get fur everywhere. And don't keep sniffing at my boots or I'll tan your hide."

Albrecht was glad to hear Jutta tell his sister she couldn't sniff the boots. They were fancy ones, with metal toes. Jutta made herself a new pair every Moon Festival. Ursula wanted boots like them, but their father said no.

Ursula ignored Jutta, took her human form, and ran a finger over the toes of each boot. Jutta tossed an apron at Ursula. "Can't have naked little girls running around either. 'Specially not when they're princesses."

Ursula donned the apron, and Jutta took Albrecht's leg in her hand.

Ursula clasped her fingers over her heart. "Be brave."

Albrecht didn't need her telling him what to do. He was about to say as much when everything around him turned the sickly white of a lightning bolt. Jutta had put the bone back to rights. For a moment, he felt outside his own body. He feared she'd torn off his leg altogether. But she hadn't. It was still there, a burning spear.

"And now to splint it," Jutta said.

Albrecht held his breath as Jutta lashed flexible bands of metal to his leg with strips of torn cloth.

"Most people use wood," Jutta said. "But for you, my prince, only the best. You mustn't walk on it until it's healed."

"How long will it take?"

"Two moons," Jutta said. "But don't you worry. I'll bring you things to help you pass the time."

Jutta brought him bits of metal at first. Then, when she saw how good Albrecht was at making things, she brought him gears and hinges and levers. Albrecht assembled clever boxes that cranked open. Then he demanded things in certain shapes and sizes. With them, he made a crude mask with a moving jaw. A little metal soldier holding a sword and a shield that slashed his weapon down when you slid a lever.

As a special gift to help him heal, Jutta made Albrecht a smooth metal boot to hold his leg in place. He couldn't walk in it, but it made him imagine a man made entirely of metal. What a man that would be! Nothing could burn him! Nothing could stab him!

He would like to be a metal man himself. He would like to command an army of metal men. He would put wings on them, and then nothing could stop him.

Weeks passed. He healed quietly using his body's slow magic, enjoying the werebeasts Jutta brought him in secret for his entertainment. It was great fun to make a were dance, and once they'd broken the law by taking their were form outside the Row, they were so afraid that he could make them do anything.

When Jutta finally removed the boot, Albrecht's leg was withered. It ached when he put his weight on it. It would always hurt in cold weather. Flesh and blood were stupid things, he decided. What do you expect, though, from something that comes from women?

Even after he was healed, Jutta did not stop bringing him bits of metal, and Albrecht did not stop building.

IV

Ursula loved the woods. Loved to be far from the hard lines of her father's kingdom in a place full of soft edges, of light-dappled shadows, of rich and layered scents. Moss and lichen and new soil. The breath of animals. The forest music: bone-haunting, beautiful.

It was there Ursula felt most alive. And that was where she returned after she delivered Albrecht to Jutta. She needed to collect the clothing she'd left behind.

Poor Albrecht. But also foolish Albrecht. He had no one but himself to blame. He'd chosen to climb so high. He'd fallen asleep. He'd probably find some way to make it her fault, some way to get her parents to scold her.

But for now, she had the woods to herself, and that was good.

It was spring. Cool air thick with evaporating dew. She needed to run. To shed the numb weight of winter. To fill her body with the freshness of the season. She angled her face to the leaves and roared. She was alive, awake, hungry, moving on instinct and in joy, unlike in the castle, where it was lesson after lesson, correction after correction, and always, always, always fighting with her brother.

She bore it as well as she could. She had no choice. She would be queen and needed to learn how to rule well. She sometimes felt sorry for Albrecht. It must be hard to be second. Hard to be less important. He would be happier, though, if he didn't want what she had. And she wanted him to be happy. She loved him. He was her brother, her twin, her ally. Nothing in the world could change that.

The music of the woods embraced her. It felt as though there was no difference between her and the earth and the air, no difference between her and every other living thing around her. She caught the scent of something familiar and yet not, and it took her a moment to realize there was another werebear in the woods, one who smelled musky and sweet as grass.

She stopped running.

She'd never talked to another werebear. Never even met one. Moving cautiously, she approached a clearing in the center of the woods. And that's where she saw her—not a bear, but a girl with dark brown skin, as glossy as a wet river stone. Her black hair frothed around her face, and it looked light and alive. She appeared about Ursula's age, maybe a year or two older. Ursula could hear her own breathing. Could feel her own heart.

Curiously, the girl was wearing Ursula's clothing. She hadn't seen Ursula yet, and it was obvious she loved being in the woods too. She arched backward, her hands touching the grass for just a moment before her legs followed. A back walkover, as neat as the wing flap of a swallow. The girl laughed.

Ursula did too.

The girl spotted Ursula. She froze. Ursula took her human form and crouched to conceal her nakedness. The girl looked at the dress.

"I'm sorry. It's yours, isn't it? I shouldn't have put it on."

"It's all right."

And it was. Ursula didn't care about dresses. She had many. What she didn't have was a friend.

The werebear looked down. "The slippers were just so pretty."

Ursula shrugged. "They pinch."

The girl smoothed the rose-colored fabric of the dress. Then she stepped out of the slippers and pulled an arm out of the sleeve.

"Wait," Ursula said.

A feeling filled her and she had to act on it, even as she knew it could mean trouble. "Keep the gown. I've outgrown it. The slippers too."

The look on the were's face—surprise, delight, disbelief—made it worth it. But it was fleeting. "I couldn't."

"Why not?"

"Folks on the Row would ask where I got them. They'd think I stole them."

"Who would think that?"

"Everyone. *No one* gives things to weres. Especially not finery such as this." She started undressing.

People gave Ursula things all the time. Flowers, cakes, objects carved from wood, even jewels. They gave her things *because* she was the princess, not because she was worthy—and they did so *despite* the fact she was a were. This was something she could never not know . . . the way obligation made people act around her. It meant she couldn't be sure of anyone except herself.

The werebear handed her the dress and slippers and walked to where she'd left her own clothes in a neat pile. "I've never met another one of us. The only one I've ever heard of is—"

She stopped midsentence and dropped to her knees. "I didn't realize. I apologize. Oh, please, I—"

"Please don't," Ursula said. "What's your name?"

The bear whispered her answer. *Sabine.* A beautiful name, like two notes in a song. The sight of her on her knees, full of shame and fear, made Ursula bristle. She wanted to run away. But she took a breath and held out her hand, not caring anymore that she was naked.

"Arise."

Sabine did.

"I pronounce you my friend and my companion. And in these woods, we are equals. And from one equal to the other, please, take the dress and the shoes. I don't need them."

Sabine looked skeptical. "What will you wear home? You don't want people seeing you starkers. Do you want my clothes?"

Sabine had a tunic and trousers. She had no shoes. Though the clothes looked comfortable enough, they also looked like things Sabine needed. And Ursula's mother would ask her where she'd found them, and she didn't want to tell anyone about Sabine. She wanted her all to herself.

"I'll go home as a bear." She'd have to sneak past her mother, but she'd done that many times.

"You can *do* that?"

Ursula nodded. She wasn't supposed to, but no one would stop her, just as no one had stopped her running through the kingdom. Other weres couldn't, even though it was normal enough to be a were. Lots of common folk had two aspects, especially the ones who had been born in the farm district, where her mother came from. Something about being in contact with the earth seemed to bring on a dual nature. Some people called werefolk *frissers*, but Ursula's mother forbade that.

"It's a slur. They are *performers*," she said.

As soon as baby weres could walk, they were taken from their families and brought to Cage Row, which was named for the lines of cages filling the empty land between the farm and town districts. Werechildren were to be left there, or their families would be sentenced to the dungeon. Weres could only take their animal forms on the Row. Anywhere else was prohibited. They made their living performing there for pennies. Acrobatics, juggling, fighting. Whatever people wanted to watch. Ursula would change this law once she was queen. No more dungeon. It was dark and smelled wrong, and nobody ever came out. If she could live in the castle, then weres could live with their families. She intended to be a just queen, one who didn't make special rules that only some people had to follow.

"It's fine," Ursula said. "No one will know."

"All right." Sabine had agreed so quickly that Ursula wasn't sure whether it was because she also wanted to be friends, or because she thought she had to obey. Sabine folded the dress neatly and set it on a flat stone. "I'll leave the clothing here, just to be safe. It can be something I try on when I feel like it. And you can fetch it if you need."

"Take it," Ursula said.

Sabine started and Ursula realized that her words came across as more of an order than a gift. She had been trained by her diplomacy instructor how to pivot away from such awkward moments: with a subject change.

"Do you want to race?"

Sabine nodded.

"Bet you I'm faster." Ursula smiled so Sabine would know it was all in fun.

Sabine smirked. "That's what you think."

"Try and catch me!"

Ursula dove forward, landing as a bear. From behind, she heard a roar, the thump of feet, and the forest's music urging them onward. They wound through trees, splashed across cold spring streams, and filled their lungs, running side by side until both were exhausted. They lay down in a patch of moss, panting. Ursula had never been so happy to be who she was. There was a reason after all for her to be a werebear—to be with Sabine.

When the light in the forest dimmed, Ursula knew she had to go, but she didn't want to. What would it be like to live in the woods with Sabine forever? It didn't matter. She couldn't. She would be queen. She had to do what was right, always. And she wanted to, perhaps above all else. She touched Sabine's nose with hers. Then, slowly, she took her human form again. She lay on her stomach, her hands making a pillow for her chin. "I need to return home."

Sabine shifted and lay the same way. "Me too."

"I have more dresses if you want them." Ursula studied Sabine's profile. Even though Sabine's skin was dark, Ursula could still make out a smattering of freckles on her cheekbones. They were like stars in reverse.

"Oh, I couldn't. I'll keep this one safe, though," Sabine said, "in case you change your mind."

"I won't," Ursula said. "I never do. My mother and father say I'm stubborn."

Sabine laughed. "People say that about me too. They say I should have been a weremule. Can you imagine?"

Ursula laughed, but she couldn't imagine wanting to change a single thing about Sabine.

<hr />

To return home, Ursula traveled through the woods until she reached the wide river that wrapped around the kingdom's north edge. A branch of the river had been diverted to make a moat. It was guarded, but if anyone saw her crossing it, nothing was said. What could they say to the girl who would be their queen? She climbed out, shook the water from her fur, and headed to a little-used door on the far side of the castle. She debated making her entrance as a bear but never could get the hang of undoing latches with her paws.

She took her human form again, shivered, and dashed inside, hoping no one would see her naked body streaking up the back staircase. No such luck. The first person she saw was her mother, coming out of a little room she sometimes used to do her needlework.

"Ursula." The queen sighed, and Ursula knew she'd disappointed her mother yet again. "What's done is done. It's story time. Make yourself presentable and then go to your father's study. You know how he gets when he's been kept waiting."

<hr />

That night, Ursula lay on her back, mulling the tale her father had shared. All around was darkness; she could not even see the gold of the cage overhead.

"Once upon a time," he'd said. All his stories started that way. She'd come to believe there was no such thing as once upon a time. The same things happened, again and again.

This tale had been about the daughter of a lord. A wise man had predicted she'd prick her finger on a spindle and die, and so the lord had outlawed spindles. She found a long-forgotten one anyway. And because she didn't know what it was, she touched it, pricked her finger, and fell into a death-like sleep. Her parents abandoned her, and then a king—Ursula didn't even want to think about this part—found her and planted his seed in her.

Albrecht had wanted to know what kind of seed, the ninny. Ursula knew how such things worked; her mother had told her. What she hadn't said, though, was that a king might do such things to a girl as she slept, a girl whose parents had abandoned her, a girl who was not awake to choose. It made her feel sick. If even the daughter of a lord did not have a choice, what girl did?

Unable to sleep, Ursula felt grateful for her cage. No one could reach her there.

The story got worse. The king already had a wife who could not bear children. The useless queen, as King Tyran called her, was so angry at her husband's infidelity that she demanded their cook turn the twins into a stew. But the cook wouldn't, and the useless queen was banished.

"And they all lived happily ever after," her father had said. "And what do you think of this story, my children?"

"The best part was where the queen wanted to cook the babies," Albrecht had said.

"That was terrible." Ursula hadn't been able to hold her tongue. "The babies did nothing wrong."

King Tyran scratched his whiskers. "And who did wrong in this story?"

Ursula had wanted to please her father with her observations, but she also wanted to say what she truly thought. It was rarely possible to do both.

Albrecht spoke first. "The lord should not have left his daughter alone. It is a man's job to protect women and girls."

"Truth," the king said.

Ursula needed protection from no one. She was a bear. But she did not wish to call attention to the fact.

Albrecht continued. "And the girl was foolish for touching the spindle, even though it all turned out well for her because she became queen, which is better than a lady."

"Also true," the king said. "Very good."

"Everyone has done wrong in this tale," Ursula said. "Everyone except the daughter and the babes."

Her father had looked surprised. "Do say more."

"The lord should have told his daughter to avoid spindles. She could have avoided it and been saved the injury."

"But then she would not have been queen," her mother said. "And then where would she have been?"

Had they heard the same story as she? There was no safety in being a queen. The original one was cast aside because she could not have children. The king was selfish, and the girl's father was foolish. Both had abandoned women they were supposed to love. Could no one see the wrongness of it?

Happily ever after, her father had said.

That's how all his stories ended. But that wasn't true. Not everyone lived happily ever after. Not the banished wife. And who knew what would become of the replacement queen or her babies? She'd been born into a world where men could claim or discard her without remorse.

When Ursula was queen, she would make sure no children were harmed by the foolishness of adults. She would be wise and just. Her subjects would be safe. She knew what she was about, not Albrecht.

That was why fortune had seen to it that she was born first.

V

Seven years passed. A werewolf named Hans was twelve. His sister, Greta, was thirteen. It was winter, bitter and white.

The children knelt by their parents' bed, watching them sleep. Their father and stepmother shook with fever, which had turned their skin clammy and gray. The sound of their chattering teeth made Hans want to sob on the floor.

"Hans," Greta said, "what are we going to do?"

"I don't know," he said. "I keep hoping they'll wake."

Hans crept to the fireplace and put another log on the flames, just a small one, so that Greta wouldn't scold him about their short supply. He could always find more wood.

He leaned against the window by the kitchen table, cupping his hands around his eyes. Moonlight silvered the snow. It was a full moon; his bones told him so. Ordinarily that made it the kind of night he liked to be outside, running on four paws, breathing in the whole world.

Not tonight. He'd never leave Greta and their parents alone. Not now. Hans kept his face against the glass. He didn't want Greta to see his tears.

The forest was always quieter during winter, as though it needed a season to rest and replenish. That's usually what winter was for Hans and his family.

But not this year. Father and Stepmother had taken ill at the change of seasons. A cough into their fists, then blood spat into their palms.

He pricked up his ears. Full moons always sharpened his hearing. His sense of smell too, though it was hard to detect anything over the sickness.

Cappella's pipe pierced the night. Her music had drawn him that first day. He'd been so lonely for a friend who was not his sister, and Cappella was exactly what he'd wished for. She still didn't know he was a werewolf, though. He'd been forbidden to tell anyone lest he be taken by the king.

There was so much he wanted to say, so much he wanted to ask, none of which was possible when he was in his wolf form. She didn't even know his name.

"I know that song," Greta said. She knew about Cappella. She'd never asked to meet her. She understood that would ruin Hans's secret. She was a good sister, in that way and every way. "I made up words to go with it."

Greta made up songs so often their parents used to joke that she was really the daughter of the woods, halfway to being a tree herself.

He looked to their parents. "I think they'd like for you to sing."

Greta knelt by the bed and held her stepmother's hand. "Do you think they can hear us?"

He nodded. He wasn't sure, but he wanted her to sing. He wanted to feel something like normal again, and he also loved when his sister's voice and Cappella's pipe found each other. His two favorite things made into one.

Greta stood by the bed. Her song was sad, but somehow the words she'd come up with made it feel like sadness was necessary and beautiful, the way seasons were for the trees, the way the night was for the sky, and the way valleys were to hills.

He moved to the table, which held the last of their bread and their empty soup bowls. He and Greta usually tidied up straightaway, but they hadn't that day, as though putting off the task would stop time.

As Greta sang, his father's breathing changed. It had been rattling for days. Now it ceased for long stretches. Greta noticed and stopped singing. The sound of Cappella's pipe continued, faint but clear, as though the coldness of the air had sharpened it to a fine point.

Father's last breath was nearly soundless. A whisper, a sigh. Then the song ended. In the silence afterward, as the fire burned itself to ash, Stepmother followed Father into the beyond.

"Hans." Greta sagged to the floor.

He knelt next to her, sliding his hand into hers as he had when he was learning to walk. He needed her hand then to keep from falling down. He needed it now too.

She squeezed his fingers. "What are we going to do?"

"I'll take care of us," he said. "Always."

"We'll take care of each other. That's our promise."

When the first light of dawn seeped through the windows, their parents looked as though they were sleeping peacefully, dreaming of spring. The awful chattering of teeth had stopped.

He looked into Greta's dark blue eyes. "Now what?"

"Ash for the earth. It's what they would have wanted."

"I'm hungry," he said.

"You're always hungry." Greta hung the kettle over the fire and sliced a dry husk of bread into two pieces. As the water heated, she toasted the bread over the flames. Hans made tea from dried dandelions.

It had been quiet since the sickness arrived, but the quiet felt different now. It felt endless. There would be no more of Stepmother singing harmonies with Greta as breakfast was made. No more of Father talking about which part of the forest he planned to tend.

The woods were quiet too. Hans supposed they knew. He finished his toast and tea and went outside. He needed to pee, and he needed to cry, two things he didn't want to do in front of his sister.

When he returned, Greta was combing the tangles out of their stepmother's long black hair. Greta handed him a damp cloth, and he wiped his father's face and smoothed his beard.

"His hands too," she said.

Father always had dirt under his nails. His fingertips were so dirt stained they looked like tree rings.

"The trees are everything to us," he'd often said. "Our home, our heat, our livelihood."

Whenever Father had to cut one down, he always thanked the woods for their sacrifice, and he made sure to plant replacements.

Hans set down Father's hands. "I think we should leave them as they are. The dirt was part of him."

"True enough." Greta had braided Stepmother's hair and fastened it around her head like a crown.

"I don't want to do this," he said.

"You know what Father always said."

"Ash for the earth, for the plants and the trees, and all of those for the yous and the mes."

Hans swallowed. That meant they had to do the next thing, the hardest thing.

Wood was scarce. They'd been too busy caring for their parents to gather and chop it. But Hans went where he knew he could find twigs and sticks. Greta gathered their parents' clothing and bedding. It was a shame to lose it, but if it had disease on it, they couldn't have it in the cottage anyway.

By midday, everything was ready. Greta fetched a burning stick from the fire inside. "Ready?"

Hans nodded.

She touched it to the pyre and then blew. Kindling caught, burning red and orange and gold. Some of the wood was wet and sent showers of sparks into the air. They spiraled down, sizzling when they reached the snow. Hans and Greta sat side by side, surrounded by giant trees, watching the flames at work, turning the silhouettes of their parents into something else entirely.

The fire burned until darkness fell.

"We're alone now," Greta said.

"We have the trees," Hans said. "The music. We have Cappella."

Greta was silent, but he could tell from her expression she did not think much of that. "We should go in," she said. "It's started to snow again."

<hr />

The next morning, they found three gold coins on their doorstep—as bright as tiny suns. Greta picked them up.

"Are they real?" Hans said.

She nodded. "As far as I can tell. Where do you think they came from?"

"I don't know." Theirs was the only house in the woods; the king would permit only one to be built. Cappella and her mother lived in the hollow tree. But surely they had no gold. They didn't even wear shoes.

"Should we keep them?" he asked.

His sister was matter-of-fact. "If we don't, we'll have a hungry winter. Think of all we didn't do to prepare while Stepmother and Father were ill."

"Someone must have wanted us to have them," Hans said.

Greta wrapped her shawl around her shoulders and looked into the woods. The music was soft and gentle, comforting even. "Do you see anyone?"

It had snowed overnight, enough that the remains of the fire had been buried. He saw no footsteps. He would have expected some leading up to the porch, unless the delivery had been made just after they went inside.

He pointed that out to Greta. "I don't smell anyone either."

"Bundle up," she said. "If we leave now, we can be back before dark."

VI

Hans and Greta started the long walk to the kingdom. He remembered what his father said of it.

"The smell of too many people and not enough trees."

And that was true. But it was also exciting. Half the kingdom was farmland with animals and growing things. The other half was where things were made and sold. Wagon wheels. Horseshoes. Bread. Boots. So much.

They stood in front of a baker's cart piled high with honey cakes and seeded loaves and things Hans didn't even have names for.

"I wish you could see how wide your eyes are," Greta said. "Like saucers."

"All the better to see everything I want to eat," he said.

"Be patient. You must keep your wits until we've bought the necessities."

She gave him a look that he understood—she was telling him he couldn't lose control. He couldn't become a wolf. Not here.

He dragged his feet and pulled the little cart they'd brought with them to carry their purchases home. She was right. That didn't make it easier.

After they finally found someone who'd make change for a gold piece, they loaded their cart with potatoes and flour, onions, dried meat, salt, cloth, and a pair of boots for each of them. They'd bought cloaks too. Greta's was dark blue, Hans's as green as new leaves, and as a special surprise, Greta let him choose a beautiful red one for Cappella.

"It's easier spending money that was never yours to begin with," Greta said. "Do you think she'll like it?"

"I know she will." For a moment, he even forgot about his hunger.

Everything they'd purchased had cost them less than a single gold coin. It made him feel hopeful for the future. Whatever they needed and couldn't make, they could buy.

"Greta?" He looked at her.

"All right," she said.

They were headed back toward the bakery cart when a commotion rose in the cobbled street. Someone important was coming. People pointed, and two golden flags with lions on them fluttered on poles carried by men in shiny clothing. Then came soldiers in heavy boots, and after that, the prince and princess.

The prince had blond hair, like Greta's. But they looked nothing else alike. Where Greta had dark blue eyes that reminded Hans of the sky just after sunset, the prince's eyes were so light they looked almost white. Meanwhile, the princess had pale brown hair with reddish undertones. The prince might have been showier, but he also seemed like the jagged mountaintop behind the kingdom, shoving rudely at the sky. The princess was more like something grown of valley earth, solid and true.

With so many people around, Hans thought about what Father had said about not being able to breathe in the kingdom. Then Greta cried out. Someone had bumped into her.

She pointed at a thin, ginger-haired man in a fine silk tunic. "My coins! He stole them!"

The man thrust his hips at her. "Do you want to reach into my pouch for them?" He laughed, turned, and then pushed through the crowd.

That money was theirs. It was their future, their security. Hans was hungry and he was angry, and he could not stop the wolf. His clothing ripped, and his shoes slipped from his feet, and he was on all fours, snarling. People screamed. He lunged and sank his teeth into the man's wrist.

"Help me!" The man kicked Hans in the ribs and jerked free.

Hans snarled and prepared to bite the man again, but suddenly, he couldn't breathe. Someone had slung a rope around his neck, squeezing his windpipe. The more he struggled, the tighter the rope got.

"Hans!" Greta cried. "Hans!"

He hunched his back, the rope taut, all thoughts of coins and breakfast forgotten. Now he wanted one thing: air. If he held very still, he could pull a thread of it through his nose.

The prince crouched in front of him. "Do you know what happens to frissers who shift outside the ghetto?"

"Albrecht, leave him alone. Can't you see he's not even full grown?" The princess clamped her hand on her brother's shoulder.

The prince shrugged her hand away. "He's big enough to be dangerous."

"Watch your words, brother. Weres are no more dangerous than any other person."

"He shouldn't be here. Look at the little beast. He's torn that man's shirt and flesh."

"Albrecht! Enough."

"It's nothing personal, Ursula. This is a dangerous frisser who's hurt one of our human subjects. If you weren't so emotional, you'd see the truth."

Hans snarled, and the rope tightened. He swayed, his tongue thickening. Then the princess was next to him, steadying him, as she loosened the rope.

The prince scolded her. "I'll tell Father you did that."

"Shut it, Albrecht. You," she said to Hans. "Stay here. Don't move. Don't let anyone provoke you." Then she turned to Greta. "What are your names, and what happened here?"

Hans sat on his haunches. The crowd loomed.

Greta's voice trembled. "That man stole our money."

"She lies," the man said.

Hans growled. The princess shot him a glance, and he lowered his head.

Prince Albrecht circled Greta. "Your frisser needs better manners."

"Albrecht, enough. You know what Mother says about that word."

"Mother isn't here," he said.

The princess turned to a guard and pointed at the thief. "Search him."

One guard put his arm around the man's neck, while another patted his pockets.

Greta had moved close enough to Hans that they were touching. She smelled salty and sour. Fearful.

The guard produced two gold coins, a few silvers, and a bounty of coppers.

"Is this yours?" the princess asked Greta.

"Not all of the coppers. Just some. But the gold and silver are."

Albrecht picked the gold out of the guard's palm. "I think it doesn't belong to either of you." He showed the princess the coin. "Same markings as Mother's."

Her brow furrowed. "How did you come by it?"

Greta's face reddened. "It was a gift."

"From whom?" Prince Albrecht asked.

"I—I don't know," Greta said.

"Oh, so I suppose it just magically appeared on your doorstep?" The prince had lifted Greta's braid from her shoulder and was examining it.

Hans sat as still as he could, hoping the fur rising on his hackles wasn't too obvious.

"It's ours. I swear it." Greta stood tall, and Hans was proud of her.

The prince and princess exchanged glances but said nothing.

"She's lying," the thief said.

"One of you is lying," Princess Ursula said. "That is certain."

"It's our father's gold, made by our mother." Prince Albrecht dropped Greta's braid and addressed the thief. "How did you come by it?"

The man reared back. "Ehh, the truth is—it *was* hers. She dropped it and I was trying to give it back."

Greta's whirled toward him. "I didn't drop it. And I didn't steal it either. It was given to us."

"Enough," the princess said. "Take the thief to the summer castle, remove his trousers, and let him walk home without them. He can think about what telling a lie and showing his ass have in common."

"Such language, Ursula," Prince Albrecht said. "What would Mother say?"

The princess shot him a fierce look and turned to Greta. "You cannot explain how you came to have this gold?"

Greta lifted her chin and squared her shoulders. "It was left for my brother and me after our parents died. I do not know who left it. That is the truth."

"We should tell Father," the prince said.

"Their parents have died and it's two coins. Hardly anything. Let's leave them be."

"We should enforce the laws of the kingdom," the prince said. "This one had the king's gold, and that one took his frisser form outside the ghetto and bit a man. That's three laws broken."

Princess Ursula pointed to Hans. "He can go back to the Row. The sister can come with us to the castle. We'll ask Mother and Father what to do."

The prince stepped close and squatted low. His face was inches from Hans's.

The prince smelled of many things: meat, bread, metal, ash, and death. It was unmistakable, that little whiff. Hans's heart raced.

"Don't taunt him, Albrecht," the princess said.

"I'm not," the prince said. "I'm taking the measure of him."

"Hans," Greta said. "Go. I'll sort all of this out and then find you."

The prince looked at Greta as she spoke. The way he watched her made Hans's legs feel oily and weak. He'd seen hunters in the woods before. They had exactly that look.

"Both of them should come with us," the prince said. "I've always wanted a pet."

"Albrecht, *stop*."

"Perhaps we should leave it up to the cub," the prince said. "Do you want to go with your sister into the nice, warm castle? Or do you want to cower on the Row with the rest of the frissers? What do you say, little dog? Oh, I beg your pardon. *Animals* can't speak. Woof, woof."

Hans wanted to take his human form again, but his wolf aspect resisted. It said to him, *This is who you are. This is how it feels to be fully alive . . . how it feels to smell the world . . . the breath of humans . . . the scent of smoke on the wind . . . of soil and the cycle of decay and rebirth. You are a wolf, a wolf, a wolf.*

But Hans knew he was human too. He was both at once. And who he was at any moment ought to be his choice and his choice alone.

His spine straightened, his fingers stretched and became sensitive at their tips, his tail slipped back into his body, and then he was crouching, unclothed, before the prince and everyone else. Cloth fell around his shoulders. The red cloak. The one he'd meant for Cappella, placed there by Greta. He stood and spoke his wish.

"I'll go with my sister."

VII

Ursula and Albrecht stood before their parents.

"Show me the gold," King Tyran said.

Albrecht fished it out of his purse.

Tyran leaned forward in his throne. "Is that all of it?"

"That's all," Albrecht said. "Just these two coins."

"There were also silvers and coppers," Ursula said.

The king waved away the small change. He held the golden coins up to the light. Then he handed them to the queen. "What do you think? Are these of your making?"

"I—I am not sure," the queen said. She coughed into a handkerchief. She'd been coughing a great deal lately. "Where did they say they got it?"

"The woods," the king said. "And I would think you'd recognize your own gold. But we could test it."

"We haven't any blood," the queen said.

Ursula was puzzled. What would blood do?

The king gestured at Greta and Hans. "We have plenty right here."

"Oh, Tyran. They're children."

"They have plenty to spare."

"I have a knife," Albrecht said.

"Use mine," Ursula said.

"*You* have a knife?" Albrecht laughed. "Since when?"

"I meant use my *blood*," Ursula said.

"Darling, no," her mother said. "You don't want a scar."

Albrecht looked both girls over. He hesitated, as if deciding which one he wanted to hurt. He took Greta's hand. "The blade is very sharp."

"Please, no." Greta pulled, but his grip was stronger.

"Stay still. Unless you like it when things hurt." He sliced her palm, dipped his finger in it, and offered it to his father. "Is this enough?"

"Plenty," Tyran said. "Touch it to the coin."

Albrecht ran his finger against the gold. It started to bubble.

"Your mother's gold has a flaw," the king said. "Blood weakens it."

Albrecht laughed. "It figures that the creation of a woman weakens at the sight of blood."

Ursula wanted to smack her brother, but she had to look like the one in control, the one meant to rule. There was always talk that Albrecht should get the throne. Any mistake she made could destroy her future. A boy must only be born first to rule. A girl must be born first *and* prove herself, and that still might not be enough.

Greta closed her fist around her wound. Ursula took a handkerchief from a pocket. "May I?"

Greta nodded, her eyes bright with tears. There wasn't too much blood. For all his faults, Albrecht knew how deep he needed to slice. He'd cut no more.

The king addressed Greta. "How did you come to be in possession of my gold? Think carefully about your answer."

"It was left outside of our cottage," Greta said. "I assumed it was alms after the deaths of my parents."

"Who were your parents?"

"The woodsman and his wife," Greta said.

"Pity," the king said. "I liked that fellow."

"And you two children are now living all alone?" the queen asked.

Greta nodded. "Yes, Your Majesty."

"That is no way for children to live," the queen said.

Greta looked apprehensive. Ursula could tell she wanted to say something but did not dare.

"Her brother is a were," Albrecht said. "He has a wolf nature."

"A wolf," the king said. "He'd be no match for our Ursula. Would you, boy?"

"I could kill him," Albrecht said.

The queen coughed again, this time more violently. "The children need a place to live."

Ursula could see resistance in Greta's eyes, and also fear. It made her admire the girl, whom she might have written off as nothing because she was so pretty and fair.

"They could live here, Mother," Albrecht said.

Her brother didn't have a generous spirit, so he had to have something he wanted out of the arrangement. *Oh, mercy.* Albrecht liked how Greta looked. It was obvious.

"Girl," the king said, "can you do kitchen work?"

"Yes," Greta said. "But—"

"Then it's settled. We grant you a position in the kitchen. Albrecht will take you there."

"What about the brother?" Ursula said.

"Her brother belongs with the weres," the king said.

Ursula bit her tongue. They probably thought she belonged there too.

"I want him," Albrecht said. "I need an assistant."

"That settles it, then," the king said.

Ursula was astonished. Her brother hated weres. He was always mocking them. She worried for the boy in the beautiful red cloak.

"Jutta must make him a cage," Albrecht said.

The boy looked horrified.

"Well done, Albrecht and Ursula," the king said. "You are excused."

Ursula could not help but notice that her father said her brother's name first. She curtsied. On her way out, she overheard her father ask her mother where she thought the coins had come from, if not the royal treasury, where they were carefully guarded and tracked.

"I couldn't begin to guess," her mother said, her voice husky as it had been so often lately.

Ursula could not help but hear the fear in her mother's voice, followed by a coughing fit that echoed long after she'd left the hall.

VIII

Cappella hadn't seen her wolf for days. In all the years they'd known each other, this had never happened. She thought he might be hiding, playing some sort of new game. She looked everywhere. At first, it felt exhilarating, but those feelings soon gave way to confusion and then anxiety.

Had she done something that made him angry? She couldn't think of what it might be, and any misunderstandings they'd had in the past—a stepped-on paw, a nipped finger—they'd resolved in seconds with gentle head butts and steady gazes.

Pipe in hand, because she was too upset to play, she returned to the tree where her mother waited.

"What's wrong, Pella?" her mother asked. "It's not like you to look so sad."

"The wolf is gone."

The look that crossed her mother's face told Cappella she was right to worry.

"You've tried calling him?"

"Of course."

"And you've looked everywhere?"

"Yes. I'm afraid something terrible has happened."

Her mother held out her arms, and Cappella moved closer for a hug, even though she was getting too old for such things.

"What about the cottage?" her mother asked. "Did you look there?"

"Why would I look there? He's a wolf. He lives outside."

"All the same," her mother said, "I think you should check. Would you like to go together?"

Cappella nodded and followed her mother outside their great tree. The day was a fine one. Sunlight shot through the canopy and sparkled on the snow still left on the ground. The bright light made for extra shadows, and behind each one, Cappella thought she saw her wolf. But it was never him. It was a rock. Or the frond of a wind-brushed branch.

They reached the cottage. Her mother knelt as though she was looking for something on the threshold. Then she stood and peered through the windows.

As she did, Cappella noticed two pairs of depressions in the ash-gray snow. "Look, Mother. Footsteps."

Her mother exhaled. It was a long sound, the kind she made when she had a lot to say and didn't know where to begin. "Headed toward the kingdom, it looks like."

"But why?" Didn't they know it was dangerous there? She looked at the footsteps again. "Why did they not return?"

"We need to go home, Cappella. There's something I must tell you."

⌒⌒⌒

They sat on soft cushions in the center of the tree, where a little fire crackled merrily in a ring of polished stones beneath the grate they used for cooking. Her mother heated water. It wasn't very often that they had serious conversations, and Cappella could tell that her mother was moving slowly and deliberately so she could gather her thoughts. Cappella couldn't stand the tension, and the way the music of the forest was always a little louder inside the tree made everything worse.

"Do you think he's dead?"

Her mother poured hot water into two cups. "I don't know." Then she reached into a clay jar and removed two dried flower blossoms, which she dropped into the water.

Cappella counted on her mother to know everything. That she wasn't certain, that she couldn't offer reassurance, made it hard for Cappella to breathe. She wrapped her hands around her mug. "Why did we go to the cottage to look for him? Do you think they hunted him?" She'd seen a golden-haired hunter in the woods, and her mother insisted Cappella remain in the tree whenever he was on the prowl.

"Oh, no," her mother said. "That wasn't what I was thinking at all. Do you remember the morning, not too long ago, when I left before sunrise?"

Cappella nodded.

"The day before that," her mother said, "there was a death. Two, actually."

Cappella held her breath, fearing what would come next.

"The woodsman and his wife passed away, as all living things do."

Cappella breathed out. Not her wolf. She felt terrible for those people, but she didn't know them, so her sorrow felt more like a shadow than something real. The dried flower in her tea, its petals unwound, spun slowly in her cup.

"They passed away, but their children lived."

Their children. Cappella had seen them on occasion, a brother with gray eyes and a sister with the longest, most beautiful hair she'd ever seen, the color of winter sun. She'd never spoken with them because her mother had told her not to. She'd always been curious about them, though, especially the boy. He was just her age and his face was so kind. She felt sad for them. If she'd lost her mother, she'd be alone in the world.

"I went to the cottage with a gift of gold coins for the children."

"How did you come by gold coins?"

Her mother sipped her tea and took her time in answering. "I made them."

That didn't strike Cappella as that surprising at first. After all, she and her mother made their own clothes.

But as she thought about it, questions emerged. "Is it difficult to make a coin? And where do you find the gold?"

"I summon it from the soil."

"Like a potato?"

"Yes, but like one I did not plant."

"Did you make my pipe as well?"

"I did," her mother said. "When you were just a very tiny thing, humming along with the music of the woods. And you learned to play it so quickly, as if it had been meant to be."

"Did you make me that way?"

Her mother's expression changed, and Cappella wished she hadn't asked, even as it had been in jest.

"Of course not," her mother said. "You know where children come from."

Cappella did. She wanted to ask why she had no father. Had he died? Had he left? She sometimes felt angry not to know, but she always quelled that feeling. Her mother was all she had. She couldn't afford anger.

"I don't see what any of this has to do with my wolf," she said.

"I know, my darling," her mother said. "I was thinking out loud. But this is what I truly believe . . . that your wolf is all right. He just might not live here anymore."

Cappella was speechless. Why would he leave? And without saying goodbye?

"Is that what wolves do sometimes?"

"It's what many creatures do," her mother said. "Leave home. Make their way in the world."

Cappella had finished her tea, but she held on to the cup so her hands wouldn't be empty. "I would have liked to say goodbye," she said.

"I know," her mother replied.

"I'll never leave you," Cappella said.

Her mother set her teacup down, stood, and brushed soil off her clothes. "I'm going for a walk. Join me?"

Cappella shook her head. She was confused about so many things, and she felt worse than she had before. Something important had been unsaid, some secret her mother wasn't telling her.

After her mother left, Cappella put her pipe to her mouth and listened to the woods. When she found an opening in their song, she joined in. And she hoped that, wherever he was, her wolf could hear her play, and that he felt less lonely for it.

Her song, as always, was for him.

People love the stories the man with no eyes tells, children most of all.

"Tell us the one about the little man," they shout. "The little man who spun straw into gold!"

"But I can't remember his name," the eyeless man lies.

"Rumpelstiltskin," the children cry, for they know the tale by heart, and they love the part where the strange little man tries to steal the queen's baby. They find it endlessly exciting when the brave guards discover the man's silly name, and they laugh when Rumpelstiltskin stomps so hard he splits the earth in two. They love it most when the earth devours him.

Little children can be so vengeful. The man with no eyes adores it.

"Ah, but you already know that tale, my beautiful ones," he says. "Let me tell you one about wicked bears who lived in a cottage in the woods."

The children move close enough that the storyteller can feel their sweet breath upon him, the closest thing to human touch he's had in years.

They listen hungrily as he unspools the tale of the wicked bears, their cottage, and the golden-haired beauty unlucky enough to cross their path.

They revel in the destruction that follows.

PART
TWO

IX

Three more years passed. The queen died. The king fell ill. The grief and sickness faded his golden lion's mane to one of silver. But he seemed made of hooves and leather, and he still looked as though a boulder could fall on him and split into gravel. It would take more than a single sickness to snuff such a flame.

Even so, Ursula could smell his death coming. She worked harder still to be worthy of the crown.

Albrecht had not done the same. If anything, Ursula believed, he'd lost interest in all but his mechanical devices. He and his apprentice, Hans, had set up something like a smithy in the castle. All day long, they pounded metal. They made levers and gears. They assembled monstrosities.

The smithy meant the air outside Albrecht's rooms always felt hot, even in summer. Ursula had no idea how he stood it and why he didn't just use Jutta's forge. But she supposed it was easier for him and less of a bother for Jutta if he took his building elsewhere. And of course, he would never take Hans out of the castle.

It was strange, their relationship. Albrecht had always *hated* weres—and now he had one at his side like a second shadow. She wondered how Hans was faring with the arrangement, but there was something in his eyes that made her not want to press.

She feared him, she supposed. His size, his silence, that wary look, as though something inside him was coiled and ready to spring.

In addition to the smithy, Albrecht had taken over their mother's former needlework room, the one with a hidden staircase to the dungeon below. Ursula wasn't allowed inside. Albrecht had promised Father it was for the security of the castle, and he'd also waved away Ursula's plea that she ought to know of everything security related.

"That is a man's concern," her father had said.

"But I am to rule," Ursula replied. "Is it not also my concern?"

"Your brother will always tend to your safety."

⟞⟝

Harvest season arrived, and with it another Moon Festival.

Ursula felt alive with excitement. She and Sabine had seen each other regularly in the woods for the past eleven years. A lifetime, it felt like. But today would be the first time that Ursula would see Sabine perform in the fighting cage. There were many types of performances the werefolk put on, but this was the match between weres that everyone talked about, and Sabine was finally old enough to compete—and had beaten many other weres on the Row for this spot.

Sabine and Ursula had practiced for years, with Ursula sharing everything her own combat instructors had taught her. They moved together so effortlessly it often felt to Ursula as though they were halves to a single whole. Even so, on the morning of the festival, Ursula was nervous. She wanted Sabine to win. To be adored by the crowd.

If Sabine won, she'd have money enough for everything she needed. That had always been an issue between them—Ursula's desire to give things to

Sabine, and Sabine's refusal to accept anything more than that dress and those shoes, both of which she'd long outgrown.

"If we are to be friends, Ursula, we must be equals." She'd said it so many times that it had become a joke between them. But it was never really funny. The closer Ursula got to the crown, the greater the tension between them. Sabine hated that Ursula was going to be queen. Sometimes Sabine even said their friendship would end—must end—when Ursula took the throne. But Ursula had never believed it. Nothing could end a friendship such as theirs. She wished Sabine could be more open-minded, would try harder to understand how difficult Ursula's life was, how much better she planned to rule over her people.

That morning, Ursula dressed with care as she had to for public appearances. She couldn't stand the trappings of royalty: the uncomfortable gowns, the stiff hairstyles. Since her mother's death, she'd developed her own solution to the problem of looking like a queen without feeling like a trussed fowl: a long tunic over finely worked leather leggings and high boots. They weren't the sturdy ones she wanted—boots like Jutta's, decorated with metal. But they were better than cloth slippers that flew off the moment she tried to run. Even Sabine thought those were silly now.

Ursula wore her hair in two braids, and they looked rather wonderful, she thought, beneath her simple gold crown. No one else dressed quite this way, and if anything, that reinforced the notion that she was both the queen *and* that she would be sensible and fair. Sabine was wrong. There *could* be justice with Ursula as the head of a queendom.

Her father wasn't well enough to stay for the entire festival; at breakfast he'd asked Ursula and Albrecht to represent the family.

"You'll watch the fights, will you not?"

"Of course, Father," Ursula said.

"Excellent," the king said. "I do love to watch the frissers clawing away at each other. So amusing."

Ursula bit her tongue. Since the queen's death, her father had used the slur without hesitation.

"Did you hear about the change to the fight this year?" Albrecht flipped a gold coin over his knuckles as he held a roasted goose leg in his other hand.

Ursula shot him a look. She had not.

"This time, it's not were on were. It's were on *human*. Best fighter wins the largest prize ever offered."

"Who's offering it? What's the prize?" she asked. That, she should also know. Sabine was the top fighter. This would affect her.

"I believe it's gold." Albrecht laughed.

He was obviously making a joke at her expense, and all she could do to ruin his fun was ignore it. She spread butter and honey on a slice of bread and pretended to be engrossed in the pleasures of eating. She could find out from someone else what was happening.

"Don't eat too much, Ursula," her father said. "You are getting very large." He coughed into his napkin.

She chewed the bite in her mouth and swallowed. Her father meant to help her with these comments. It was true that she was large. She was also very strong. Were she a man, these qualities would be celebrated. This was the endless struggle she felt. She was too much and never enough for her father and for the kingdom as a whole.

Albrecht eyed her and sank his teeth into the goose leg. Its skin crackled;

his lips glistened with juice. It was so Albrecht to pick the piece of meat that looked most as it did when it was still attached to an animal.

She stood and curtsied. "Be well, Father, brother. I have much to do to prepare for the day."

She needed to find out more about the fight with the prize attached. It was one thing for Sabine to best a were. It would be another thing for her to best a man. Ursula could not let that happen. She'd die first.

X

After breakfast, Albrecht stopped by his workshop to check on Hans's progress. The shaggy-haired boy was feeding wood to the forge. The windows were open wide, the only thing that kept the place from being an oven.

Albrecht stood before his mechanical man—or what would be one, once Hans managed to do as he was told. "Did you get the leg working?"

Hans opened his mouth, and Albrecht could see the excuses coming. He held up a hand. He wasn't in the mood. He crouched before the leg, examining it. From the outside, all looked in order. And it was a beautiful thing. A metal foot attached to a flexible ankle. A sleek shin so glossy he could see his own face. The knee, the thigh, the pelvis: all clever, all superb. This leg was the mirror image of the other, which worked perfectly. There was no reason this one should not as well. But something was amiss.

When Albrecht had been young and healing from his fall from the tree, he'd thought that all he needed to do was build the outsides of a creature and it would come to life. That its insides, its natural levers and gears, would magically manifest. Jutta had laughed at him for this. He'd punished her for days afterward with surly silence. Once he'd made her sufficiently remorseful, they'd worked together to develop a system for movement. It was a bit like the waterwheel powering the mill, only their operation was fueled by the winding of a key. If everything worked properly, Jutta said, their device would move of its own accord. It would, in its own way, live.

Ever since, he'd wondered what made something live. He knew parts of him were not alive. His hair. His fingernails. He'd cut these without feeling pain. But he knew parts of him were alive. The bone inside his leg, for example. It had hurt. It still sometimes did. Therefore, it lived.

To hurt was to live. He believed this. And therefore, to make something live, he had to find a way to create pain. To harness it. Someday he'd be able to build a vessel that could hold pain, and in holding it, his creation would live. He knew this would not be easy. He'd caused pain to many animals. Too much pain meant death.

He'd built practice vessels from metal. Small things. A rat with wheels instead of legs. A duck that could eat and defecate. Eventually his designs grew more complex, needing more parts, first hundreds, then thousands, each one of them needing to fit perfectly with the others. This was why he'd needed the forge. So he could build more and faster.

"Think of it, Father," he'd said. "I can build us soldiers who will never die. Who will never bleed. Who'll need neither food nor water."

His father had set down his pen and looked into Albrecht's eyes. "If you can do that, my boy, then the world's kingdoms will fall to you."

"But you're still giving our kingdom to Ursula just because she was born first. That isn't fair."

"Your sister will need someone to defend our land. To lead armies. The kingdoms will fall to you; but, yes, your sister will be the one on the throne. This is your mother's wish. I would have thought you'd enjoy the part with weapons and such. Most boys do."

Albrecht had wanted to scream. But he knew it would not help his cause.

63

Instead he reached into his pocket and pulled out the little windup rat. He'd made improvements to it. Now it was covered in the fur of a rat that he'd killed in a trap. It didn't smell nice, but it looked very much like the real thing. He set it on his father's desk, wound it, and watched as the little metal animal shot into his father's lap.

His father had leapt up. When he realized the rat was mechanical, he'd lifted it off the floor. "The wheel didn't stay on, Albrecht."

"I can fix that. It's easy."

His father placed the rat in his palm.

"Very impressive, my boy. Very impressive. But will you command an army of rats? Come to me when you've built an army of men."

Come to me when you've built an army of men.

The comment had bubbled like acid in Albrecht's mind for years. Despite his best efforts, he still didn't have a single metal man who could walk, let alone swing a sword. Hans had been useful. He'd even come up with an ingenious solution for keeping the metal man perpetually powered: wings that would flap and rewind the mechanism as they simultaneously allowed the metal men to fly. If *that* didn't impress his father, nothing would.

Albrecht unlatched the leg. He examined the inner workings. He couldn't see any problems. He opened the chest. One by one, he studied the pulleys and gears, examining them for flaws. He saw none.

The only thing to do was to wind the metal man and inspect the gears in motion. He hated to do it. Any part out of alignment could be damaged or destroy the parts around it. They'd have to start over. They'd done this more times than Albrecht could count. It was wearisome. It was also worrisome.

Albrecht walked behind the metal man. He wound the crank between the device's shoulder blades, gears ticking as the mechanism grew taut. Hans, sweeping the corner of the room, stopped to watch as Albrecht released the safety.

The man heaved to life. Albrecht stared into his open chest as the man lifted his right arm and then his left. All the gestures were smooth so far. The man turned his head this way and that. He lifted his left leg. Albrecht held his breath. The right leg moved. There was a screech of metal and then a clunk, and the man lurched, his gears grinding.

At once, Albrecht saw what was amiss. He stepped behind the man and fastened the safety. The grinding stopped. He pointed to the offending gear. "This was upside down, Hans. What were you thinking?"

Hans gripped the broom handle until his knuckles turned white.

"Come and look at what you've done."

Hans put aside the broom and came closer.

"Not there. Here. Stand here." Albrecht pointed to a spot on the floor. Slowly Hans stood where Albrecht wanted.

"Did you put it in the wrong way on purpose?"

Hans swallowed. "No, Prince Albrecht."

"Are you certain?"

"You were the one who assembled that portion, Your Royal Highness. Don't you remember?"

Albrecht struck him, fist to belly. Hans folded forward. "What mechanism inside you allows you to become a wolf? Where is it?"

Hans wiped saliva from his mouth. "I don't know."

"You're lying."

Hans shied back, clearly expecting Albrecht to hit him again. "It is the truth. I don't think about it any more than I think about making my heart beat or my lungs breathe. It just happens."

"But you can control it, can you not?"

Hans nodded. "Most of the time."

"I would like nothing more than to cut you open when you're turning so that I can understand how you function."

Hans's face paled, but he did not blink.

"The truth is, though, I would have a very hard time putting you back together, and you are more valuable to me intact. If you sabotage any of my work, though, I will do it without hesitation.

"It's a pity your sister also doesn't have your affliction, or I'd be inside her in a moment." Then he realized another way that remark could be construed. "I'd like to be inside her in that way too. How would you like that, Hans? Your sister, the consort to a future king?"

Hans's eyes narrowed. He snarled and fine hairs sprouted on his face and the backs of his hands. Albrecht loved watching this transformation. It never grew old. But Hans disappointed him by returning to his full human aspect.

"Why did you stop?"

"I thought you'd rather I fix the damaged gears," Hans said.

Albrecht stepped back, surprised at Hans's insight. He supposed he and Hans could have been friends, had Albrecht wanted it. If Albrecht were going to have a friend, having one as useful as Hans might have suited. He didn't talk too much, and he displayed good sense.

But no. Friendship was dangerous. You couldn't count on someone made of flesh and blood the way you could a man made of metal. Everything Albrecht wanted for himself depended on the metal man.

"Fix the gears," he said.

And then he went to ready himself for the festival.

XI

Hans stood away from the workshop window, watching Albrecht leave the castle. He'd been waiting so long for this reprieve that when it finally arrived, he felt briefly numb, like a limb pinned in an uncomfortable position.

The presence of the full moon, hidden by the brightness of the sky, wasn't helping. It whispered to him all the time, but especially when it was full. *Become the wolf, Hans. That is your nature, your freedom, your joy.*

In truth, his happiest moments had been as a wolf. Those years he'd spent running through the woods with Cappella. Lying by her side as she played her pipe. Leaning into her as she stroked the fur on his head, his back, beneath his chin. She'd touched him with hands that loved him.

His worst moments had also been as a wolf. That day in the square when the man had stolen Greta's coins, when Hans had shifted and ruined their lives. Since then, he'd shifted only when Albrecht forced him to.

At first, Hans had refused, even when the prince used devices that caused him pain and cost him blood. He resisted until Albrecht threatened to use his tools on Greta. After that, Hans submitted, again and again, as Albrecht watched. Took notes. Made cuts on his human skin and peeled back his fur to see how they'd shifted.

To keep Greta safe, Hans submitted, but only when he had to. Today he did not.

"I miss the days when you resisted," the prince once told him. "The look you got in your eyes when you held on to your human form was so delicious, like goose liver. And do you know how they make that? The chef feeds the goose until it can't eat anymore, and its liver gets so fat it's liable to burst. I'll feed it to you someday, so you know what I'm talking about. It's fantastic. Pain is a marvel. It's the secret to life. Nobody but me will be honest with you about that, but I don't expect you to be grateful."

As physically painful as Albrecht's abuse was, seeing Greta in the kitchen was worse. The prince wouldn't let Hans speak to her. Not a word, or she'd suffer. To survive, Hans turned inside himself. He feasted on memories and wasted no hope on the future. He felt no more alive than one of those things they'd made. He too was at the mercy of malevolent hands, winding, winding, winding.

Hans surveyed the devices he'd been tested on and even helped build . . . the chair, the thumbscrews, the masks of metal. These worked as designed. But the metal man and windup animals always wound down and stopped moving. He'd figured out how to fix this and then blurted it to Albrecht. It had been a stupid thing to say aloud. A stupid idea to give away.

Albrecht had, of course, embraced the idea of self-winding wings. He'd even tried to attach a set to the backs of living rats. It was so gruesome, Hans had to force himself to forget what he'd seen.

What he'd heard.

What he'd smelled.

You are clockwork. You feel nothing.

All he could do to slow Albrecht's progress was to sabotage the gears when the prince wasn't looking. Clot them with dust. Put them in upside down. Snap off their tiny teeth. Hans had known what would happen when he was inevitably caught. But he needed to hold Albrecht back. It was the one thing he could do to have any control at all.

Hans pulled on thick leather gloves and opened the metal door of the oven. It blasted heat: a plea for wood. It was always hungry and the wood sang when it burned, music that reminded him of Cappella's pipe and his sister's voice.

Behind him, rats chittered in their cages. Hans knew they wanted their freedom. But the prince would only have him capture more. Besides, some of them were badly scarred. They seemed unlikely to survive on their own. To keep them caged might be considered a mercy.

The moon tugged at him like a hook in his heart. He wanted to become the wolf. To howl. To run in the woods. To find Cappella and spend a quiet hour by her side. A single hour would be enough. His heart pounded a message. *Become the wolf. Become the wolf.*

He had one way of fighting this feeling, and with Albrecht gone, he could avail himself of it. He said goodbye to the rats. Closed the workshop door behind him. Walked partway down the flight of stairs and pulled back a tapestry covering a hidden room. This space was his. In it, his most precious thing. His only thing. He locked himself in his sleeping cage, lay down on his straw mattress, and slid his hand beneath it.

Out came the red cloak he'd bought for Cappella. It was no longer the beautiful thing it had been. Its edges were frayed, and it was a bit dingy. But it was soft, and it reminded him of who he'd been. Of what he'd once had. Of whom he'd loved.

He laid his head on part of it. The rest, he held in fisted hands, breathing it in, remembering.

XII

Greta stood alone, knife in hand. She felt relief at the solitude the festival had given her. It was usually so noisy in the kitchen, so hot, so full of people plucking fowls and kneading dough, putting things in ovens and pulling them out again. It was like a mouth grinding away, and in the end resulting in nothing but shit.

Greta had adjusted to despair. She'd become expert with a knife after spending years of days breaking down birds, pigs, and cows into parts that would be cooked into various dishes. They were long days spent wrist deep in flesh and blood and bone. Time had become like a dream to her, the repetitive motions, the sounds, the smells. So much of the world was meat, wrapped in skin, bound by sinew. All it took to unknit everything living was a blade.

She didn't like to look at people anymore, because she couldn't help seeing them as their parts. Dark meat and light. Skin and fat to slice away. Soft organs, safe for now in the darkness. She assumed people could tell she was thinking this about them, which was why they stared. She couldn't help it, though. You become what you do repeatedly. She was a blade, an unmaker.

Greta liked to sing as she worked, softly, to the music of the forest she could still hear. Was it inside her head, or did everyone hear it? She had no one to ask. She couldn't even ask Hans, who had become something of a valet to the prince. He was valued, which meant he was safe. There was nothing more she wanted for her brother, even as it hurt her feelings that he never spoke a word to her.

She also knew why the prince liked to watch her in the kitchen: She too was meat. He looked at her the same way she looked at the flesh in front of her, as though he was imagining how it could be rendered and transformed into something useful neatly and efficiently.

It was no secret he desired her. He occasionally brought flowers and gifts, such as soft animal skins to keep away the chill at night—the maids' quarters were drafty in winter. He touched her too sometimes; his unwelcome hand cupping her bottom or the curve of her breast. More than once, he'd pinched her hard. The look on his face horrified her. He liked seeing her in pain.

The first time he made her cry, he gave her a little clockwork device afterward: an egg that cracked open to produce a tiny winged creature. It was strange and hideous and also beautiful at the same time. She'd never owned anything like this, useless and ornate. She supposed it was good to attract the attentions of a prince. But she didn't want it. She didn't want that sort of attention from anyone. She never had. She wanted to be amid the trees and their music. That was home. Her only home.

Still, he was the reason she got to see Hans, so she accepted the attention without complaint. It was worth it for her to see that Hans was well, even as he always looked at her with sad eyes. He was well, and he was tall, taller than their father had been. He had very nearly become a man.

Her life had once been different. *Their* life had been different. But that life felt distant now, like something someone else had lived. She hadn't known then that it had been as fragile as breath, as impossible to hold as a song.

She stretched the plucked wing of a chicken and brought the knife down on the ridged joint that kept it attached to the bird. *Thwack.* The limb was free. She lifted the blade, ready to move it to the next joint, when she heard something more clearly than she had in ages.

Music.

It was the woods.

She set down her knife, closed her eyes, and listened. Strange how that helped her hear better, as if releasing the blade and the awful sight of butchered meat left her more open to the effects of the song. Her body ached. But she stood still in spite of her grief, as steady as a tree. Sorrow hadn't broken her. It meant there was hope. That she did not always have to live this way.

No one was coming to save her and Hans. Life was not going to get better. Not unless she made it so. Her chance was now.

Hans was almost certainly with Albrecht. He was valued. Protected. He'd never go hungry. She had no right to ask her brother to leave that behind. And yet she could not bear the thought of escaping without him.

Willing herself to move, she sneaked into the tower where he and the prince worked. Heart in mouth, she peered into the prince's chambers. She saw many things so awful they rooted her to the stone floor.

She did not see her brother. He must have gone to the festival after all.

The woods called to her. A strand of music, a high piping harmony no doubt played by Hans's friend, brought to mind the image of a bird gliding on an updraft. Effortless freedom. When had she last felt that?

She considered going back for her clockwork egg. Imagined the weight of it in her hand.

But it was not a bird. Not the real thing anyway. It was monstrous by comparison.

She didn't need it. A blade, though, was another story. She returned to the kitchen and dropped one into a sack, along with all the food she could carry.

It made her a thief after all these years. So be it. Maybe the things people said about you had a way of becoming the truth.

XIII

Albrecht arrived at the outdoor arena before his sister. He and Jutta stood side by side. She was well into her third ale, swaying in her boots. Albrecht had sipped a bit of one, but it was mostly to be polite to the man who'd handed it to him. He hated the taste, and he'd never liked the way it made him feel, like the bolts that held him together had been loosened. His devices couldn't operate if they weren't just so, and neither could he.

He'd come up with the idea to give an irresistible heap of gold to whichever man could defeat the werebear at the Moon Festival. The fight was always the best part of the celebration, and it was always between the top two weres from the Row. That was a missed opportunity, and he rather suspected they weren't really fighting. Better, Albrecht knew, would be a battle between a were and a full human. A real fight to demonstrate once and for all which was superior.

He intended to be the one chosen to fight. When he won, the message would be clear: Full humans were superior to frissers, and he was stronger than that top-ranked black bear. It wouldn't take a genius to understand that meant he was also more fit to rule than his sister.

All this time, he'd let Ursula think he had no interest in the throne, that he was content to work on his devices, that he'd someday lead her soldiers, something he'd already begun doing on behalf of their father. He'd have the kingdom for his own, and he'd do it by persuading the people that he was better, and by winning the loyalty of the soldiers who would defend him on his ascent. He was confident that even some of the weres would choose him over his sister. Strength and decisiveness—that's what he would bring. And once he had his army of flying metal men, he and by extension the kingdom would be unstoppable, a force that could take over the world.

Albrecht elbowed Jutta. "What do you make of her?" He pointed to the warrior at the edge of the ring.

"Wouldn't want to meet that one in an alley," Jutta said. "I understand her were aspect is a bear."

Jutta's pupils dilated. Her irises, usually a deep gold with the telltale black ring, were nearly all black. She feared the bear. That was the trouble with weres who were prey animals.

"Think you could take her?"

"As a human, yes. It would be easy. I am much larger than she, and I would run her through with one of my fine swords. As a horse? I'd hate my chances, even in retreat. A black bear can outrun water. Their bodies don't look it, but it's the truth."

"Are you going to enter the contest?"

"Gold is as useful as a wig on a rat," Jutta said. "I prefer iron and steel. You'll never change my mind on that, young prince."

"Oh, but it *is* useful," Albrecht said. "With it you can command hearts and bodies."

"You've got the whip on mine without needing gold," Jutta said.

He gave her a gentle punch in the arm. "You're not like most of the other weres. That is why I like you so."

Jutta smiled. "It's not true what they say about you, that you hate were-folk. Your two closest comrades are weres."

She meant Hans and herself, and she was right. It wasn't hatred he felt. It was more complicated. Weres disgusted him with their unstable, shifting bodies. The strong ones fascinated him. But they were not superior. His devices, especially the weapons, made him superior. And he was close to creating a better sort of human. A more durable life-form, and one that never had to succumb to the rude humiliation of being a thing with blood and bones, one who could fall and not be broken.

The black werebear warmed up, moving her limbs quickly and precisely. He studied her face. He was an expert in the matter of beauty, and she was one. Unquestionably.

When he fought her, he would concentrate the damage elsewhere. It was criminal to harm a beautiful face: theft from the bearer, and theft from those who'd been deprived of a pleasing vista.

"They're announcing the contest." Jutta trembled, from fear or excitement Albrecht could not tell.

Ursula stood at the far edge of the crowd. As usual, she was alone. Even though people were shoulder to shoulder across the square, Ursula had a ring of space around her. The people did not love her. This was very good for him.

He didn't need to listen to the announcer call out the terms of the fight. He'd designed them. Whoever won would earn fifty pieces of gold. This was more money than any of these people would see in a lifetime, but Albrecht felt no shame that none would get the prize. Instead they'd get the excitement of seeing him win, a fair trade.

Man after man stepped forward, and more than a few boys.

"Anyone else?" the announcer called.

Albrecht watched Ursula's expression. She was staring at the werebear. He almost thought for a moment she was going to volunteer, but that would be ridiculous. She didn't qualify. Besides, it would require her to shift in front of the crowd. To be naked before her people. To show her animal nature. She'd never do it.

"Last call!" the announcer said.

Albrecht climbed to the platform where the fighting cage sat. "I'll fight."

There was no sound other than the demonic music from the woods. And in that moment, Albrecht wondered if he'd miscalculated. If perhaps his people did not relish the specter of their prince facing a beast.

But then the shout rose, a thick wave that thrilled his skin.

"The prince! The prince will fight!" the announcer said. "Who would like to watch?"

If the earlier wave of sound had been large, this one sent shivers through his blood. This was what it was like to be loved by your people, what he imagined flight would be like. To be weightless. To look down on the world. Glory.

He dipped his hand into his purse and plucked out silver coins for each of the commoners he'd supplanted, pinching the winking metal between his fingers and making a show out of each gift because the crowd loved it so. The volunteers, happy to have money for nothing, left the platform, and Albrecht assessed his foe. He could read nothing in her eyes. Not fear. Not bravado.

It was a pity. He had excellent instincts for weakness, a talent he'd honed hunting. Some animals hid. Some struck first. Some tried to lead you away from their offspring and mates. This was true for human beings. There were the fearful ones. The ones with hot tempers. The ones with everything to lose.

She looked away first. He followed her gaze and, in Ursula's expression, learned everything he needed to know.

"Ready?" the announcer said.

The bear stepped out of her clothing, dove through the open door of the cage and landed on four paws faster than Albrecht could have said his own name.

Oh, this was going to be wonderful.

He walked inside after her, but he didn't like being in a cage, even one as large as this. The bars were bad; worse was the black metal overhead, like a low sky on a starless night. He hated darkness. Hated the way it made him feel small.

The werebear moved her head from side to side, as if to assess him. Her mouth was closed, so he could not see her teeth. But her paws weren't even as large as his hands. This was good. She was smaller than Ursula. He never would have admitted it out loud, but he was terrified to face Ursula in a fight. They'd scrapped as children and he was always relieved when their mother intervened and told Ursula it wasn't fitting behavior for a princess.

He flexed his fingers. He'd strapped a pair of hidden blades to his wrists, blades that would spin once he snatched them out and released the spring-loaded catch. They devastated flesh, even through fur. He'd never tried it on a bear, but if he stabbed hard, he anticipated no problems.

The announcer hoisted the bag of coins. "The fighters compete for these—and for the honor of being the strongest warrior in the kingdom! Who will win? The powerful Prince Albrecht? Or the beautiful werebear Sabine?"

There was the crowd noise again, and any fear Albrecht felt about being in a cage vanished. The cage was a sheath. He was the weapon.

"Touch palms," the announcer said.

The bear ambled over, as if she hadn't a care in the world. She stood and held out her paw. Albrecht placed his hand against it. It felt dry and rough, like tree bark. She had a scent of smoke and earth to her. Wouldn't he love a cloak made of her fur so he could smell that every day? No wonder his sister couldn't take her eyes off her. She could probably smell her a mile away.

Ursula had moved to the edge of the platform. As usual, no one stood near her, a gap in the crowd that made her form even more conspicuous. She was ridiculous. So tall, with those braids and that totally unsuitable clothing. Their mother would have wept to see her like that. But if Ursula wanted to watch so badly, he'd give her two eyes full.

The announcer exited the cage, locked it behind him, and hung the key from his belt. "Fight!"

Albrecht crouched low, his arms out wide. The were struck, and he hopped back. Her claws snagged his vest, but it was thick leather. It would take more than a swat to shred it.

She dropped to all fours, snarling and baring her impressive teeth. He considered taking out the blades, but those were meant to be a surprise. A grand finale. No, the initial fight would be him versus the were. No weapons beyond strength and cunning.

He rose from his squat and looked down on her. Then he turned and hit her jaw with a flying back kick. His boots connected solidly, and the sound of the soles against her teeth was almost as satisfying as her grunt. He would have liked a roar of pain, but it felt like a good start.

He turned to the crowd, locked eyes with Ursula, and bowed. This, the audience loved most of all. He could feel the were approaching from behind, so he rolled to the side and she rushed past, barely avoiding the bars of the cage. He hadn't thought it would be this easy. He also hadn't considered how much he'd love the thrill of this particular crowd. He'd heard cheering before, all his life. Everybody loved royalty. But this version of love felt different, as if the prospect of pain made it more fevered, more real.

He flexed his wrists to be sure of the blades. There they were, more solid than bones, more reliable than breath. With practiced fingers, he flicked one of the straps free. Then he turned toward the bear. She looked wary, having missed twice and taken a solid blow to her jaw. When she snarled, her teeth were red. He bided his time, letting her wonder when he might attack, letting her wonder whether she should.

He considered where he would stick the knife. She roared, spraying him with hot, bloody spittle. The roof of her mouth, he decided. The soft palate. He'd shove the blade up through her brain and she'd die instantly, leaving a perfect were form.

He couldn't see Ursula. She probably didn't want to watch him triumph. He pulled out a blade. The people near the platform gasped.

The black werebear froze when she registered the knife. They hadn't been prohibited; indeed, nothing had been said about weapons by design. Weres never used them in their fights, for obvious reasons. Only a fool of a human would fight a bear without having a bit of steel on him. He smiled. There was nothing like watching an animal that's realized it's looking at its own death.

The bear stood rooted on the floor of the cage. He flung his knife. It flew, end over end, slicing the air. She stepped to the side and it missed—as he expected. It was a ruse. Real warriors never threw their weapons unless they wanted to arm an enemy. Given that the bear had no thumbs, this was not a concern.

She roared and rose on her hind legs. For a moment, he feared she would take her human form and hurl the weapon back. She seemed like the sort who wouldn't miss.

She remained a bear, however. Albrecht wanted her to think he'd thrown away his only advantage. He wanted her to come at him, mouth open. So did the crowd. They made so much noise he couldn't hear anything, not even the woods.

The bear obliged, snarling and bounding. Albrecht reached for his other knife, unfastened the strap, and whipped it from his sleeve. Just before she attacked, she startled and skidded to a stop, as if she'd seen something terrifying behind him.

There was so much noise now, a great churning like the river that rushed down the mountain. As Albrecht brandished his knife, pulse racing, something hit him from behind. He flew forward, glancing off the black bear, grazing her cheek with the tip of his blade. He hurtled, spinning, making a scream he could feel but not hear.

He crashed onto the metal cage floor, skidding until he hit the bars. His vision tunneled. Every inch hurt.

Breathe.

Breathe.

His brain had to remind his body to do this most basic thing, and even then, it felt as though his lungs had been wrapped around his ribs and simply could not expand. His breath, when it came, tasted of blood. He'd bitten the tip of his tongue. He spat, wiped his chin, and then remembered where he was.

With a curse, he stood.

The door of the cage was open. A pile of clothes and a golden crown lay by it. In the distance, he saw two bears, one brown, one black, bounding away. Ursula had made a fool of him in front of the entire kingdom.

People were laughing at him. Even the forest sounded as though it were laughing. Its music had taken on a bright, staccato tone. Albrecht strode to the announcer, whose jaw hung open wide enough that Albrecht wished he still had his knife.

"Give me the coins." Blood droplets flew from his shredded tongue.

"But—" the announcer protested, his face flecked with red.

Albrecht slammed his fist into the man's stomach. The *unnnnh* that followed was exactly what he hoped to hear. He snatched the pouch of gold and stuffed it into the purse at his waistband. He picked up his sister's crown, ignoring the throbbing in his tongue when he bent. Wouldn't Father like to know she'd left it behind like a piece of trash?

Albrecht jumped off the platform, landed gingerly out of habit, and spat a mouthful of blood. As he looked for Ursula, a flash of golden hair caught his eye. Greta, slipping furtively through the crowd. What was she doing out of doors? That was forbidden.

She headed toward the road to the farming district and the forest. She was escaping. Leaving the castle. Leaving *him*. He took a moment to think about what he'd do, which woman he'd pursue.

He turned after Greta. Coiled on the edge of the platform was a rope. He took it. He swallowed the blood in his mouth.

Ursula could wait.

XIV

Ursula and Sabine ran as bears until they reached the abandoned cottage in the woods. They'd been going there for years, tidying the place and making sure creeping vines never fully swallowed the walls. They'd drunk pots of tea there. Eaten bowls of porridge. They'd even stocked it with clothing, blankets, medicine, bandages, and other such things, as if to make it seem less like a hideaway and more like a home.

They shifted to their human forms, and Ursula fetched them clothes. Sabine held her hand to her cheek, and blood oozed between her fingers.

Sabine showed Ursula the cut. "Is it bad?"

Ursula wrapped a blanket around Sabine's shoulders and examined the wound. She never should have let the fight happen. She could have volunteered herself. If the kingdom wanted to watch a man fight a were, why should it not have been her against her brother? But the truth was, it had never occurred to her. She couldn't imagine fighting him. Not for real. Not in front of their people. That wasn't what a prince and princess did.

In failing to do this, she'd failed to act, and Sabine would wear this scar for life.

"Hold still." The gash was deep, but the edges were smooth and would knit neatly. Ursula fetched the medicine kit and unrolled it. She took a bottle of spirits and poured it over her fingertips, cleaning them. Then she offered it to Sabine for a sip. She declined.

"I'm definitely taking a sip after this is done." Ursula dampened a cloth and pressed it into the wound.

Sabine winced but held still.

Ursula's eyebrows drew together as she poured spirits over a needle and threaded it. "Ready?"

Sabine's lips made a teasing smile. "What if I say no?"

"I would probably light a fire, make myself some tea, and watch you bleed to death."

"So no tea for me?"

"No. Gore only."

"In that case, I suppose you may embroider my face."

"Luckily for you, I am very good at stitch craft." Ursula pinched the needle and tried to quell her trembling. Being close to Sabine always made her feel not quite firmly fixed in her own body, neither the human nor the bear version. But being this close? It had never happened in their human form, not in all these years, not at all how Ursula had wanted and imagined it.

She cupped Sabine's uninjured cheek in her left hand and pretended everything was fine. "This will hurt."

"I'm shocked," Sabine said. "The injury itself was such a delight to receive."

"Do I need to sew your mouth shut?" Ursula looked at Sabine's lips. Those lips.

"At this rate," Sabine said, "the cut's going to heal all on its own. Just start. I can take it."

Ursula closed the wound with her left hand. With her right, she pierced Sabine's skin and saw the flash of pain in her eyes. Ursula winced.

How could Albrecht have done this? What had he hoped to achieve? She wouldn't consider the possibility that he'd meant to do more than injure Sabine. Even Albrecht wouldn't be that monstrous. He'd probably been scared. She could smell his fear every time she took her bear form. Sabine was no less fierce a warrior.

She tightened the thread on the first stitch. "Only a few more."

Sabine said nothing. Ursula took the silence as a wish that she hurry, so she did, piercing the skin as swiftly and gently as she could. Soon she forgot that she was so close to Sabine. That her fingers had Sabine's blood on them. That she was causing her pain, even with the intent to heal. She was focused on the wound and what it would take to make it right and nothing else.

She finished. Tied it off. "There. I should probably confess now that I actually can't sew at all."

"I should probably confess now that I'm not surprised. Stitch craft. Honestly."

Ursula set down the needle. She knelt before Sabine, gathering Sabine's hands in hers. She lifted them to her lips. She looked up. Tears spilled onto Sabine's cheeks. Ursula rose and reached for them. With a fingertip, she wiped away one tear, and then the other. And even though there were no more tears to dry, she pressed her hand against Sabine's uninjured cheek. It was so warm. So soft. So dear.

Ursula's breathing changed. It was faster now. Sabine gave her a look that she'd never seen before. At first, Ursula didn't understand it. And then she did. There was an intentness to it. A purpose that was so clear in her deep brown eyes. Ursula's insides sped up. She felt as though she was turning to liquid, threatening to spill.

Sabine leaned forward. "Ursula."

That was all it took. Her name. A request behind it. An invitation. A promise. Their lips touched. Ursula was gentle. She did not wish this, of all things, to hurt.

Ursula was used to transformations. Her body went from bear to human and back all the time. This transformation was something else, something beyond. She'd become lips, hands, a beating heart. She couldn't get close enough to Sabine, not with her mouth, her tongue, or the rest of her body. Was it like this for everyone, this ravenous hunger, or did Ursula's bear senses make everything more acute? She couldn't tell. She had never kissed anyone else, had never wanted to, and never would again.

Sabine cupped her hand behind Ursula's head and Ursula followed suit. She'd always loved Sabine's hair, since the first day she'd seen it, and it felt even more wondrous than she'd imagined, soft and strong at the same time. It was exactly like Sabine.

Time passed, but she couldn't measure it. She could kiss Sabine forever. What she'd imagined for years didn't measure up to what was real, what was happening, what was turning her body into something entirely new. She felt like the night sky, infinite and sparkling with stars. Like something that could hold the entire world in its embrace.

Sabine's hands moved to Ursula's cheeks and then to her hair again, and it felt as though both of her bodies, bear and human, had been awakened for the first time at once. Ursula wanted more. More, more.

But then Sabine pulled away.

Ursula's eyes opened. Sabine's were wide, and she held up a hand.

"Did I hurt you?" Ursula's gaze shot to Sabine's wound. "I—"

"Shh. Listen."

Ursula's senses flooded. She couldn't focus at first. Couldn't hear anything. And then she did. Someone was coming. They were running.

"What do we do?" Sabine had already taken her bear form. Ursula shifted too. When the door swung open, she moved in front of Sabine to protect her. And she growled as though she wanted to rip the high white sun from the sky.

Ursula needed a moment to recognize Greta. She knew her, of course. She'd seen her working in her corner of the kitchen many times since that day in the square. But now it was as though every last scrap of childhood had been carved away by the bladed edge of the world. Her face was bone white, frozen. Ursula backed away, bumping into Sabine as she did.

Sabine took her human form first. Ursula followed, glad Sabine's stitches had held. Greta brandished an enormous knife.

Ursula, not one to be embarrassed by her own nakedness, realized something. "This house. It was yours, wasn't it?"

Greta nodded.

"I didn't know." And that was true, although Ursula could have figured it out, had she thought about it. This made her blush.

"We've been looking after it." Sabine, who'd slipped into a tunic, handed Ursula clothing. "Come in. Sit."

Greta hesitated. Ursula knew that if she had given the invitation, Greta would have come in. But that wasn't how she wanted it to be, with her giving commands that must be obeyed. This was Greta's own house, for goodness' sake. Sometimes the burden of her birthright was more than she could take.

"Greta," Ursula said as she pulled a tunic over her head. "Would you like to come in?"

Greta put the knife in her satchel. Her face was hard to read, but Ursula thought she could understand the calculations behind her eyes. Greta wanted to come in, but she was also afraid. Afraid of Ursula and Sabine. Afraid they would harm her.

Ursula had power. She'd wielded it badly when she didn't insist Hans and Greta be set free that day. She'd been stuck then between pity and the law, and she thought she'd struck a fair balance. She'd been wrong.

"Where's your brother?" she asked.

"I came alone." Greta eyed the satchel over her shoulder. It bulged with food. "I apologize. I shouldn't have . . . I—"

Sabine put an arm around Greta and led her to a chair.

"Here, sit. Rest. You've had a journey." She took the bag and set it on the table. She removed a loaf of bread and some cheese and sliced them both, making a pretty arrangement on a plate.

Leave it to Sabine to know the right thing to do. The human thing to do. She needed Sabine for that. For so much more. It made her want to kiss Sabine all over again. She felt her body start to glow with heat. With pride. Sabine was hers. *Hers.* In every way.

Ursula knew she ought to leave. If she did, Sabine could heal in the safety of the forest. Greta could have company and protection. Neither would have to contend with the presence of someone who complicated everything. Reluctantly, she put on boots. Much as she didn't want to leave, she excused herself, closed the door gently behind her, and walked into the woods.

And that was it. That's what leaders did. The right thing. The difficult thing. The thing they did not want to do. She hoped they understood.

It would be night before long. She needed to return home in time for her father's benediction, which would happen when the moon reached its peak. She needed to make things right with Albrecht too. He'd be angry with her for interfering. But it wouldn't be the first time and it wouldn't be the last time. They were siblings. Twins. And the bond of that blood would bear out always.

XV

Albrecht followed Greta all the way to the cottage in the woods. He'd noticed the place before on hunting trips and such, but he hadn't cared about it. Why take interest in a hovel? If there wasn't game inside, it meant nothing. The place interested him now. He had her cornered.

He was in the midst of planning his attack when Greta opened the door and was met by two bears—Ursula and the black were.

If they killed her, he wouldn't stop them. Greta deserved it for leaving him. What's more, he could use that as justification to slit their throats afterward. He'd say they were on a wilding in the woods, attacking a humble kitchen maid—that he'd had no choice.

The knives in his boots wouldn't have been his preferred weapon to go against a werebear. He'd rather a crossbow. Death from a distance—that was the smart move. But then they became their human selves again, and Greta went inside, closing the door behind her. What now? Surprise them? Accuse them of treason?

That could work. Greta had a knife, and in his experience, the person who carried a weapon intended to use it. He'd have to come up with a plausible story. The perfect idea struck. The three of them were meeting to ensure that weres in the kingdom would become the favored variant under Ursula's reign. Greta's brother was a were. What more incentive did she need? The story would scare people, and people were quick to believe what they feared.

He adjusted the rope on his shoulder and decided he ought to set a snare. It might work, it might not, but when he returned, he could always chase someone into it. Much as he wanted to apprehend Greta, that would be difficult in the presence of two werebears, to put it mildly.

The cottage door opened, and Ursula stepped out. He ducked behind the tree again and watched her stride toward the kingdom, her hair still in childish braids. Had she even realized she'd left her crown behind? Undoubtedly not. Their father would be livid; it had been their mother's, made of gold she'd spun the night before they married. His mother might have been common born, but her magical gift meant she was worthy of being queen. For Ursula to be reckless with this proved she was not.

He followed, walking quietly like the hunter he was. She went east instead of passing through the frisser row. It didn't surprise him. Most of the cages would be empty because everyone was enjoying the most raucous part of the Moon Festival—when the moon hit its apex. From that point until dawn, all were feasting and drinking and watching the frissers change and run wild through the kingdom on the one day a year it was permitted.

She carried her head at a surprising angle, and it struck him: She knew he was behind her. He coughed.

She turned, arms crossed. "It's rude to follow people."

"I only just now saw you," he lied. "I wanted to clear my head."

"How's your tongue?"

"It doesn't bother me." And it was true. He had a high threshold for pain. It still smarted, but Ursula's intervention and Greta's abandonment hurt far worse. The tongue would heal on its own. Those wounds would heal only with vengeance.

He kept his distance as they walked toward home. His anger made it hard for him to be near her and remain calm.

"Albrecht," she said. Her voice was soft. Weak, even.

He left her opening unanswered. She glanced at the sky, no doubt assessing how much time they had. She probably itched to let out the beast inside her.

"It was wrong, what you did," she said. "I was trying to spare you from a mistake you could not recover from."

"What mistake was that?"

"Killing a were. Those fights aren't ever to the death. We don't want any of our people to think of you as unjust, or worse, a beast. You're the *prince*."

"You know better than anyone that frissers aren't fully human. Each of you literally contains a beast, and you're accusing *me* of being one."

"Albrecht. That's cruel. I'm your sister, not a beast. And I will be your queen. You and I must be loyal to each other."

"You don't even think about the kingdom."

"That's not true."

He scoffed. She'd left her crown behind. What better evidence did he need? They stood at the drawbridge, where the crowd would flow as soon as the castle bells were rung, where their father would join them soon. It was a beautiful place always, but especially after nightfall of a Moon Festival, where reflected white light turned the moat into an enormous mirror.

"Sabine is my *friend*, Albrecht. I couldn't let you hurt her."

"I'd say you're more than friends." He'd seen the look the frisser had given her. They cared for each other. How would a frisser on the throne and another as a queen's consort look? Terrible. It would destroy the kingdom. Destroy its history. Its heritage. It was bad enough that Ursula had forced her way out of the womb first, upending the proper order. This development would end the world as they knew it.

"Time to put on our crowns, sister."

Ursula brought her hand to her forehead. "Oh no."

"You haven't lost it, have you? There's a lot of history in that crown. You might say it's one of the most valuable objects in existence, a symbol of the kingdom itself. Pity." He pulled his own out of his purse and arranged it on his brow. "Look, here comes Father now."

The king walked slowly, supported by guards at each elbow. His skin was slack and pale, and his silver mane limp, but his eyes were sharp.

"Ursula, what on earth are you wearing?" the king said. "And where's your mother's crown?"

"She left it behind at the fighting cage, Father," Albrecht said. "But it's all right. I took care of it for her." He produced it. Ursula seethed beside him. He could practically feel her anger.

"Come to my chambers after my speech," Father said, coughing into his fist. "I have something to tell you both."

~~~~~

When they arrived at their father's chambers later that night, the king waved them in. His hands and ankles were so swollen they looked as though a well-placed thorn would rupture them.

"Sit, sit," the king said.

Albrecht took the chair across the fire from his father. It was too hot there, but this chair was the better one. Ursula was left with the smaller one.

She didn't even look at Albrecht, so he knew he'd gotten under her skin.

"It's a fine thing I took care of Ursula's crown, wouldn't you—" Albrecht stopped when his father held up his hand.

"I'm tired, Albrecht. Enough. I have a story for you both."

A story. His father and his stories. He knew the reason for them: To test his potential. To gauge how he'd rule. It should have been clear by now what kind of king he'd be. Decisive. Strong. Exactly what the people needed. He'd look after the crown and what it represented, unlike his sister, who sat at attention. Albrecht suspected she *liked* these stories, even if she invariably got the meaning of them upside down.

"There once was a king who lost his wife," Tyran said.

And he had a son and a daughter, Albrecht thought. *The son was meant to be the king.* He glanced at Ursula. Her expression was hard to read, but Albrecht suspected she was nervous. As she should be.

"The wife had a sister," Tyran said.

So much for Albrecht's theory that his father was finally telling the story of their family. His mother had no sister.

"The wife had a sister, and the king invited her into his bed. He'd been lonely. He missed his wife, and of all the people left on earth, the sister was the one most like her.

"But she refused the king, and he felt as though his heart had been sliced out by her tongue. In return he took her hands. She wept and held the stumps up to him, and he showed her mercy. He replaced her hands with ones made of gold from his late wife's dowry.

"The king set a wedding date, but when the day came, the sister was nowhere to be found. Her window, which was above the sea, had been left open. They found her body on the shore, drowned by the weight of her hands. The king took them back, and every night after that slept with the golden hands in his.

"Ursula, your thoughts."

"The tale is tragic," she said. "The woman lost her sister and then she lost her hands and then she lost her life."

"The story is not about the woman at all," Albrecht said, "except insofar as she suffered for being disrespectful to the king, who'd just lost his queen."

Ursula scoffed. "A woman is allowed to refuse a man, is she not?"

"She is not allowed to refuse a king. Otherwise he is not king. And nowhere in Father's story did it say that the king had been to blame for the death of his wife, so if we are talking about those who have lost something, the king is the only one in the story who is blameless, the only one to have lost something through no fault of his own."

"You have both made excellent points." The king coughed, a long, rattling sound. He caught his breath. "I have made a decision."

Albrecht's mouth went dry. Ursula sat straight in her chair, expressionless.

"Your sister is the firstborn."

"And I am the man," Albrecht said. "And there has never been a frisser on the throne."

His father waved his hand and coughed again. "Yes, yes, as you have said many times."

There was only one logical argument about succession. Albrecht was the male heir. He was the full human. A natural-born leader. Strong and canny enough to protect the people of the kingdom. He ran his wounded tongue against his teeth so that he'd have something else to think about besides his dense father and overly ambitious sister.

"In light of the time I have left, and in light of certain traditions, I have determined what is to become of my throne."

Albrecht's heart lightened. Traditions. Maybe all was not lost. After all, it had been their mother, a commoner, who wished for Ursula to take the throne. She was dead and so were her wishes.

His father wrapped his ringed fingers around the arms of his chair. The jewels caught the light of the fireplace.

"Take a knee, Albrecht," his father said.

Albrecht couldn't breathe. He did as his father commanded.

"You too, Ursula."

Albrecht started and Ursula caught his gaze. She clearly had no more idea what was going to happen than he did.

The king reached for a sword leaning against his chair. He touched it to Albrecht's left shoulder, and then his right.

"You shall be the king of the East."

Then two wobbly taps on Ursula's shoulders. "While you are the queen of the West."

Albrecht looked up. King of the East? Queen of the West?

"I have split the kingdom in two," the king said, laying the blade across his lap. "From the forest to the farm district, including the frisser row, is Ursula's. Albrecht will rule the merchants and tradesmen. Your kingdoms"— he coughed into his hand, which came away bloody—"your kingdoms will be allies, dependent on each other."

"Thank you, Father. You are wise and just," Ursula said.

Albrecht couldn't feel his arms or his legs. This was ludicrous. An injustice. A betrayal, not just of him, but of the people of the kingdom. While the king lived, there was nothing to be done to change it. His word was law.

Albrecht clenched his jaw. Swallowed. He would master his rage for now.

His father leaned back. He looked spent. His eyelids drooped.

"Is that all?" Albrecht said.

His father's eyes opened. He looked displeased. Albrecht didn't care. His sister, the flatterer, stood and kissed their father's forehead.

"You may go." The old king bent double and coughed.

The new king and queen did as they were told. They did not look at each other. They did not speak until they reached the top of the tower, where their chambers were.

"Good night, Albrecht," she said. "Let us discuss this decision tomorrow. We can make plans and share them with Father."

He grunted. His tongue hurt again, and he decided she'd have to be satisfied with a sound that she could interpret however she wished. He had more important work to do than talking, namely locking Hans in the dungeon.

It would be a shame to be without his assistant, of course. But he needed to make sure that the werewolf did not leave the way Greta had.

There would be work for him later, a great deal of it.

XVI

King Tyran sat in front of the fireplace.

My boy, my beautiful boy. Golden hair, blue eyes. Tyran often thought that if he'd been the initial sketch for a masterpiece, Albrecht was the final work. Everything about the young man was bigger and bolder, like a sun that had burned through the morning's gauze of clouds. His hair so thick and shining. His eyes so pale blue they were almost white.

Though he was not yet done growing, he was already taller than most men. He could outshoot them with his crossbow. Disarm them of their swords.

And the things he built . . . The bridge monkeys! The clockwork swans in the garden! The room with the false floor! He'd made the castle a wonder. Albrecht was a fine man. The finest of men. Yes, his son would be a good king. Had he not loved his wife so much, he might have given Albrecht the entire kingdom.

But he'd surprised himself by also loving his daughter from her first breath, and he had not stopped when her dual nature was revealed. He knew there was still time to civilize her, and he would help by giving her the portions of the kingdom that were soft and wild. The farmland. Was she not a ripe young thing herself? A field to be plowed? And then the forest too. Did she not love the music of it? Did a bear not need land to roam?

She would be a fine queen and had, after all, been the firstborn. She was intelligent and paid close attention to what her instructors had taught her. And she'd kept the bear in control so that she didn't embarrass the family. She'd done well enough at that. And she could fight. He'd had to put an end to her sparring with her brother to save the boy's dignity. Ursula was worthy. That business with the crown—that was unlike her. Most likely that was due to Albrecht's shenanigans.

Ah, his children. He knew their ways. He'd loved them as well as he could. The decision was a good one. He was certain.

Tyran had never been this tired. Tired in his mind, his bones, his flesh. Tired of pissing blood. Tired of coughing it up. There had been so much lately. He felt like he was becoming a woman in his last days, oozing red from every orifice. It struck him as an undignified end, this leakage; but then, his feelings about it didn't matter. Feelings never did. He was the king, and if this is how his body was going to cease its business, on a tide of red, then so be it.

The more he thought about it, the more it felt a fitting way to go. Warriors rode the river of blood to the beyond, did they not? So would he, and not at the hands of any enemy but time. He wanted to write these last thoughts, capture them, that a bit of himself might live on. He gripped the arms of his chair and stood, swaying on the soft tree trunks his legs had become.

The window framed a black sky above an even blacker smudge of forest. And there was the moon, perfect and round, the crisp white eye that gazed unblinking on kings throughout time. Tyran could scarcely see his hands in front of him and suspected it was not just because the hour was late. The horizon inside him had swallowed his light too.

He eased off his rings. The metal was rough from where he'd coughed on them, rough where the blood had devoured the gold. Then he lowered himself into his chair, opened a book, and dipped a quill in the ink pot.

The king departed on a river of blood.

Spent, he set down his pen and leaned back. His life was ending. His story was ending.

And his children ruled side by side, happily ever after.

It had been a perfect solution, one that arrived in a dream: His wife was still alive, wearing her dress from their wedding day. She was young again and laughing. She'd taken an apple in her hands and split it in two, a trick she'd loved performing when the children were young. She held out the two halves to him, and he awoke with a gasp that turned into a terrible coughing fit.

But that had been it. The solution. All would be well.

Tyran closed his eyes. He wanted to see his wife again. He wanted to inhale the scent of her. To feel the softness of her body against his. His lips parted. Something warm and wet issued from his mouth. More blood.

The darkness was complete now, even after Tyran opened his eyes one last time. He could smell the fire, the scent of centuries of growth being reduced to ash. He could hear the pop of wood—the protest against this indignity. It struck him as funny, that he had become so like a log, bloated and inert. So many years, so swiftly erased.

The king sighed, a single note, the last of a song. Then he was gone.

He never did learn who'd made all his gold.

A woman approaches the storyteller. He can smell her. He can hear her quiet breathing. The rustle of her skirt in the breeze. Everything about her seems soft and pliable, like warm bread.

"Come closer," he says. "There's nothing to fear."

She clears her throat. It is a delicate sound, and he imagines her white neck. Her tongue, her teeth, her rose-petal lips. He wants to ask her what color her hair is. Gold, he hopes, and long.

There is a shuffling. Feet against sand-covered stone. She is closer now. Not close enough to touch, but it will do.

"Once upon a time, there was a golden-haired girl who was told to stay on the path," he says. "Would you like to hear what happened when she left it?"

The woman hesitates. She is licking her lips, he imagines.

"The girl was given a basket of food: bread, meat, crisp apples, soft cheeses. Her mother wrapped her cloak around her shoulders and warned her: 'Stay on the path. There are wolves in the woods.'

"But the girl did not stay on the path. Not long after that, she encountered a wolf."

The woman gasps. He wants to be the air in her lungs, feeding the blood that travels through her red insides all the way to her heart.

Others join the woman. They too are hungry for a bite of story. They shuffle close. Touch shoulders. But he speaks for the benefit of the woman and the woman alone.

He wants her ears. He wants to make her feel things. He wants to change the rhythm of her heart and lungs. He wants to write his breath into her memory.

So he tells her what the wolf did to the girl. What he did to the food in the basket she carried.

"Wolves devour," he tells her. He is generous with the details.

"And this is why you must stay on the path. Or better yet, avoid the woods altogether."

PART
THREE

XVII

The new kingdoms, cheek by jowl, were half circles, with the winter castle at the east end and a smaller, less fortified summer castle in the west. Stone mountains rose behind Albrecht's castle, hard and high enough to sometimes pierce the clouds. The singing forest wrapped around Ursula's portion of the kingdom. Beyond lay other lands. Distant. No more a part of daily life than dreams.

The dead king's body was burned at the spot where the two kingdoms met, the center of a curving stone bridge that had guardhouses on each side. Below, the silvery river rushed by, turning autumn sunlight into bits of glass. Albrecht's clockwork monkeys squatted on the railing. Had they been wound, they would have jeered at the spectacle. In their silent state, their open mouths made them look as though they too wailed in grief.

People from both sides of the kingdom solemnly watched the body burn, the farmers and weres from the west and the merchants and tradespeople from the east. Between them, the smoke rose, a black finger scratching the blue sky. Together, the people said farewell to their king. They stood along the streets quietly, whether exhausted from the Moon Festival or stilled by grief, Ursula could not say.

She couldn't find Sabine. She was disappointed but not surprised. Sabine was most likely still in the cottage with Greta. Meanwhile, Albrecht stood beside her, his feet stepping on the long shadow she cast across the cobbles.

He nudged her ribs. "Where's your favorite bear?"

Two could play at that game. "Where's Hans?"

"My dog? He's working, as usual." Albrecht was lying. She could tell. But it was a strange thing to lie about.

Around his neck hung a lion mask made of golden metal, a nod to their father. The mask had a hinged jaw and teeth that looked entirely real. They probably were. He was good at making such things. Rumor had it he was working on an army of metal soldiers, a way to keep the kingdom secure without risking the lives of any men. That felt hopeful to her—something that would benefit all their citizens.

It made her uneasy. People admired her brother. It was easy to see. They listened to him, as much for the beauty of his voice as for the substance of his speech. He had a confidence that she didn't, a certainty that let him do things like imagine a device that did not exist and then build it with his own hands. It was as though he knew how to make his own space in the world while she only could only follow the path set forth by lessons she'd been given.

He might be a fine king after all. She'd always dismissed this possibility. She was firstborn. He was flawed. She was to inherit; that was that. He'd protested, but she had set that aside as envy. Maybe she'd always feared that he'd make a better ruler. He was just so *commanding*.

Still, she'd never wavered in her desire to be queen, and she had every intention of being a great one. And now this. She was queen of half, ruling alongside her brother. And if he proved to be the better ruler, what then? Would she retain her throne because it was what she'd always wanted, or would she reunite the kingdom for the good of the people?

She had no answer. But she said to her brother, "Father divided the kingdom and made us dependent on each other, that we might always have peace between us. A treaty will formalize our close relationship. And I am all in favor of this, even as I am firstborn. I see wisdom in his choice, surprising as it was."

Albrecht looked at her and Ursula felt a sudden ache. They were orphans now. He put his hand on her shoulder. It felt heavy, hard.

"Later, sister. For now, let us focus on what we must do."

When the fire burned down, they split their father's ashes. Each received a golden bowlful. Ursula dipped her hand in deep, scattering hot plumes of it into the air over her kingdom. Some of the ashes flared red on the currents of wind, flame blossoms spiraling through the darkness. She wanted them to travel all over, returning her father to the place he'd ruled, the land he'd loved, so that his remains could nourish the soil.

"Should we sing the dirge?" she asked.

Albrecht scoffed. "That's for peasants."

He flung his portion of the ashes quickly, perfunctorily, as if the pain were nothing. He finished before she did, and he rubbed the last of their father's remains on his cloak. He looked as though he'd wiped away tears too; ashes streaked his cheeks.

Ursula knew better than to speak. Albrecht wouldn't want to be caught feeling emotion, and even though he wasn't as good about concealing his pain as he thought he was, there was no need to antagonize him.

She felt an urge to embrace him.

But he was too far away. One by one, he wound his mechanical monkeys, and they clicked into action. They shrieked and clapped, and Albrecht raised his lion mask to his face and headed away from her.

Ursula hesitated. The air tasted of ash, and the monkeys' metallic voices scraped like metal against stone. But her brother didn't give so much as a backward glance, so she walked toward her castle, on feet that did not feel quite her own.

She would call on him later, when he'd gotten his bearings. Then they'd forge their pact.

⟜⟞

At the summer castle, a group of servants fussed over Ursula. She tried to summon all their names but couldn't. There were so many of them.

"Forgive me," she said. "My mind has been much occupied."

As she soaked in a tub of hot water, being scrubbed clean by two maidservants, she wondered where the guards were. She did not begrudge them taking part in the king's funeral, even as it would have been safer for the women left behind to have protection. She would speak to the men in the morning. In the meantime, she was protection enough.

She glanced at the high ceiling of the castle, which had stood for generations. It had always been her favorite place to stay each summer. She loved its huge timbers and its windows that could open to the clean air blowing from the woods. She felt lucky that it was hers. Lucky to be the queen of the West, lucky to look after the farmers and the forest. She wanted to share it all with Sabine. She ached to see her again. Her first act would be to free the werefolk from the ghetto. They could sleep anywhere they wished on her side of the kingdom. This meant that Sabine could sleep with her. Her skin grew hot at the thought of it, at the memory of their kiss.

After she was dried and dressed in her nightclothes, Ursula looked at the cage she'd once slept in during summers at the castle. The room also held an enormous, richly dressed bed. She decided that's where she would sleep.

Cages were for animals, and as long as she had power, werefolk were not animals. She climbed into the bed and pulled the silky covers to her chin, marveling at how strange it felt to have so much ceiling soaring overhead. She'd grown used to a cage. This would take some adjusting.

As she struggled to fall asleep, she reviewed her more serious memories of the day. She didn't like the way she and Albrecht had parted. He'd never been good at managing his emotional side. His surliness might have been a surplus of feelings he couldn't handle.

She thought about the treaty. Her highest priority was making sure trade deals were fair. Her farmers would need tools and such in order to grow food and raise livestock, and if the prices for tools were too dear, they'd have to sell too much of their harvest, which would mean they'd go hungry. She'd make sure Albrecht understood such things. And of course, the weres. She wanted him to lift restrictions in the East too. He'd see. It would be better for everyone.

As she rolled to her side, clutching the blanket, a sound distracted her. At first, she assumed it was somehow related to her father's memorial. But these weren't revelers. She caught a whiff of smoke and sat with a start. She ran to the window and opened it wide.

Her queendom was burning.

XVIII

For his fourteenth birthday, Prince Albrecht had received a mirror that Jutta crafted with his mother's gold. It was large and ornate, and he loved regarding himself naked in the quicksilvered glass. He took pleasure in the curves of his chest muscles. The plumpness of his biceps and buttocks. The glory of his legs. His favorite tree, the one that grew between his legs, was a thing of wonder.

Now, for the first time, he regarded himself in his mirror as the king. Not of the whole kingdom, as he should have been, but of the better half. The one where things were made by men, and because of this, the one that would annex the other before too much time had passed.

He'd taken his father's suite of rooms as soon as the body had been carried away. The first thing he set up was the mirror, which he'd long made a habit of speaking to as though it might answer back. It didn't, of course, although he could easily imagine a feminine tale of vanity taking place before just such an enchanted glass. His conversations with it were a way for him to practice how he looked when he spoke. To hone his expressions and gestures. This was part of the power of kings: looking right for the role. And it was something Ursula would never be able to do.

She was impressively large, yes, but there was no disguising the fact that she was neither a man nor exclusively human. Everyone knew she was a werebear, and while this was amusing in a princess because of its novelty, it was hardly the right thing for a ruler.

"Unity!" Albrecht said to the mirror.

He'd already decided this would be the phrase he'd use to excite his men. It was simple. Easy to remember. It sounded good and right. And if blood had to be spilled, well, sometimes a man had to split bodies to restore a sundered kingdom.

He kept looking around him for Hans. Curiously, he missed the were. His quiet intensity. His competence. His solemn demeanor. But needs must. It was a shame Hans had to be locked up with only rats for companions, but it wouldn't be forever, just to keep him safe. What's more, the boy was used to handling rats. They'd keep him company, and if he got hungry, he could always eat them.

To calm his mind and occupy his hands before he addressed his guard, Albrecht decided to tinker with a trap he'd been working on, a small iron box with a heavy blade inside that dropped as soon as a rodent crawled in. So far, results had been messy. Albrecht hated a mess almost as much as he hated rats.

He dismantled the box and removed the blade. Too heavy meant it would be too thick to achieve a quick cut; too thin meant it wouldn't sink into anything with more give than a worm. He decided to try a thin blade that had been weighted. Then he fitted it into the box and baited the trap using a piece of his own dinner. He poked the meat into the mouth of the box. He felt a sudden burning, a pain so deep it pounded behind his eyes. He pulled out his hand. Half of his index finger was gone.

The wound at first was dry and deep red. He could see bone. Blood welled. He couldn't stop the flow. Astonishing. The stump throbbed, and soon his hand was gloved in blood. He heated another blade and pressed the hot metal against his stump again and again, dizzy with sensation. When he'd cauterized the wound, he removed the blade. He was sweaty, the air smelled of cooked meat, and he wanted to vomit, but he resisted. Pain was life. He'd just become its master.

He regarded his not-finger, thinking about all the ways it would inconvenience him. Unless . . . Unless he could design himself a new one. Jutta would make it. Or Hans. Meanwhile, the wound would be useful. He would claim that Ursula had attacked him. Yes, she'd attacked him in his own room using a piece of glass from the mirror. She'd informed him that her kingdom would invade his, and that she herself would command an army of weres that had been trained to tear out the throats of children. They intended to establish supremacy for werefolk.

He laughed. This accident was a gift. A gift from Fate, who was making clear her desire that Albrecht restore the proper order to the world. With his intact hand, Albrecht pitched the trap at his mirror. It shattered, and now each piece held a reflection of him, as though he'd been multiplied.

Albrecht retrieved his severed finger. The first casualty of the Great Were War. He set it aside and sketched notions for a better finger than the one nature had given him. The ideas came faster than blood flow, and one by one, he pumped them into his book of devices, ignoring the pounding ache of the wound.

With the music of the woods as a backdrop, King Albrecht—*I am king!*—worked until the darkest part of the night arrived.

And then, his stump throbbing, he rallied his men.

XIX

Night fell quickly, and Sabine stopped by the cages to make sure the children had been fed and were ready to sleep. They'd been up late for the Moon Festival and would have catching up to do.

"Nicola! Marceline! Luna!" The three little weregoats were her favorites to wrangle, not that she would ever admit it. And not that she was any less fond of the fox brothers and the quiet little raccoon twins. But Nicola followed her everywhere, and even as a human, butted her head against Sabine's legs in a way that made her feel fiercely protective love.

"Did you eat?" Sabine asked.

"Yes!" the goats said, three voices braiding into one.

"Not enough," said the fox named Sebastian.

"You ate half of mine," his brother, Simon, said.

"I was hungry!" They started swatting each other until Sabine peeled them apart and sat cross-legged in the grass, putting one boy on each knee.

"Will you tell us a story?" Luna asked.

Sabine's heart sank a little bit. She wasn't much for stories. She'd heard them told, but they were never about the likes of her. If there was a bear in a story, it was an animal. Dangerous. She knew that children liked them, but she couldn't even think of how to tell one. She was only ever able to think of true things that had happened to her, which she'd disguise a bit and pass them off.

"Once there was a girl," she said.

"Why is it always a girl?" Simon complained.

"It isn't always," Nicola said. "Sometimes there's a boy. Sometimes a girl. Sometimes both. Sometimes neither."

"Do you want a story or not?" Sabine said.

The children stopped their squabbling, and Sabine told them about a bear who kissed a princess and then turned into a puff of smoke.

"Did she ever turn back?" Nicola asked.

Sabine shook her head.

"Ugh, I hate that story," Marceline said.

Sabine laughed. "It's not my favorite either. But every time you smell smoke, you know the bear is near. She'll always keep you safe."

"I guess," Nicola said.

"Bedtime, children." Sabine slid the droopy-headed fox boys off her lap and led them one by one to their cages. As much as she hated locking them in, she was also resolved to do so on a night like this. There were always men in the world who thought it great sport to threaten and harass weres. The cages kept children imprisoned, but they also kept those men away from them.

When she'd turned the last key and blown the last kiss, she headed into the kingdom itself, keeping to the darkest shadows. She'd watched Ursula and her brother on the bridge after the ceremony. Sabine had been tempted to follow Ursula back to her castle, but she knew she couldn't. Not after what had happened in the woods. She'd left the cottage not long after Ursula, noting the first yellows and reds of fall had found the edges of the leaves. They looked like fire. She felt on fire. Her face where Albrecht had cut her burned. Her lips, her skin, everywhere Ursula had touched. Fire burned. Fire destroyed.

Sabine had known it would be this way. It was one reason she hadn't kissed Ursula before. She'd kissed other girls, some were, some single aspect. She didn't love any of them, even though she loved kissing. The taste of it. The softness. The way she could breathe in someone else's breath, feeling them and their singularity from the deepest part of her. No two people kissed alike. No two people tasted alike. And she liked how it made her feel, outside and in. There had been no risk to kissing these girls. Some she knew, some she didn't, not really. But it was always understood between them that those kisses were petals plucked, not seeds planted.

That was not how she felt about Ursula, and she'd had years to work it out. Years since that day they'd met. Since she'd mortified herself by putting on the dress and shoes of a princess, pretending to be one. She knew better, even then. The pretty dress was a distraction, the thing meant to take your eyes off the ugly truth. Everything wrong about the world came from that very place Ursula lived. The very thing Ursula was. There could be no justice in a world ruled by a single person, a single family. That was the world that sent weres to cages. The world that tore families apart.

Sabine could barely remember life before her first cage. She was lucky; most weres couldn't remember any. But Sabine had been older. Her parents had come as merchants from afar. They'd refused to cage Sabine. And before the family could leave, her parents had been taken. To the dungeon, she now knew. She waited for them to come for her. That had been the last thing her mother had said to her. A promise. *We'll see you soon.*

Sabine had to stop walking. Had to catch her breath. She put her hands on her knees and waited until the feeling of falling passed. None of that was Ursula's fault. Ursula was a baby when it happened, even younger than Sabine. But it was the world Ursula was born into. A world Ursula accepted. A world Ursula believed in.

It would have been easier had Sabine not been in love with her. Had she never kissed her. But now that she had, it felt like another promise waiting to be broken.

Hood up and head down so that no one would get a good look at her eyes, she slipped into a tavern. It smelled of sweat, ale, smoke, and men. She wasn't worried. Anyone who noticed her, who threatened or harassed her for being a were, would soon regret it. She never made trouble herself. Nor did she flee in the face of it.

She sat sipping a cider and eavesdropping, and as the night wore on, learned what she was after. The kingdom was split. Ursula would rule the west and Albrecht, the east. Sabine fought an impulse to leave right then and console Ursula, who had to be disappointed at the news. But she resisted. If she sat at Ursula's table and shared a meal, if she went into Ursula's cage and held her close all night, she would lose herself. Her integrity. Her belief that a better world was one without a crown.

Ursula was her best friend. The person she loved. But she couldn't have her without losing her soul. And as much as it hurt to live with the memory of that kiss, she had it. She would always have it. A scar no one but she could see, running all the way around her heart.

She finished her drink and was about to leave when a man burst in, his face flushed in excitement. The king was gathering forces, he announced. Rallying men to unify the kingdom behind him. He had weapons. Was promising gold. And was saying things that Sabine knew could not be true . . . that Ursula had plans to give special privileges to werefolk. To lift them up above single-aspect humans. Never once had Ursula said anything of the sort. She'd said she didn't want to separate families anymore, but that was hardly a privilege.

When Sabine realized she was gripping her stein so tight her fingers hurt, she pushed it away, stood, and headed toward the door.

"Where do you think you're going?" A man moved in front of her, large with hands the size of loaves.

Someone behind her pulled down her hood.

Another leaned close, noting the rings around her irises. "Would you look at the frisser trying to sneak out of here."

"Let me pass," she said. "I've done you no wrong."

"The wrong's that you exist in the first place," Bread Hands said.

"Look at its face," another man said. "That's the one the king was about to kill. Should we finish the job?"

"We should bring it to him. A gift," Bread Hands said.

She shoved past him, trying to make it through the door. "Let me go."

And then there was laughter, and hands on her, and they were not gentle, and she pushed her way through the doorway and into the night. In the cold air, beneath the plump moon, she let out the bear. Her clothing ripped. Her shoes fell away. She eyed the men who'd followed and surrounded her, deciding which was closest to her size. She'd save him for last and take his clothes.

It took longer than she thought, fighting each man who dared step out of that pub. She was surprised they kept coming at her, surprised that every last one of them thought he'd be the one to defeat her. It was funny and it was irritating. Could they not see who she was? What she was capable of? Did they really think their tiny man hands were a match for her paws?

They did.

She showed them otherwise. As she dressed in the clothing of the last man she'd fought, she caught a whiff of smoke. It made her think of Ursula. Made her think the story she'd told the children had become true. The scent thickened and she knew it was no figment of a story visiting. The kingdom was burning. She stepped out of the clothes she'd just taken and took her bear form once more.

The farm district was engulfed by the time she reached it. Ursula's castle too. Sabine stood in the darkness watching it, terrified Ursula was inside. If she was, she was lost. Sabine couldn't imagine that had happened. Ursula was too capable. The mere thought of a world without Ursula was also unimaginable. That would be a world without the sky. It would come undone.

Sabine turned around to check on the children. The cages of the adult weres stood empty, every last one. No doubt all had gone to fight, even the elders. The children remained in theirs, sleeping deeply the way only the very young can do. She wanted to take them someplace safe, but she didn't know where that was. The forest, probably.

But for now, as much as it sickened her, they were better off in their cages. She left them behind for the time being. She'd return for them after she fought off Albrecht's men. Their cries for unity were lies. They didn't want unity. They wanted the end of weres. She wouldn't fight for a throne or anyone sitting on one, not even Ursula. But for her people? She'd lay down her life. She filled her lungs with air that tasted of smoke and ash. And then she ran toward the fray.

XX

The dungeon was a garden of bones. They lay on the damp stone floors. Skulls and ribs and femurs of the people who'd refused to give up their were-children. Hans touched some and found them roughened by the sharp teeth of rats. He didn't blame them. They'd done what they needed to survive.

He'd done the same to keep Greta alive. He'd done everything Albrecht ordered, withstood every torture, stayed alive himself to protect her. Now that she'd left the castle, he could stop living if he wanted to. He was so tired. So broken.

And she was free. Albrecht had told him as much after he'd pulled Hans from his cage, pummeling him.

Why did she leave?

Did you know she was planning this?

Do you know what I'll do when I get her?

Hans had used Cappella's cloak to shield himself. He'd held on to it as Albrecht dragged him to the dungeon. He wrapped himself tighter in it now, just as he had the first day he came to the castle. It didn't feel quite real that Greta had left without him. She might have thought he was safer working for Prince Albrecht. Or worse, that he'd come around to Albrecht's side. That he liked it. He felt sick as he realized what it must have looked like to see him standing quietly behind the prince, never saying a word.

He should have said something. Sent word somehow, just to let her know he was still Hans. Still her brother. That he still remembered their promise to take care of each other.

He leaned against the stone wall, the cloak around his shoulders. Time passed, minutes, and then hours. He listened to the muted forest song and thought of what it had been like to live there, breathing music, growing up beside Cappella. He wondered whether he and Cappella would have been friends had she known he was more than a wolf. Whether she could have come to his house and shared soup and bread and conversation by a crackling fire.

Then it struck him that Albrecht hadn't said "when I *find* her." He'd said "when I get her." That meant Albrecht knew where Greta had gone. She'd gone home; it's what he would have done. That meant she wasn't safe, after all.

Hans cursed and threw himself against the wooden door. He felt for the keyhole, but his finger was too big. He groped around on the floor and found a bone. It broke off as soon as he wiggled it in the lock.

Enraged and desperate, he removed his clothing and welcomed the wolf. Immediately certain senses bloomed. Smell. Hearing. He began gnawing at the door. He gnawed until his gums bled, taking breaks only to pull the splinters from his lips.

There were more rats around him than he'd realized. It was easy for them to slip through the space beneath the door, and for the first time, he wished that he had a rat aspect instead of a wolf one.

He'd always been proud to be a wolf. Big and strong, with mighty claws and teeth. But it was his very size that was keeping him captive now. So much for brute strength. There was always something in the world more brutal.

He could tell the rats in his cell were curious about what he was doing. So he told them while he took breaks. It made him feel good to have someone to talk to. He liked the way it felt when their noses prodded his fur. He nosed them back.

He told them everything. About his parents. About his sister. About Cappella, and how he'd wished he'd been his human self with her, even if it was only once. He'd told her he loved her in his wolfish way, bumping his head into her forehead, leaning against her. But to say it as a human would have been something else. He'd never had the courage; he'd forever have regret.

And as he thought of regrets, he apologized to the rats for what he'd done to them. What he'd failed to protect them from. Never again would he consent to do that which he knew was wrong.

Hours after he began, he still wasn't through. He wanted to close his eyes and wish for death. But where would that leave Greta? As soon as he could, he resumed his labors. When the moon was at its highest point in the sky, when he could feel its pull on him the most powerfully, he finally broke through. His paws and mouth dripped blood. He craved food. Water. Rest. But Greta was in danger.

He snatched the cloak with his bleeding mouth and fled.

XXI

Cappella had watched the king's body burn. She hadn't known it, though. She'd smelled smoke, climbed a tree, and reported to her mother that the there was a fire on the bridge and everyone in the kingdom was watching.

"What happens in the kingdom is nothing that concerns us, Pella."

It was the answer she always gave. Where this used to frustrate Cappella, now it angered her. She didn't know what to do with this feeling or how to make it go away.

Even though Cappella was grown—as tall as her mother—she knew nothing beyond life in the woods. She'd never been allowed out. Never ventured into the kingdom. Never had so much as a friend, not since her wolf had vanished.

As much as she loved her mother and living in a forest of music, she wanted to know things. Have friends. Understand the wider world, not pretend it didn't exist. Her mother had kept secrets. She'd once lived in the kingdom, and that's why Cappella wasn't to go there.

For years, Cappella had accepted this limit. Accepted the idea that it didn't concern them. But she didn't accept that anymore. Whatever was happening in the kingdom *did* concern her. If it didn't, then Cappella wouldn't have questions. Her mother wouldn't need to lie. The truth became pebble plain: There were things her mother didn't *want* her to know. She was hiding something. She'd *always* been hiding something.

Cappella could pretend this wasn't the case, as she'd pretended her wolf hadn't died and was instead roaming another forest happily. But she didn't want to. The absence of truth felt like a wall between her and Esme. It meant her mother didn't trust Cappella to know the facts. Either something terrible had happened, or her mother had done something terrible. Possibly both.

"You're lying to me." The words were out before Cappella could really consider them, before she could find a better way to phrase things. "You know what's happened. You know why the air smells of smoke. Why the citizens have lined the streets."

"Cappella." The way her mother said her name, it sounded like a scolding. A rebuke. Esme said nothing for quite a while as she dropped nuts into her basket. When she spoke again, her voice was harsh. "You're not being fair to me. I've given you everything I have, everything you could ever want. I've loved you the best way I know how. Aren't you happy?"

"You're keeping things from me. How can I be happy knowing that?"

"I hide nothing from you. You see me every day. You have for your entire life."

"Why am I not to step foot into the kingdom?"

"Because it's dangerous."

"If it's so dangerous, why do I see so many girls my age there?"

"Because their parents aren't as careful as I am."

"Their parents. All right, then, who's my father?"

"You don't have— There isn't one."

That had to be a lie too, but she could not say those words out loud. Not without wanting to leave her mother forever. She took a breath. "Who are *your* parents?"

"Dead."

"Do you have a brother? A sister?"

Her mother didn't answer right away, and Cappella knew that she'd hit a vein of truth. "How could it possibly hurt anything if you told me about our family?"

"I had—I have a sister," her mother said. "Your aunt."

"Why have I never met her? Does she have children?"

"Come, it is getting late," her mother said. "Let us talk about this in the morning."

That was what her mother so often did. Put things off for later. This time Cappella didn't want to. Maybe it was the effect of the rising moon, one night past full. Maybe it was the smell of smoke. The ringing of the bell at the castle. She was going to keep asking questions. She was going to get to the truth.

"What if I told you I wanted to meet my aunt?"

"It's not possible," her mother said.

"Why? Did you do something terrible?" Cappella felt brave and reckless, the way she did sometimes when she climbed too high in trees to get a better view of the kingdom. "It's all right if you did. I love you. I will keep loving you. But it hurts me when you don't tell me the truth."

"I wish you would not ask such things."

There was something Cappella was afraid to know. Until this moment, she'd never imagined such a thing. Now she feared it was true. "Did you kill someone?"

"Oh!" Her mother dropped the basket. "Of course I didn't. Cappella—"

Cappella waited.

"It's so difficult to speak of this."

"It's impossible not to know the truth. I'm fifteen. I'm grown. You treat me the way you did when I was small, and I'm not that little girl anymore."

Her mother's eyes gleamed with tears. Cappella regretted her questions. They were selfish. She'd been unfair. She led her mother to a moss-covered log. They sat side by side. She felt less heated, less tight, as though her anger was unweaving itself. She slipped her arm around her mother's shoulder.

Esme leaned against her. Then she wiped her tears and sat up straight. "I can tell you this much."

Cappella braced herself. She wanted the truth. She also feared it.

"My sister is the queen. Her husband, the king. They made it clear that . . . that I was no longer welcome in the kingdom."

Cappella reeled. "But why?"

"It was many years ago."

That wasn't an answer, but Cappella couldn't bring herself to push for more.

"You have cousins. Twins, a boy and a girl. They'd be, oh, around five years older than you."

Cappella sat with the information. She'd always wanted a family. And here, she'd had one that her mother hadn't told her about. That her mother had kept from her. Her mother had concealed more than she'd imagined. Still, when she looked at Esme, she saw so much sadness that her own anger felt cruel.

"The girl is a were," Esme continued. "She has a bear aspect."

A were. Cappella sucked in her breath. She'd seen a werebear in the woods. Two, in fact. The brown one and the black one. Could one of them be her cousin? Had her mother seen the werebears too? And if she and her mother were related to the king and queen, then how could the kingdom be a dangerous place for them—unless Esme was a criminal? Cappella had so many questions, questions she hadn't the nerve to ask.

Her mother had always seemed like a kind and easy soul. A middle-aged woman who gathered nuts and berries in the forest. Who, with her green eyes and light brown hair, looked as though she'd been made of the same gentle material as the woods themselves. She was more than how she looked. She was a fugitive. Her mother had hidden much, and Cappella suddenly wasn't sure she wanted to know all of it.

"What are my cousins like?"

"They were toddlers when I left, but they both were dear to me. Ursula looked like my sister. Albrecht favored his father."

"Which of them will take the throne?"

"That's always been the question. Traditionally, it's been the firstborn. But that was Ursula. Many believed it should go to the son, Albrecht, on account of the fact that he's male."

"What would have happened if they'd had no children?"

"The king had no brothers or sisters," her mother said. "There is no heir on that side."

"But the queen had you."

"That's right. And I have *you*. You would be the next in line, if things hadn't happened the way they did—and, I suppose, if they knew about you."

If they knew about you. Her cousins must have had everything they ever could have wanted. They had each other, and no doubt everyone loved them. No doubt they had never imagined her or felt the longing that she'd felt for family. For them.

"Shall we go?" her mother said.

Cappella didn't want to. She wanted to leave the forest. She wanted to see what the kingdom was like. She wanted to meet her cousins. Perhaps whatever had divided their parents would not divide them.

"Cappella, please." Her mother looked at her as though she knew exactly what Cappella was thinking. Another thing that was unfair between them—Cappella didn't know what her mother was thinking at all.

The music of the forest shifted. There was a rustle. Cappella turned her head. A red cloth that hadn't been there a moment ago hung from a low branch a few yards away. Strange. She lifted the cloth and shook leaves and dirt from it. It was a cloak. Or had been, once. It was the worse for wear. But the fabric was still soft. She touched it to her cheek and sniffed. A bit like rat, a bit like dirt, and a bit like a scent she'd know anywhere.

Her wolf.

Cappella wrapped the cloak around her shoulders and pulled the hood over her hair, wishing she had a pin to keep it closed. She never wanted to take it off. She inhaled his scent again, and that's when she knew. Somewhere, somewhere close, her wolf was alive.

"Wolf!" she cried. "Wolf!" And then a third time.

He did not reply. He did not come running.

"Cappella—" Her mother looked afraid. "Where did that cloak come from?"

"I found it on a branch. I don't know how it got there, but—"

Her mother grabbed Cappella's wrist. "Let's go."

Cappella pulled away. "I want to find my wolf."

"No. We don't know that he's still safe for you."

Cappella stared hard at her mother, weighing her options, considering what price she was willing to pay to defy her mother. Esme had hidden so much of herself that Cappella didn't know what she would do in the face of defiance. Cappella had never tried. And then in an instant she knew. She wanted her wolf. More than anything. And she trusted him.

So Cappella ran. The music accelerated. The air felt harsh and smoky in her lungs, but the woods were with her. She knew this. She ran through the last rays of daylight, looking everywhere, her heart in her mouth.

As she came upon grouping of rocks that she and the wolf had always loved climbing, she saw a heap of gray fur.

He lay on his side, his front paws bloody, his muzzle matted and damp. Cappella put her hands on him, feeling his ribs, wondering where he'd been and what he'd endured. He was breathing hard and whining as though he was in pain. But his eyes were the most worrisome. They couldn't focus and kept rolling back in his head.

And even though she'd run from her, Cappella wished for her mother. She didn't want to be alone, not when her wolf was sick. Her mother would know what to do. And then Esme arrived, breathing heavily. She dropped beside Cappella and offered the wolf water from her leather pouch. He closed his eyes and let it drip onto his tongue and down his throat. He let out a high-pitched whine, and then his mouth closed. He shuddered and he became a boy with a bloody mouth, shredded fingertips, and a naked body covered in filth and bruises.

Her wolf. Her wolf was a were. He'd had a human aspect he'd hidden from her.

"Mother." Cappella couldn't manage anything beyond this.

Esme, on the other hand, didn't seem surprised. "Let's wrap him up and carry him home. Quickly now. Use the cloak."

Cappella wrapped it around him and tried to lift him, but she couldn't. He was too heavy.

"Let me." Esme lifted him over her shoulders, her face straining. Cappella had always known her mother was strong. Now she was seeing the extent of it.

By the time they reached the tree, darkness surrounded them. But the tinge of smoke in the air felt menacing, unsafe. All Cappella wanted in that moment was for her wolf—her were—to open his eyes. But he did not, not for hours. And as he slept, the scent of smoke grew worse.

XXII

Ursula's castle had been built atop a small hill. She could see the whole of her queendom, from the dark scribbles of the forest to the stubbly quilt of farmland to the bridge to her brother's domain. Fire was everywhere.

Men on horseback dipped their torches as they galloped through the smoke, leaving more fires in their wake, as though destruction was the crop they were planting. She had only minutes before they reached her.

She ran down the stairs, where she found her servants cowering in the hall.

"Where are the guards?" She looked about. No one offered an answer. "Tell me!"

The cook spoke. "They've left. There was talk of joining Albrecht's unity army. We thought it was nonsense. Just ale and bravado."

"What talk?" She'd heard nothing and felt sick. She'd not been paying attention. She was a fool. This was her fault.

"That your brother—King Albrecht—would take your queendom sooner rather than later. That he was rallying men to unify."

He wouldn't.

But as soon as she had the thought, she knew that he would.

"Run," she told the women. "Run to the woods. Take what you can carry." When she looked at them, she knew some of the women would do as she said. And she knew that some wouldn't. She could see the doubt in their faces. The resistance. The fear. Even now, when they'd seen him attack unprovoked, they would join him.

Her brother's men were coming for the summer castle. Its ancient timbers, dried for ages, wouldn't stand a chance against their torches.

Ursula ripped off her nightclothes and flung open the door, becoming the bear before she'd even crossed the threshold. A world of scents assaulted her, all violent, all wrong. Without a village full of people with buckets and deep wells, they could not extinguish these fires. The only thing she could do was find Albrecht and talk sense into him.

She crossed the burning farmland, running straight through flaming bushes and grass, moving too fast to be burned. She mowed down Albrecht's men without missing a stride. Albrecht, she knew, would be somewhere he could see all of it. Somewhere he didn't have to risk his own hide.

He might have been good with weapons. But he always made sure the advantage was his. He used snares. He shot arrows from afar. He'd sent men in masks after her rather than coming himself. Albrecht was a coward.

She'd never let herself think in such stark terms, always chalking it up to that day he fell out of a tree, a day that made him afraid of being hurt by the world. But she thought it now. His fear had made him dangerous. It had made him develop bows that shot harder. Arrows that flew farther. That mask he was wearing—the lion. He'd probably also made armor that covered every inch of his skin. His metal men. That's what they came from. It wasn't genius. It was fear.

His fear and what he would do to avoid it made him unlike her. She knew this in her bones. Whether as a bear or as a woman, she could brave anything.

Wind blew from the north—this was why she hadn't smelled the smoke earlier. It also meant she couldn't track her brother by scent alone. The most likely place he'd be, she realized, was the bridge where his stupid monkeys were. She'd head there if she wanted to stay above the fray. He'd be in one of the watchtowers, looking down on things, out of harm's way, ready to descend when victory was his, ready to wind the monkeys so they could shriek into the wind.

She'd see to it that this never happened.

When she reached the bridge, she spied him in the west tower. His golden mask, lit by a lantern, gleamed through the smoky air, his pale hair wild around his head, exactly like a lion's. She supposed that's what he would have wished to be, had he been a were. A lion. A nod to their father, to the line of men stretching back like an arrow through time—and of all animals, perhaps the only one that could take on a bear.

She managed to surprise the four men stationed at the tower, two with spears and two with swords. A hastily thrown spear whisked through her fur as it sailed past. The other missed. She leapt, spinning midair, taking out one with her front paws and the other with her rear. One of the swordsmen, a man in an owl mask, escaped across the bridge. The other feinted. She had him on his back before he knew she'd even left the ground. She batted his sword toward one of the monkeys. It crashed into it, denting the clockwork before flying into the river. She didn't care that she'd cost the man such a precious thing. He'd cost her more. Stepping hard on his chest, she reached for the ladder and clawed her way up. Wood squeaked overhead. Albrecht, aiming an arrow.

"Not one inch closer," he said.

She shifted back to her human form. She'd give him a chance to end this with words. He'd of course have to atone for what he'd done. The things he'd destroyed. The lives his men had taken. But she could make him see that he'd made a mistake.

"I'm coming up." She reached for the next rung.

There was a twang and then a sharp pain in her shoulder. He'd shot her. He'd actually shot her. "Albrecht!"

"I told you not to. You have only yourself to blame. Don't make me do it again. Next time, I'll shoot to kill."

The wound wasn't deep, though it ached. She clung to the ladder. Albrecht nocked another arrow, and she noticed his bandaged stump.

"What happened to your hand?"

"Not your concern."

"You're my brother."

"You're my enemy," he said. "Surrender your territory and you can keep your life."

She pulled the arrow out of her shoulder and felt better immediately, even as she was now gushing blood.

"It's not too late," she told him. "We can fix this."

"That's exactly what I'm doing," he said. "Fixing a kingdom wrongly split by a man who'd lost his sense to age and disease." He drew his arrow back. She wished she could see his eyes, but it wasn't possible. She became her bear self again and released the ladder, dropping into the night. The bow zinged and an arrow sank into the hump on her back.

She tumbled through space, spiraling so that she could land on her feet. The impact knocked the wind out of her. The arrow burned. One more shot would finish her.

She crawled beneath the tower, out of range of Albrecht's arrows. She couldn't believe he wanted to kill her. But he'd shown her his intention, so she had no choice but to accept the fact.

In the distance, people clashed swords and limbs and teeth. Some of these people, she knew, were fighting for her. Their lives were her responsibility. Her queendom was lost. But they might live to fight another day if they fled in time.

She burst from her hiding spot and rushed toward the battlefield, what once had been acres and acres of apple and pear trees. Now the smoking silhouettes of burned stumps raked the sky. A few last men and weres fought on. The sun would rise before long. She stood on her hind legs and bellowed. It was the biggest, most ferocious sound she could make, and she thought she would split into pieces from the pain.

Her people answered back. Some with the voices of men, some with the cries of weres. And that's when she remembered the cages. Weres—children—would have been locked inside them and would not be able to get out unless they managed to keep their human form, which would be impossible for children in the midst of the madness. She couldn't leave those children to be found by Albrecht and his men. He would show them no mercy.

All around, fires burned. Many were crops, but some the cottages of farmers. She hadn't a moment to waste. Ursula turned and heaved herself to the cages. Every time she found one, she shifted to her human form so she could work the locks. She freed raccoon twins. Two fox brothers. Three tiny goats.

"Run," she said. "Flee to the woods."

She caught the scent of Sabine but couldn't see her anywhere. Nor had she seen her on the battlefield, though with her coloring, she would be impossible to see if she'd fallen. Ursula grew queasy at the thought. When she could find no more trapped werechildren, she became her bear self again and headed toward the woods. The forest was vast. Albrecht would not have had a chance yet to secure it. There would be plenty of space there to hide. And she needed to. She could fight no more. She'd lost too much blood.

The music called to her through her pain as she ran, and she let it fill her with purpose and urgency. She crossed into the woods. Moving in time with the music, she weaved through trees, unaware of anyone else who might be near. She ran toward the cottage, hoping Sabine might still be there. Or if not, that Greta would take pity on her.

The world darkened. Her senses faded. Her mind traveled to her father, wondering if his death felt like this, a great easing of the self from the substance of the world.

She felt nothing at all as she took one last leap forward, not even the shaking of the earth as her great body fell.

XXIII

Greta woke up alone. Sabine had left the cottage not long after Ursula, with a promise to return. Greta recalled nodding and saying, "That would be welcome."

But they'd just been words. Words spoken by the mouth of a girl gone numb. She imagined this was what stones in the river felt like in early spring, when the frozen runoff from the mountains rushed over them. Perhaps these stones had once been living things too, shocked into stillness by the rude assault of cold.

She stood on the bare wood floor. She'd forgotten how much she missed this soft warmth. She never wanted to feel anything else with her feet than wood beneath them. There was a smokiness to the air that worried her. She dressed and fixed her braid, wrapped a shawl around her shoulders, and stepped outside. Wind came from the kingdom—something there had to be burning. Something huge enough to bind the woods in a foul white gauze that tasted like ash.

She had no desire to leave her cottage. But she had to know what was on fire. Had to know if Hans was in danger. She felt sick, dizzy. The air, the worry. She slipped on her shoes and resolved to go to the edge of the woods, just to see. It wasn't too far. She wouldn't risk much.

The trees were quiet; she could hear every footstep, feel every thud of her heart. Even the birds held their songs in closed beaks. Now that she was jolted from numbness, every sensation felt sharpened, her sense of foreboding included.

The forest floor dipped into a tiny clearing thick with brush. Greta stepped into it and nearly tripped over the body of an enormous brown bear who'd sunk into a thick patch of ivy. The bear had been wounded; the broken shaft of an arrow emerged from her back, and the fur around it was matted with dried blood. There was another wound nearby. Greta knew very well who this was. She wished she could walk away from the princess. But she couldn't.

She crouched by Ursula's side, reluctant to touch her. Was she dead already? Then the princess moaned and opened her light brown eyes. She curled a lip and snarled. It was a plea. *Help me.*

Greta had never butchered a bear, but she knew enough about animals to understand how bodies came together. She knew how much pressure a muscle could take before it tore. She also knew that there was no need to be squeamish. Bodies were skin, they were meat, they were bone. She could get this arrow out. It might be safer to let her die. But then, that would make Greta cruel, and she was not that.

The bear's back was a mess, the arrow a full finger's length in. Greta winced as she pulled. When the arrow came free, the princess whimpered. Greta dropped it and gently pressed the opening. Beneath her, the princess slowly took her human form again.

"Pack . . . the wounds," she said, her speech labored. "Moss . . . and . . . burdock if you can find it."

Burdock had heart-shaped leaves. The moss was everywhere. Greta pulled some together. The princess shuddered as Greta pressed them into the wounds.

"I'm sorry," Greta said. And she was, even as she had no love for her.

The princess grunted. "I'm lucky. Help me sit."

Greta said nothing as the princess told her what had happened. The news was shocking. Unthinkable. That one half of the kingdom should be set against the other . . . It meant families had been divided. She was even more afraid for Hans. He was the right hand of Albrecht. Everyone knew that.

Greta stood. She'd made a decision. "Come to my home. Take what you need. Food, clothing. Even a knife."

"Sabine," the queen said. "Is she still there?"

Greta shook her head. "She left yesterday. Said she had to go home."

"You haven't seen her since?" The queen's face was pale.

"I haven't. Is it your wound? I can sew it up."

"I'm fine. It's fine. Weres heal quickly. But we must hurry. There are surely people who'll need our care. Other survivors too."

Let Hans be among them, Greta prayed. *Let him come home.*

⚬⚬⚬

They found them all over the woods—weres, farmers, the wounded, the dead. Smoke thickened the air still, stinging Greta's eyes, souring her stomach, making her head throb. The search was miserable, and every time Greta saw a body, her heart seized. In all, they'd gathered three dozen corpses. Some had been burned. Some bled to death. Others looked as though they'd been trampled by horses. The bodies were all ages. All sizes. Many werefolk. Some single aspect. But each of them was someone's loved one. A sibling, a parent, a child. Hans was not among them.

By the time Ursula had gathered the survivors in a clearing not terribly far from the cottage—a place Greta's family used to picnic on long summer nights—she felt fouled in a way she never had when she was butchering meat. That was orderly. Methodical. Nearly bloodless. War was anything but. She wished she could be one of the trees rising up around her. Tall, strong, made of stuff that could not be brought down so easily by men.

Even among the survivors, she didn't find Hans. She chose to take relief in that. Perhaps he was neither dead nor wounded. Perhaps he was perfectly safe. Greta fed the fire twigs and dry leaves. Little children had gathered around her. A pair of redheaded brothers. Three weregoat sisters with jet-black hair. Two tiny girls who kept shifting into their raccoon forms. None had parents anymore. Werechildren never did.

"Careful, children," she said. "Fire bites."

Counting the seven children, there were not quite three dozen refugees in all. Mostly women. Some rather on the elderly side. If they were supposed to wage any sort of war against the kingdom with this lot, it would be short and sad.

As Greta built up the fire, the queen and some of the other adults tended the wounded and cleaned the bodies of the dead. These they lined up so that grievers could make their farewells.

If Greta hadn't known who Queen Ursula was, she might have liked her. Despite her injury, she had easily taken command and was arranging bodies with respect as well as making sure the wounded were triaged and tended. She wasn't lazy or weak-willed, that was certain.

Relieved to have something to do, Greta fetched the food she'd pilfered from the castle, along with water and some things she'd foraged, and she set about preparing porridge. The task helped keep her mind off Hans.

When the food was ready, Ursula beat a wooden spoon against the pot. People looked up.

"I am sorry for all of your losses. For what has become of my queendom. This is what we know."

The queen paced as she walked, her shoulder seeping blood. "My brother has stolen our land. Burned much of it and many of the homes. He has taken many lives in the process. But we will fight back. We will restore justice."

It was meant to be a stirring speech; Greta could tell. But none of the adults cheered in response. The red-haired brothers, in their werefox forms, were nipping each other in the face. The other children were sleeping in a heap. Only a fool would think a few dozen survivors, especially ones like these, could take on the king and all the soldiers he commanded.

"With respect," said one man, who had the rough hands of a farmer, "we're sunk. We'll be lucky to make it through the winter."

The queen's expression tightened. She looked the man up and down. Then she looked away, as if dismissing him. "I am your queen. I will see to it that justice is done. We will make it through winter. That is a promise."

It was a tense moment, and everyone watched closely, taking note of what happened to people who challenged the queen.

Greta broke the silence. "Who's hungry?"

People lined up, children first, and Greta filled cups and bowls, and people ate. There were sounds of slurping and hushed voices, and over that, the music of the woods, and something she hadn't heard so close in ages—the pipe. The one that Hans's friend played.

It pierced her like a knife. It took her apart. She had no defense against it. She bowed her head and wept. She would have to find that girl someday, just so she could talk with someone who had known and loved her brother.

It was the closest she could come to acknowledging she might never see him again.

She felt a presence next to her. The queen. Greta wiped her eyes and nose.

"Thank you," Queen Ursula said. "The porridge is just right."

Greta knew she had to acknowledge the praise. All she could do, though, was nod and offer more. Ursula waved her off. Then she cocked her head. Greta could hear nothing, but she knew the ears of werefolk were sharper than human ones. Ursula stood, her body angled toward something Greta could not see. Through the waning smoke, a figure approached. For a fraction of a moment, Greta thought it was her brother.

But it wasn't. She knew who it was as soon as Ursula took off running: Sabine, returned, and in her human form. The queen embraced her, and Greta felt the sting of envy. She wished Hans had been the one who'd returned. She would have given anything for that; she would even have continued to serve Ursula and tend these refugees. Heart aching, she stood, brushed debris from her apron, and turned toward home.

XXIV

By dawn, Albrecht was back in his chambers. Out of habit, he glanced to where his mirror had stood. The frame was empty. Shards of glass littered the floor. But he didn't need a mirror to know how he looked. Triumphant. Filthy. Dressed in the blood of his enemies.

Like a king.

His mask still hung around his neck. He removed it and set it on his desk. It was pitted now where blood had touched it, but that only made it look better.

The kingdom was unified, and it was his. His sister was dead. He'd watched the arrow hit. Seen her fall. He'd also watched her run off like the fool she was. The injury wasn't survivable.

What's more, the frisser row was burned; nothing but ash-filled cages remained. The fields were full of their bodies. Some frissers had escaped to the woods, but it would only be a matter of time before he and a team of men hunted them down. The surviving farmers had sworn their fealty, and he'd promised them help replanting in the spring. Many of his soldiers had at one point been farmers, so they'd be good at this. What's more, they would be there to crush insurrections before they started.

This was what swiftness did. This was what decisiveness did. It was how you made the world what you wanted it to be. It was a shame that it had required bloodshed, but that was not his fault. Had his father done the right thing in the first place, Albrecht would have taken the throne without requiring a single spilled drop. Likewise, Ursula could have stepped aside. He had not asked her to directly; that was true, but she knew he wanted it. Asking would have alerted her to the attack, which would have made it more dangerous for all. He'd had no choice, really. Others had taken that from him.

"Jutta!"

With Hans in the dungeon, he'd moved Jutta into the castle to help him build a replacement finger. More than one, actually. His wound would need to heal first, but he was eager to try the devices he'd sketched. He'd thought of several ideas, each a better finger than the one nature had supplied.

"Jutta!"

He poked his head into the corridor and there she was, rubbing her eyes, as though he'd woken her. Understandable. It had been a long and eventful night, and she'd worked nonstop, sharpening blades and pounding out arrows. He hadn't slept himself, but he was so exhilarated from his victory that he couldn't imagine putting head to pillow.

He led her to his desk and showed her the sketches.

"And what substance will we use?" she asked.

"Use the metal you think best. I trust you. Just make them perfect." She'd never let him down, not once. He felt a rush of gratitude. He put his uninjured hand on her shoulder. "You're special. You could be among the last of them, you know."

"The last of them?" Her eyebrows drew together.

"The last of weres. What if they all perished last night, all but you and Hans?"

"I—" She paused, as if choosing her words with care. "I do not think that is possible or likely. Many of them were—are—children. Surely . . ."

"You're probably right, friend," he said. "The children are especially difficult to kill. Smaller targets. And I'd forgotten that more can always be bred."

Jutta closed her eyes and shuddered, a very equine gesture.

"I will never let anyone harm you," he said. "Where would I be without you? Rest if you'd like. You can start work in a few hours. Meanwhile, I must fetch Hans. I'm sure his time below has taught him everything he needed to learn."

On his way to the dungeon, Albrecht remembered that Hans would need food and drink before he could work. So Albrecht set a kitchen maid to work on a tray.

The kitchen angered him. It reminded him that Greta had left him. After all he'd done for her these past three years. After the visits and the compliments he'd paid her about her golden hair and lily-white skin. He'd saved her from a life of coarseness and roughness. Singled her out. He'd even planned to bed her when the time was right. And she'd left. She'd left him. She'd rejected his favor. She'd rejected . . . him.

It hurt worse than the loss of his finger, not that he would ever say it aloud. It had not occurred to him, though, that a woman could wound him without a weapon—simply by withholding her affection. What dangerous creatures they were, and the more beautiful, the more lethal. Greta was, in this way, the greatest menace of the kingdom. She would have to be brought to heel.

"Are you all right, Your Majesty? You look unwell, and your hand . . ." The kitchen girl stood in front of him, the tray laden with food and a jug of ale.

He glanced at his not-finger. Yes, it bled. But he was fine, and she was impertinent even to ask. He took the tray from her and ventured to the dungeon.

It had been clever of his grandfather to build a new castle atop the old. It meant the new castle was higher, and higher was better.

It also left solid rooms to hold prisoners. The old doors and windows had been filled in with stone. Escape was not possible. Rumor had it one person *had* made it out over the years, but that was before Albrecht's time and could very well have been nothing but a story the gullible chose to believe.

When he reached the bottom of the staircase, the light was weak, but there was enough to make out debris at the base of the door to the room where he'd locked Hans. Bits of wood.

No.

He rushed forward. The door had been ravaged. Hans was gone.

Albrecht threw the tray against the wall, bumping his hurt finger in the process. But he had mastered his rage before he'd reached the top of the stairs. He knew, of course, where Hans had gone. The same place Greta had gone. He'd need Jutta's help, but he could catch them both. In the meantime, he had a kingdom to run.

O nce upon a time," the storyteller says, "two children lived in the woods with their father and stepmother.

"When hard times fell on the family, the stepmother decided they could no longer afford to keep their children clothed and fed.

"'Husband,' she said, 'lead your children deep into the woods. Leave them there. The forest spirits will care for them.'

"His wife had a harsh voice and an unkind face. The man did not want her to use either against him. So he led his children away.

"But his son had overheard the woman's ugly voice and made a plan of his own. The boy dropped white pebbles behind him as they walked, and that was how the boy and his sister made it home again."

"And then what happened?" the children ask.

"Are you certain you wish to hear it?" the storyteller says. "It gets far grimmer from here."

The children were certain. For what child does not wish to hear terrible truths told in a beautiful way?

PART
FOUR

XXV

As the kingdom burned, Cappella slept next to the boy who was her wolf, waking up every so often to check on him. He did not stir. She knew he lived from the slow rise and fall of his chest.

Her mother didn't come home during the night. She'd said she was gathering supplies, but Cappella didn't believe it. They had plenty in their tree. Food, water, bandages, and even candles they'd made from beeswax. Her mother was inspecting whatever the source of smoke was. Something terrible was happening.

Despite the lie her mother told, despite the anxiety she felt, Cappella was glad to be alone with the wolf. She'd always known they were bound. Some part of her must have perceived he was more than a wolf, that they could be more to each other. This was not something she wanted to talk about with her mother. It never went well. When Cappella first had begun to menstruate, she'd asked her mother the purpose of this uncomfortable, messy thing.

"It shows that your body is ready to have children," her mother had said.

"Do you bleed too?"

"No." Her face took on a pained expression that ended the discussion. At first, Cappella thought perhaps a mother stopped bleeding after she had a child. That a child was the cure. But then she recalled that the woodsman's wife had had two children.

The woodsman. Now she understood what had happened. Her wolf was his son. His parents had died. He'd gone into the kingdom afterward and only just returned. Her mother had known this all along. She'd known and hadn't told her; she hadn't let Cappella try to find him. She didn't want Cappella to have this wolf, this boy. She wanted to keep her hidden away in their tree. For how long? Until Cappella's hair had turned all the way white?

She studied the boy who lay beside her. She would have known that shaggy hair anywhere. He'd always intrigued her, always darted off when he came near. Talking with him would have been against the rules, and Cappella had tried to be a good daughter.

Cappella had accepted her mother's rules, but she hated them. She *needed* other people. She wanted others. Someone to listen to the music of the trees with. Someone to walk with to the edge of the woods, where the leaves were thin enough that they could hold hands and count stars. She wanted to love someone, and she wanted to feel loved in return. Day after day for years, she'd played that yearning into her pipe. It was in every song she ever played with the trees. The wish for love.

Did her mother want love too? Cappella would never ask. Her mother would never say. It would become one more thing she and her mother did not—could not—talk about.

When day broke, Cappella smoothed the boy's hair. It was softer than his wolf fur, with edges that curled around her fingertips. She blotted the blood from his mouth and then saw to his fingertips. His nails were shredded, and it hurt to look at them. She poured clean water over them, hoping to dislodge anything that might prevent them from healing. Then she wrapped them gently in bandages woven of moss. As she did, his eyelids fluttered. Opened. She watched his face as he took her in: fear, then relief.

"Where are we?" His voice was exactly as she'd imagined it would be, sweet and rough.

"This is where I live," she said.

He sat, holding the red cloak around his waist. He touched the cloth as though it was a comfort to him.

"Careful," she said. "You're hurt."

He glanced at his fingertips. "It's not so bad."

"You're the wolf," she said. "My wolf."

His face reddened and he looked into his lap. "I wasn't allowed to tell anyone. And you told me your mother wouldn't let you talk with people. I didn't think we had a choice. And I didn't want you to be scared of me."

When she was younger, she might have been afraid. Watching him shift from his wolf form to his human one had been shocking, perhaps in part because of her great surprise at seeing him and her horror at his injuries. There was no denying that the transformation itself had been astonishing to witness; she could hear his bones rearrange themselves and watch fur sink into his skin. But she didn't fear it. She didn't fear him. She couldn't. Not ever.

She felt nothing but tenderness. She wanted to put her palm to his cheek. To tell him she was so glad he was back. That she'd missed him.

"Are you hungry?"

He nodded.

She made a bowl of dried berries and nuts, along with some bread that had been cooked over the fire. He put a berry into his mouth and chewed slowly.

"I'm sorry I don't have anything softer. Does it hurt?"

He nodded.

"Eat all the berries. We can gather more. I'm afraid they won't last you very long."

He ate two more. "I've missed these."

It had always been so easy to talk to him when he was a wolf. Words flowed like notes from her pipe. Whatever she thought, she'd said. She edged away from him until her back was against the bark of the tree. There was the solidity she needed.

He gestured at the cloak across his lap. "I bought this for you. It used to be . . . it used to be cleaner."

She laughed. "You mean it didn't come with moth holes and a sort of rattish odor?"

He laughed too. "It's seen some things."

She touched the edge of it. "I love it."

"I've held on to it for a long time."

She thought he might say more. But he didn't. He finished the berries, and they sat in silence.

He wrapped the cloak around his waist and moved toward the opening, peering out. "It's smoky out there."

"You're not leaving, are you?" She felt a sense of panic, though she didn't want to show it. "You should rest. Heal. And my mother is bringing herbs that will lessen the pain—"

"I have to," he said. "My sister."

"You should at least finish the berries and a full skin of water." She would have done anything to keep him with her. A thought struck, one that made her blush. "You haven't any clothes."

He grinned, and it was somehow exactly the expression it was when he was in his wolf form: mischievous, sweet, and wonderful. "That's where it's convenient that I can travel as a wolf. I need to find my sister. It's urgent."

"Is she in danger?"

He nodded.

"Will you be back?"

"I don't know," he said. "I want to be. I'll try."

They were both silent. The smell of smoke was thick, and the music of the forest sounded strained, troubled.

He stood in the opening of the tree, his form darkened by the daylight behind him. "I missed you, Cappella. Sometimes I could hear your music from where I was. Or at least I thought I could."

She didn't need to ask whether he'd liked it. She knew he had. He always had. He used to tip his snout to the air when she played, tongue lolling. Or sometimes he'd roll over on his back, paws folded on his chest. But she wanted to hear him say that he'd liked it. That he'd thought of her as often as she'd thought of him.

Her heart ached. "Wait—I still don't know your name."

He looked at her with his gray-and-black eyes. "Hans. My name is Hans."

And then he was the wolf again, and he was leaving, limping on his injured paws, and Cappella felt as though an arrow had been blasted through her chest.

A minute passed.

Hans had traveled far enough away that Cappella could no longer hear him. The woods played soft music, as if they knew her heart needed something tender to bind it.

What do you want? she felt them ask her. *What do you want?*

She knew her answer the moment she felt the question take shape. She wrapped the cloak around her shoulders, flipped up the hood, and then she stepped out of her tree, pipe in hand. She knew where he'd lived, once upon a time, so she set out in that direction.

He was too fast for her to catch up. When she arrived at the cottage, the door was closed. He had already gone inside. She looked in the window. He was there, dressed now, embracing a girl with a braid of golden hair that ran all the way down her back. Their shoulders shook, and she knew they wept, and she felt like an intruder. They were a family. She was not part of it.

She stepped away from the window, mortified at the thought she'd be seen. Then, not far away, she heard voices, and through the smoky air, she smelled food being cooked. Was this the danger Hans had spoken of? She turned, intending to run home and hide.

She nearly crashed into her mother.

"Oh, thank goodness," Esme said. "I returned home, and you were gone. I was terrified something had happened to you."

"I'm fine. But what's going on? Why are people here? Why is the air so full of ash?"

Her mother carried a bag that looked full to the brim. "I'll tell you on the way."

"On the way? Are we leaving?"

Her mother, she knew now, was a fugitive.

"Nothing like that."

Her mother walked so fast Cappella had to trot to keep up. They turned toward the clearing, keeping out of sight. As they observed the people gathered there, her mother whispered, "There's been some sort of battle. There's a group of three dozen or so refugees, some wounded. There are also bodies. And one of the survivors—" She paused. "I believe one is your cousin Ursula. She moves just as my sister did. Even their voices sound the same. Whatever happened in the kingdom, whatever has created all of that smoke, was terrible."

"I thought you said what happens in the kingdom has nothing to do with us."

Her mother closed her eyes. "I know what I said. I was wrong. These people have run from the kingdom, as I once did. One is our kin. They all need our help."

"What if they want to hurt us?"

"It's a possibility," her mother allowed. "But it never works to stand aside and hope the hand of power passes by. In the end, it finds us all unless we resist. And sometimes it finds us even then."

Something sparked inside Cappella. "How do you know this? And why have you never said such things to me before?"

"Hush, child." Esme stepped toward the clearing.

"No!" Cappella hissed.

Her mother took a deep breath and then let it out slowly. "I didn't tell you because there were things that I didn't want you to know. Didn't want you to *have* to know. I wanted your life to be joy and music in the woods. I wanted you to know nothing but happiness."

Cappella believed her mother thought this was the way to happiness. But it had been a path to loneliness. It had been a lie. She hadn't known her family. She'd missed out on the fullness of friendship with Hans that would have been possible. Maybe even his sister too. If her life had been happy, it was incomplete, a fraud, a lie.

"All right." Cappella would do what she could to help for now. But later? She did not yet know what she would do.

But she wanted more than this.

XXVI

After she failed to find Sabine among the early survivors, Ursula had been afraid to hope. She'd been more afraid to face her fear—that her brother's act of war had killed her. Sabine's survival made her feel as though she had a second chance at being queen. That she could undo this wrong.

They stood away from the camp, between trees whose leaf-laden branches curved overhead, washing them with red-gold light. Ursula was so relieved she no longer even felt the wound in her shoulder. She took Sabine by the sleeve and tugged her close.

Then she stepped back and examined Sabine's ash-streaked face. "Your stitches are nearly ready to come out." She traced the line of them with her finger. "Do you have any fresh wounds in need of attention?"

Sabine stiffened. "Nothing too bad. Some burns on my hands. A sword nicked my shin. I don't need anything, not really."

"Let me look at them anyway."

Ursula wished they still had the cottage. She wanted to sit Sabine in a chair. Heat water. Tend every inch of her and follow it up with kisses. But in truth, the cottage had never been theirs. They'd been playacting. This was real, though. She was queen, and they were together, and side by side, they would fight back. Someday they would build a home together. A castle of their own, with just-right beds and chairs. Fine things, comfortable things.

She would give Sabine everything she'd never had on the Row, everything she wanted. Sabine needed only ask and the world would be hers. The memory of their kiss had made everything that followed survivable. Ursula was counting the moments until they could have another.

She took Sabine's hands in hers and her heart responded, beating against her rib cage, urging her to kiss Sabine again, but Sabine didn't return her gaze. She was no doubt exhausted and bewildered. Even so, it stung. Trying to remember that she'd had probably been awake most of the night and had no doubt seen horrors, Ursula led her to a nearby stump.

She gestured for Sabine to sit. "Your throne."

Ursula reached into a bag of supplies slung over her shoulder. She set a bottle of liniment on Sabine's lap. She took Sabine's hands again, turning them so that she could examine the contours of every finger. Her skin had been turned shiny by burns. It would peel away. But her hands would heal. This was good.

Ursula rubbed them with liniment, tenderly, so that she wouldn't cause Sabine any pain—but also because she loved holding her hands.

"Now the leg." She examined the shin. A cut ran straight across it. "I ought to sew this or you'll have a scar."

"I don't mind a scar. It's fine. Let's finish this." Sabine looked around, as if she'd just woken up. "It's strange."

"Strange?"

"Last night was the first night I can remember sleeping outside of a cage. And it scared me. I kept waking up and seeing the leaves and bits of sky and I've never felt so small. So alone."

"I know what you mean. But it's because you were used to the cage. You'll get used to this. And if you still want a cage, I'll have one made for you. You can have anything you want." She brushed the skin of Sabine's wrist with her lips. "You might have been alone last night. But you aren't now. You'll never be alone again. I promise."

Sabine's hands stiffened. She pulled them away. "Ursula, I told you this would happen."

"What—that my brother would attack my kingdom? You never told me that."

"I told you that things would be different between us."

"I will make things right again. I promise."

"That's just it. You can't."

When Sabine looked into her eyes, Ursula knew what words were coming. She knew, and she was powerless to stop them, and she had no armor to protect herself from the wounds they'd cause.

"No, Sabine. Please. I'm not ready."

"You're queen now," Sabine said.

"I'm a queen without a queendom. Nothing has changed."

Sabine's voice was rough, impatient. "Everything has changed."

"But I'm going to make things better for werefolk," Ursula said.

"That's exactly what your brother has been telling people—that you planned to assert new rights for werefolk, rights that would 'put them ahead.' That's how he described it."

"I never said that. That's not what I meant by . . . How could he—"

"He's been whispering for months. Telling people about the metal men he's working on, how he and he alone can make the kingdom stronger than ever. He's told people that you would destroy everything great about it. You never noticed because you'd been spending your time with me instead of your people. It took your brother a single day to take your queendom.

'Unity,' he told them. Your brother told his people a better story than you did. He was ready. You weren't."

"You sound like him." The words stung. Ursula fought back tears.

"It's partly my fault. I took you away from your duties, and I regret it. It never should have gone this far, not when we both knew I will never be the partner to a queen. Because I was selfish, you've lost your throne, and many weres and farmers have lost their lives."

Ursula struggled to catch her breath. This blow, at this time. She'd wanted to count on Sabine. She had. She still thought she could, if only she could make Sabine understand.

"Sabine."

"I will not be in your service as queen. I cannot be. You are my friend. I will fight alongside you. Defend my people. Build new homes for us all. But we could never be equal partners, and I would settle for nothing less."

Ursula felt something inside her collapse. She could not speak. She could scarcely breathe. If she'd given up her throne, if she'd let Albrecht rule, none of this would have happened.

But she hadn't wanted to give it up. She'd wanted her birthright, her crown, the chance to lead. She wanted to make good decisions for her people. To be just to all. To improve the lives of weres. And she knew she'd be better at this than Albrecht, who cared only about proving his superiority to her. She'd had no choice in this. That was the truth.

She wanted to be angry with Sabine. Wanted to go full bear and snarl and claw. To fight her the way Albrecht had fought her in the cage. Not to hurt her, no. She would never hurt her. But to win. To show her that she was wrong.

But she knew Sabine. Ursula could roar all she wanted. Sabine was stubborn. That was one of Ursula's favorite things about her: how steady she was, how forthright, how consistent. Sabine wouldn't change her mind because of an argument. But maybe Sabine would change her mind once she saw the sort of queen Ursula was.

"All right," Ursula said. "I think we're finished here."

Sabine opened her mouth as if she was going to say something else, but Ursula didn't want to hear it, especially if it was going to be something kind and gentle. That would make her cry, and that was the last thing she wanted.

"Keep the liniment. Put it on your burns until they don't feel tender anymore. The scar on your leg shouldn't be too bad. We weres do heal from our wounds quickly, after all."

She left Sabine. She had survivors to focus on. Werefolk who needed her. And there was the matter of the dead as well. Their bodies would need to be burned. Sent back to the dust and ash they came from.

By the time Ursula returned to the clearing, two new souls had arrived. One looked familiar, a woman who would have been about her mother's age. She'd seen her before, but where? Had she been a maid? A merchant? Her clothing was no help—it didn't look like anything made in the kingdom. It was far rougher, dyed the exact shade of moss. It might even have been moss, though Ursula had not known hands that could weave such stuff.

Meanwhile, the girl held a golden pipe in her hand. Where had such a thing come from? Then it struck her. That piping sound she'd sometimes heard on her trips to the woods—that had been the girl, and this had been her instrument. More than once, Ursula had felt her mood change because of this girl's music. Anger dissipated. Feelings of tenderness emerged. She'd attributed it at the time to the presence of Sabine, and maybe that was partly the case. But she could recall times that the music alone transformed her.

This music might be something to fear. It might be something else. But the most chilling realization that struck Ursula was that if she'd heard this music in the woods, then this girl and their mother were forest dwellers. She did not know them. And she had no idea if they were friends or foes.

XXVII

Cappella felt a thrill, part terror and part hope, when Ursula approached. She didn't know whether she feared her more for being a princess, a were-bear, or her cousin. What's more, she'd gone her whole life without talking with others, and here she was, among so many. Everyone looked exhausted. Some wore dirty bandages. Others held raccoons and other small animals in their laps. *Werechildren.* She had to force herself not to stare. The prospect of being among them, being surrounded, made her tongue feel as dry as bark.

"Mother," she whispered, "do we kneel?"

Her mother shook her head.

Cappella wanted to, though. She dropped to her knees and tried to bring her mother with her, but only succeeded in pulling Esme off balance. Ursula stopped a few feet away.

"You have your mother's mouth," Esme said.

Ursula's expression went blank. "Who are you to speak of my mother, to speak to me without being addressed?" She produced a knife.

Cappella's eyes widened.

Esme didn't flinch. "I am one who changed your cloths when you were small. I watched the first time you became a bear. I've known you since before you knew yourself."

"So you were a nursemaid?"

Esme shook her head. She looked defiant, proud. Cappella regretted kneeling. She'd never seen anyone interact with her mother. Never seen any conversation up close, really. But she didn't like the look on Ursula's face. Didn't like anyone to challenge her mother. And she really didn't like the knife. She stood.

Esme took a half step closer. "I'm your aunt," Esme said. "Your mother's sister."

"My mother never had a sister."

"Untrue. She does."

"My mother is dead," the princess said. "Any real sister would know that."

Esme closed her eyes. She said nothing. Seeing her mother in a moment of grief, Cappella took her hand. If Esme had not even known of the death of her sister, then perhaps she'd held less back from Cappella than she'd thought. Either way, she didn't trust Ursula.

Esme opened her eyes at last. "I am sad to hear this news."

"She never spoke of you," Ursula said.

Cappella felt a flash of anger at her cousin. How dare she? Then she remembered that Esme had never spoken of her sister either. Two sisters, silent about each other. Cappella had lifted rocks before and seen tiny bugs writhing in the muck. This felt like that, ugly things, too long hidden.

Her mother spoke. "I suppose that's because she believed me dead."

"Why would she believe that?"

It took a while for Esme to reply, and Cappella felt each moment crawl past. She hated not knowing what her mother was going to say. Being here, with all these people, was overwhelming. To discover things her mother had long concealed this way was humiliating. Enraging.

"Your parents and I had a falling-out," Esme said. "They said I wished for things that were not my own. They sent me to the dungeon to die. I escaped and have lived here since. I am Esme. This is Cappella. Your cousin."

Ursula's eyes traveled up and down Cappella. Her gaze rested a moment on the pipe. "That is no small quantity of gold. Tell me, what happens to the gold when blood touches it?"

Cappella brought her pipe to her chest. Did her cousin mean to wound her?

Her mother spoke. "It's never seen blood. But, to answer your question, blood would undo it."

"Is that why you were banished? Because you stole the gold my mother made?"

"No," Esme said. "That is not what happened."

She said nothing else. Even the forest held its song. Cappella wondered whether her mother would fill the void with an explanation, a story, a justification. But she didn't. People stared. The silence felt like forever.

Ursula broke it.

"Why are you here? These woods are mine, and if you mean any harm—"

Esme interrupted. "The woods are our home. We came to offer our help. It looked as though you might need it."

Cappella stole another glance at the people. They all looked so tired, so hungry.

"We need nothing from you," Ursula said.

"Ursula!" A tall, thin girl with dark brown skin looked at her with astonishment.

Ursula shot a look at the girl and then uncrossed her arms.

She turned again to Esme. "What skills do you have?"

"I know the forest and its food sources," Esme said. "I also have healing skills."

Ursula's expression changed. She looked relieved, although she didn't say as much. She turned to Cappella. "And you?"

Cappella struggled to work her mouth. She lifted the pipe. "I play music."

"Any useful skills?" Ursula asked.

The girl who'd chastised Esme spoke up again, clearly trying to smooth things over. "I love music," she said. "I'd love to hear you play."

A look of shame crossed Ursula's face.

"I'm Sabine," the girl said. "You're the piper in the woods, no? I've heard you play."

Cappella nodded. And then she realized something. This was the black werebear. And Ursula was the brown one.

"In truth, we could use your skills," Ursula said to Esme. "Will you lend them to us?"

Esme nodded. "For the time being."

"And I suppose music wouldn't hurt," Ursula said. "As long as you know when to be silent."

Cappella's face burned. She wasn't a child. And her cousin wasn't that much older than she was. If this was how queens made people feel, Cappella understood more and more why her mother had stayed in the woods.

"Perhaps she could play a tune now," Sabine said. "She could lift our spirits."

Ursula shrugged. "Fine."

⌒⌒⌒

Cappella had never played for anyone besides her mother and her wolf. She didn't much feel like playing, not after Ursula made clear what she really thought of musicians. But Sabine had asked. Cappella liked Sabine, she decided. She wanted Sabine to like her. And maybe Sabine and Hans knew each other.

She took herself to a flat, moss-covered rock away from the fire, away from the smoke and the people. It felt strange, to play her pipe for people knowing they expected to be entertained. She'd never thought of music as that before. It was what she did to say what was on her mind when she didn't have the words for it or another person's ears to hear her. She sat, put her pipe to her lips, and found an opening that she could make work. A short song. That's what she'd play. One Hans liked.

She played a few lines, but then something took hold of her, and she shifted into a song that expressed how she really felt: like telling Ursula where she could shove her crown.

It felt good to get it out. Probably the way Ursula and Sabine felt when they were running through the forest roaring at each other, being their wildest selves.

When Cappella finished, she looked up. The flames of the campfire flickered, but that was the only motion. Her mother was still. Her cousin, still. All the people from the kingdom, still. Behind them, looking at her with his wide gray eyes, was Hans, along with his sister. All those eyes on her, especially his, felt like too much.

She couldn't be here. Not another second. She excused herself and headed home. First slowly, quietly. And then as fast as her feet would take her. Not too far behind her, making enough noise that she could hear him, Hans followed.

XXVIII

Cappella ducked into her tree. Hans hesitated a few yards away, something he never would have done as a wolf. Had this been years ago, before all this, and had she been upset by something, he would have lain next to her, his head in her lap, until he felt her sadness lift. Back then, he'd always known how she was feeling. It was partly his wolf nature and partly a result of how much time they'd spent together. He was fluent in the language her body spoke. Every gesture, every nuance, he knew.

It was different now. Time had made that so. He'd been in the cottage with Greta when he heard her play. The song at first was one he knew. He wanted to bring Greta to her, to introduce them. But as they approached the camp, Cappella's music turned angry. Livid. It was at him. It had to be. She'd saved his life and then he'd left her—he had a good reason, of course. But why hadn't he brought Cappella with him?

He had to make things right. He didn't know if it was possible. She wasn't the same girl he'd once known. Her music told him so. She'd always been very good. Now she was transcendent. The anger she played burrowed inside his heart. He'd do anything not to have to feel it.

"Cappella!" he called.

He approached her tree but could not bring himself to enter without knocking. After three light taps, he stuck his face inside.

The heart of the tree glowed gold, sketching beautiful shapes on the charcoaled walls. He said her name softly, as a question. She looked at him and then into her lap at the pipe that lay across it. When she looked at him again, he knew it was all right for him to enter.

They faced each other across a lantern with their knees close enough to touch.

"I'm sorry," he said.

"You didn't do anything."

He knew that was untrue. "Why did you leave when you saw me?"

"I didn't want to be there anymore," she said. "Why'd you follow me?"

He tried to choose words as carefully as she'd chosen notes for her song. "I followed you because I *had* to."

Cappella's eyes narrowed. "Who made you? Did my mother?"

"It wasn't like that. No one made me, no one but myself."

She pulled her cloak around her shoulders. "We don't know each other anymore, Hans. And you've been gone for so long. I got used to it. I had to. And it turns out, I didn't know you the way I thought I did."

"Cappella." He didn't want to cry, but he couldn't help it. Albrecht had mocked him every time he cried, which hadn't been often. But still. He let the tears flow. "Forgive me. Please forgive me."

"I'm not angry with you," she said.

"But the music."

"That was for Ursula. I want her to eat bees."

He snorted at the image of that. Her face had softened, and he knew she wasn't mad at him, but he couldn't stop crying.

"When I was in the castle, I had only one thing of my own. I'd bought the cloak for you the day we were taken. I held on to it. Every night, I slept with it."

She started to cry too. And then she laughed. "That would explain the smell."

He laughed with her, and it felt so good.

"Look at us," she said. "We're ridiculous. I haven't cried like this since I was little. Not since you left."

"You grew up," he said. "If not for your pipe and your hair, I might not have recognized you."

"I think if we are talking about who has changed the most, we'd be talking about you. And I don't just mean that you've become a far bigger wolf."

"What do you mean, then?" He was still careful, but it felt as though words between them were coming more easily.

"I mean that you revealed yourself to be a complete scoundrel."

He blanched.

"All that time we were children," she said, "you could have carried our food and water and you made me do it."

They laughed again, even as he was still sobbing. She put her hand on his knee and they were silent awhile.

Then he said, "I never meant to fool you. It wasn't like that."

"I know why you hid your human aspect. I am angry that you were taken away, that you were kept from me. This was because of the king, was it not?"

It was. The king and the queen. Albrecht too. And, he supposed, Ursula.

"I'm also angry that my mother knew who you were and didn't tell me. I thought you'd died, Hans."

He'd sometimes wished he had, though he didn't feel right saying it out loud.

"And I'm angry that my cousin isn't more like you. She's awful." Then her expression turned avid. "Was she like that in the castle? Or was she saving that for me because I'm a lowly musician? And was the castle extraordinary?"

Hans shrugged. He knew a lot more about Albrecht than Ursula. And Cappella was no doubt wondering about a different sort of castle life than the one he'd had. He didn't want to talk about what his time there had been like. Not at length. To talk about all that Albrecht had done to him, all that Albrecht had made him do . . . that would make it all real again. Telling the story made it harder to forget.

She reached for his hands. His breath caught. It felt so intimate, so tender. More than he could bear. She turned his palms up and looked at his fingertips and his torn nails.

"Does it hurt terribly?"

He swallowed and shook his head. Other things hurt worse.

"Your fingers are warm," she said.

"Yours aren't." Hers were like ice. His, in contrast, were sweating. He hoped it didn't bother her. He didn't want her to let go. Her fingers touching his felt like he'd swallowed the night sky and was holding starlight in his chest. He wanted to burst.

When he dared, he stole glances, memorizing the way the light of the lamp found the edges of her, bathing them in gold. He'd never looked at her face like this. He knew her features, of course. She had black hair with a white streak on the side. Brown-black eyes. Skin the color of raw wood. But he'd never seen the beauty in her. Not like this.

"Thank you for following me," she said.

"It was because I had to," he said again, trusting that this time, she'd understand.

"What now?" she asked.

He knew what he wanted to do: pull the cloak with Cappella in it toward him. He wanted to kiss her. There was the matter of the lamp between them, which would probably set them both on fire, but he felt that way already. Even the tips of his ears burned. But did she want him?

Their physical relationship had been so much easier when they were little. Then, every touch did not have so much weight, so much tension. He wouldn't trade those days for this one. He hated feeling like this, and he loved it too. He had never felt more alive than in this moment.

He also knew, all the way in his marrow, that he wouldn't kiss her until he was sure that she wanted that too. And he couldn't know unless he asked. And there was simply no way he would. He didn't have the nerve.

He set her hands in her lap, wiped the sweat from his own, and stood. "We should go back, I think. People will want more music."

XXIX

After Albrecht had reunited his kingdom and vanquished his sister, he took stock. His side had suffered losses, yes. That was a shame, a shame to see good men brought down by beasts. A shame to see productive farms reduced to ash, especially at harvest time. But they would rebuild. In the meantime, he'd dug into the treasury. A gold coin for every family who'd lost a man.

He had plenty for now, although with his mother dead, replacing them would be difficult. He would find a way, though. He would mint coins with his face on them so that people did not forget who'd given them so much.

The days passed. Jutta remained in the castle. He needed her more than his people needed horseshoes and nails. She made a decent replacement for Hans. And she'd redoubled her efforts to prove she was loyal. She'd already handed over every sword in her shop. Promised to make more if they were needed. She'd even apologized for her were nature.

Albrecht had thumped her back. "It is not necessary, my old friend, I know you know man from monster and right from wrong."

Some weeks after the battle, after the smoke had finally cleared and the sky had stopped snowing ash, he and Jutta were eating a meal together when a visitor was announced. A farmer, it seemed, making wild claims.

"I know where your sister is," the man said.

"My sister is dead," Albrecht said. "I shot her."

"Beg your pardon, Your Majesty. She lives."

Albrecht picked up a roasted leg of chicken and tore into it. He thought best while chewing.

"I'll tell you for a price," the man said.

Albrecht swallowed. The man had brought knowledge, but he'd contradicted the king. And his request for money—astonishing. He blinked slowly at the farmer. Assessed him. Large. Appeared to have been well fed over the years. Not a were.

Albrecht's curiosity won. "Where is she?"

"Not just she," the man said. "Everyone who's left. Near about three dozen, including children. Many weres. Goats and foxes and such."

That was interesting. A handful of survivors was one thing. But a handful, including weres, with Ursula? That was different. It meant she was plotting. Undoubtedly intending retaliation. He could wipe all of them out. He'd have to before too long.

"Show me," he said.

Jutta pushed her plate away.

"Not you," he said. "You have other work to do."

⸻

Albrecht and the farmer set out for the woods. He should've known Ursula was there somewhere. It's where she always went. He'd been preoccupied distributing coins. He should have considered the possibility of her survival. Nonetheless, knowing exactly where they were would save him time and effort.

The farmer pointed at the remains of a campfire. All around, the soil was gray with ash. "This is the first place we camped. Before the queen found us.

But she moved us to a place near a cottage where they have all sorts of supplies laid in. We burned the bodies of the dead there."

If his sister had moved near Greta's cottage, a plot between them was certain. But first, to deal with the farmer. The man had embarrassed him. He'd betrayed his queen for coin. He'd do the same to Albrecht at the first opportunity. The fool had sealed his own fate.

"I suppose you'll still want to be paid for this," Albrecht said.

The farmer held out his hand. "If you wouldn't mind. I did lose quite a bit in the fighting, you see."

Albrecht flicked his right hand toward the man, quick as a blink. His knife found its mark and the man dropped, his mouth open, as if he'd had the surprise of his life. Albrecht knelt, pulled the blade from the farmer's heart, and wiped the blood on the dead man's tunic.

With the toe of his boot, Albrecht nudged the man's gaping jaw shut. The clack of his teeth was the most satisfying sound he'd heard all day.

Albrecht found the clearing near the cottage. He was glad for the forest music, which had covered his footsteps. From a distance, he studied Ursula's sad little band of survivors. A group of werechildren sat at the black were's knee in their animal form, along with some humans. Three little goats bouncing on springy legs. A pair of foxes that playfully bit each other's necks. Raccoons with disturbing black hands. It was a wonder no one had yet tripped his snare. If only he'd moved it a few yards closer.

He settled in to watch and consider his approach. Most troubling, if not surprising: Hans and Greta had joined them. It hurt him viscerally to see them there. He'd given both of them everything they had; that they had no loyalty to him felt worse than his missing finger.

As far as he could tell, Ursula seemed to have made a full recovery. He was somewhat surprised that she wasn't showing more effects of the arrows he'd sunk into her flesh, but then, she was an exceptionally large animal and those were the hardest to kill. Next time, he'd aim for her heart.

It would be difficult to eliminate this nest by himself, particularly given the presence of the second werebear and Hans. He'd need soldiers. He'd have to take his best. Anything less than a clean sweep would invite retaliation.

He'd take his time. Plan. Train men. He didn't want to outright kill any weres, not when they might have so much to teach him about pain and its connection with life. He needed them alive before he needed them dead.

He returned alone, hands empty, heart full, mind hard at work.

~~~~~~~

Later, as Jutta fitted a steel not-finger to his stump, Albrecht thought about gold. How he'd used it to make his people love him. It had its advantages, but a leader needed more than gold to hold on to power. He considered his father's stories. To tell a story was to seize power. To tell a story was to preserve the power that had been seized. His people needed tales to reassure them that all was well, better than ever, even though food supplies were scarcer than they should have been heading into the winter. He needed to tell these stories so they would stop believing their own eyes and instead believe the vision he was selling them for their own good.

Jutta tightened the leather straps that held the finger secure. "It is a perfect fit, I think. Does it hurt?"

"Hurt?" Albrecht shook his head. It excited him. Thrilled him. A better finger than nature could have designed. He inspected her work.

"Well done," he said.

Jutta looked pleased, and this, in turn, pleased him.

"You are a loyal creature," he said. "I value that. I wonder what makes you so?"

"A horse's nature is to serve. To be broken, saddled, ridden." She packed away her tools. "What's more, I have known you since you were a little boy. I know what's in your heart. You wish to protect us all. That's a thing that deserves loyalty, or so I say."

"You are rare among humans and even rarer among weres. Do you know the best way for me to get loyalty from the rest of my subjects?"

"By leading them well, I suppose. In times of war and times of peace. A good leader earns loyalty."

Albrecht laughed. That sounded like something Ursula might say. "No."

"Is it the metal men?"

"Not that either, although talking about those has been nearly as useful as if I'd actually built an army. Shall I let you in on the secret?"

Jutta nodded.

"As you know, I rallied my men. We had our battle. We earned our victory. But the loyalty that comes from such things is shallow. Such loyalty can be stolen with words—words that promise something better, words that question the rightness of the king. And do you know why that is?"

Jutta set down her case of tools. She kept looking at it, as though she wanted to open it up again, that she wanted a reason to do so. "Your Majesty, I do not."

"Because of fear," Albrecht said. "At heart, most people live their lives in fear. You should know this. You're a prey animal."

She nodded. Her eyes were wide enough that he could see their whites. He rather thought she'd bolt if she could.

"There is no shame. Humans are prey animals as well. Unlike insects, our bodies have no armor. We have no fangs, no claws. We cannot fly. Some among us have figured out how to be predators, how to dominate, even with these paltry bodies our mothers made us. The best way for a leader to remain on top is to harness the power of fear. If you make your people fear a threat from the outside, then there is no threat from the inside that will dismantle their loyalty. Fear is the engine of power."

"I suppose that is true," Jutta said.

"Of course it's true. And do you wonder how I know this?"

Jutta swallowed and licked her lips. "I do not wonder. That is to say, I trust that you speak truth and that, perhaps, you learned the art of it from your father."

"My father was preoccupied with other matters," he said.

His father had thought only of who should succeed him. He'd thought of what his mother had wanted. He had not thought about how to secure the kingdom, and it had failed. Those his father had shown lenience to, Hans and Greta, had left at first opportunity, even after all the attentions and mercies Albrecht himself had paid them over the years. He'd favored them, and they left all the same. Their father had never bothered to instill them with fear, proper fear of the forest. Albrecht would not repeat that error.

The only way to keep people, Albrecht knew now, was to make them fear life without you. Once you had someone in that spot, you had them until death.

"No, Jutta. I did not learn this from my father. I learned it from those who betrayed me. Come, it's time to head to the square. I will show you the power of fear."

They walked in silence from the castle to the square, where his people had gathered. With Jutta behind him, he stood on the platform where the fighting cage had once sat, where he'd been humiliated by Ursula. The cage had been melted down, though the memory was lodged deep, like a shard of glass.

For the occasion he'd dressed in his father's golden clothing, garments woven from thread his mother had made with her own two hands. When Albrecht had been a boy, he couldn't imagine ever fitting into them. And yet, here he was, standing before his people as their undisputed king, wearing that fine clothing the likes of which no one else possessed.

He stood high enough above the crowd that he could see every face, every pair of eyes trained on him. It was everything he'd ever imagined made manifest, and all that it had cost him was a finger. It could be argued that it hadn't even cost him that. He'd lost it in a rat trap that he hadn't needed to pick up. But the narrative he was spinning was that his sister had severed it in a fit of vanity, so he would spin that into the truth.

And he *was* spinning, he realized. Just as his mother had turned grass into gold, he was turning words into weapons. It struck him then that these things were his true inheritance. His father had taught him how to find the meaning in stories; his mother had given the ability to spin words that meant exactly what he wanted his people to believe.

He was his parents' son. He was the rightful heir to a unified kingdom. He could not be who he was without the legacies both had left him. He lifted his hands.

Mouths closed. Save for the music of the forest, there was no sound. It made his skin tingle, that absence. It was a space he could fill. Albrecht thrust his chin forth and spun words. He spun them, and with them he wove fear.

"There is an army of frissers in the woods," he said. "Legions of beasts bent on revenge. And the most dangerous one, my sister, has lived. Against all odds, she survived the shot I sank into her back."

The crowd gasped, a great sucking sound that Albrecht could feel. He gesticulated as he spoke, and it was like running his hands along the curves of a beautiful woman. Greta. His rage crested.

"Somehow my sister lived, and so long as she draws breath, the danger is clear."

"Let's kill her!" a voice shouted. "Kill the bear!"

Albrecht was not certain who started it. Nor did it matter. It could have been anyone. The important part was that the thing he'd woven had become as real as gold and just as valuable.

Soon the chant was on everyone's lips. "Kill the bear! Kill the bear!"

The sound rose. Like a sun, like a tower. He basked in it. He marveled. He raised his hands again and the crowd fell silent.

"We will kill her," he said. "We will, we will, we will."

Three times, to make it truth.

"And not just her," he said. "We'll kill them all. Every frisser. We will end this scourge. Defeat these beasts. Keep you and those you love safe from her army."

The crowd roared back, and it *was* a roar. Animalistic in the sense that Albrecht had always envied. That Ursula could make such sounds all on her own, that she had paws that ended in blades, that she was so powerful . . . that the throne was to be hers . . . it was everything he had always been denied. But here he was, the master of a much larger beast, one he'd wound with words. His face split into a smile so big it hurt.

He turned to Jutta, tapping his not-finger on her nose.

He shouted, so that she'd hear him over the crowd, "Was that not splendid?"

Jutta nodded back, red-faced. He gestured with his head so that she would know it was time for them to leave. He had plans to complete, and he needed her by his side.

XXX

Cappella and Esme spent their nights in the tree and their days at the refugee camp. Over time, the clearing felt more and more like a tiny village. The survivors had smoothed the earth and set up tents reclaimed from Cage Row in midnight raids. The work had taken weeks, and now when people woke up, they woke to visible breath and frost-skimmed grounds. No one slept in cages. No one ever would again.

Ursula had been much friendlier since that first day, and Cappella had grown to enjoy watching her cousin run things. She cared. She did. It was undeniable. She sometimes didn't show it well.

Sabine was always by her side, but there was something strange about the way they moved when they were near each other. It felt stiff and uncomfortable. They had no bruises or injuries that she could discern, but the look in their eyes spoke of pain.

Cappella had seen them together in the forest for years. She'd avoided them, of course, first because they were bears, and then because she knew they were humans. Back then, they'd seemed as close as two lips. Now all sense of that was gone. She wished she understood why.

She'd only ever had her mother to get along with; it had never occurred to her that bonds of love could break. But in the past few weeks, rifts were all she'd felt. Between her and her mother. Between Ursula and Sabine. The two halves of the kingdom. Things had fallen apart.

Cappella wished she understood what broke people apart. It was clear what Ursula believed: that her brother's violence had been the cause of all destruction, and that she could restore things with more violence.

To that end, Ursula had decided that everyone in the little village needed to learn how to fight. Cappella wanted to be good at this. She'd envisioned herself side by side with Hans, doing whatever one did to combat the forces of wickedness. But the first time Sabine came running at her with a stick, Cappella had dropped to the ground, positioned herself in the shape of an egg, and begged for mercy. Hans had at least had the decency not to laugh, but he was the only one.

Hans, of course, was a superb warrior, especially in his wolf form. He often watched over the camp while Ursula and Sabine sparred. Cappella liked watching him patrol, stopping every now and then to swish his tail at the older people who were tending their small fires, mending clothes, and preparing food.

One afternoon when he was doing this, she decided to play him a song, a soft one. As they'd started doing lately, the little werechildren gathered at her feet in their animal forms. Some rolled in the clover and swatted at each other, gently and in good fun, while the goats cracked nuts in their teeth. Cappella was grateful. There was nothing like the sight of children playing to help a person feel hope.

Hans sat down next to her. He'd shifted back to his human form and dressed. She couldn't play, not with him sitting so close.

"Don't stop. I liked it."

She lowered the pipe. "I was finished anyway."

"I'm hungry."

"You're always hungry."

"I want all the food. All of it."

They sat close enough that their shoulders touched. "What else do you want?"

"Don't even ask," he said.

She bristled. Information withheld felt like a lie. But maybe he didn't want to hurt her with the truth. Maybe he'd left someone behind in the kingdom. She knew he'd suffered there. She could see it on his face whenever the subject came up. There might be someone he missed. She wanted to console him, even as it broke her heart.

"What's wrong?" he asked.

"Nothing." She pretended to polish her pipe on the hem of her tunic. Two people could withhold truths.

He squinted, as if to examine her face more closely. He looked ridiculous. She couldn't help but smile.

"Do you want to practice fighting?" he asked.

"Oh, I think I've perfected my technique."

Hans laughed. "All the same, it would be fun, wouldn't it?" He stood and offered her a hand. She let him pull her up slowly, to make it last.

"Not here, though," she said. The last thing she wanted was for everyone to see her in her humiliation.

"Lead the way," he said.

Cappella brought him to a clearing at the far edge of the woods. Beyond it was a plummet to the river; its churning meant that even the forest song was distant, muted. The trees would be the only witnesses.

Hans brought two fighting sticks. It stung to be struck by one, but Cappella wasn't ready for swords or knives.

"Ready?" Hans tossed her a stick.

She caught it one-handed. "See? I'm a master."

Hans shook his head, half smiling. They faced off. He started with the pattern they'd practiced. She kept up as well as she could, but trying to remember the moves took so much of her focus that she became clumsy.

"It's all right," he said. "Keep going."

"It's not as though King Albrecht's soldiers are going to come at us with sticks," Cappella said.

"True," Hans said.

"Then why are we trying? What's the point?"

"When you first started on your pipe, could you play the songs that you can play now?" Hans jumped back and she just missed his knuckles.

"No."

"Learning new skills takes time," he said. "You have to master the basics first."

"You mastered them in a single go." She was whining. She knew it. But it was true. She sliced down at him.

He parried her neatly. "You don't turn yourself into an egg anymore."

"If anyone came at me with anything more dangerous than this stick, I would turn into an egg, hatch as a chicken, and promptly perish."

She lost track of the move she was supposed to make and pulled the stick into her chest. Hans stopped short of whacking her on the shoulder.

"You never feared me when I was a wolf," he said.

"You were a cub! You were fluffy and small. How could I resist?"

"I'm irresistible. I know."

She laughed. "Modest too."

"All right," he said. "Let's see how you do against a wolf."

Before she could fully register his meaning, he was out of his clothes and stretching into his wolf form, tongue out, tail wagging.

He ran at her, and she brought her stick down swiftly, not expecting to hit him but hoping at least for a tap. He jumped back just in time, caught her stick in her teeth, and wrested it from her grip, knocking her onto her bottom.

Do not become an egg. Do not become an egg. She very much wanted to become an egg.

He looked as if he might pounce, so she rolled away before he could pin her. She pushed herself up. He dropped her stick, and she wasn't sure if she was supposed to pick it up or defend herself with her bare hands. Then she remembered her pipe and pulled it out of her pocket. That was better than a stick. Much harder.

She was breathing hard, part from exertion and part from the thrill of being alone with Hans and not having to worry about touching him. She was *supposed* to right now. She brandished the pipe and then lunged, as if she meant to strike his snout. He fell for it, and the second he leapt up, mouth open, she pulled back and spun away. He skidded as he landed, and she could tell she'd unbalanced him.

He turned, head low, creeping closer. She was glad she knew him as well as she did; otherwise it would have been terrifying to stand before a wolf with a mouth full of such large teeth. What would Ursula do? Cappella wasn't sure.

She'd watched Ursula and Sabine spar—the only time lately the two women hadn't seemed at odds. They were so big that when Sabine flipped Ursula, the earth shook. And it wasn't just their size. They also looked so well matched when they fought, as if they had been made for it and for each other.

And what had Cappella been made for? Entertainment, she supposed. How feeble. She ran toward Hans. He rose on his hind legs. Then he put his paws on her shoulders and licked her face. Her knees buckled. She fell on her back, still holding her pipe. He pinned her in the dirt. So much for being like Ursula.

"You killed me," she said. "I am slain. Let the mourning commence." She wiped her wet face. "Ew, Hans."

Hans lay down on top of her the way they sometimes had when they were little. She'd felt the weight of him on her before, but it had never felt like this, not with the soft earth beneath her and the solid weight of him on top of her. She was out of breath from exertion, but also from the thrill of his heartbeat against her chest.

She had no idea what to do with her hands. One still held the pipe and the other she finally decided to rest in his fur, caressing him gently as she had when she was a little girl and it had seemed a safe and natural thing to do. Neither one of them moved for the longest time. She loved him. She knew it to her bones. She loved him in every way a girl could love a boy. Her throat caught. Then, before she could say anything, Hans's ears pricked, and he turned his head toward the woods. He stood, lip curled.

The little fox brothers, Sebastian and Simon, tumbled out of the bush. They were in their human form, yet she couldn't help but think of them as foxes because of their deep orange hair and clever eyes.

"Queen Ursula sent us to find you," Sebastian said, his cheeks bright.

"And we did." Simon laughed and touched his fingertips together and made kissing sounds with his lips.

Cappella sat and brushed dirt from her hair.

"Hans was helping me with combat," she said.

"That's not what it looked like," Sebastian said.

Hans growled playfully and leapt at the brothers, who scattered like leaves. They were still giggling when he took his human form and dressed. Cappella didn't mean to peek as he did, but he was so quick about it she could hardly have looked away.

Then his hand was on hers, pulling her up. They stood almost as close as they had been when they were lying down. She liked this too. The slice of space between them crackled the way the air does before a thunderstorm. She watched his gaze travel from her eyes to her lips.

She remembered what was in her other hand. Her pipe. She smiled wickedly and jabbed his ribs.

"Oof, Cappella!"

"You said it yourself. Albrecht doesn't fight fair."

Hans snatched the pipe away and stuffed it in his pocket. "You're unarmed."

"At your mercy," she said.

He laced his fingers through hers. "Shall we?"

She couldn't speak for the thrill of it. They headed back to camp.

XXXI

Jutta and Albrecht sweltered in the workshop. She gave Albrecht a pair of metal wings the size of his hand. This was the lightest set they'd made, a curved filigree of steel so thin it sang when he swished it through the air. He tested its hinge, an ingenious thing triggered by pressure, powered by small gears. In a gust of wind, it would give just so. The creature wearing it would fly. That, at least, was the plan.

"This is good work," he said.

Jutta shrugged. She was looking tired to him, tired and older than ever. "I still feel that attaching it with a leather harness would be less risky."

"Then it is no different than a piece of clothing or a boot. It's not an achievement."

Jutta's insistence on this point irritated him. He wished he didn't need her help, but without her, he couldn't work nearly as fast or as well. His not-finger was strong, but clumsy. He would continue to improve it. But for now, it was an obstacle.

He strode to a large cloth-covered cage in the corner. He whipped the cover away, and the small creature inside turned its head. In anticipation of a bite to eat, it extended a pair of wings and flapped them. And then it stood on its four rat feet and walked to the edge of the cage. It was still healing where the wings had been stitched into its flesh—a pair of crooked red-black seams.

"What do you think? Should we test this one?"

Jutta peered into the cage. "It is promising that the wings are remaining in place. But perhaps we wait until the creature is fully mended."

Albrecht unlatched the cage and removed the rat. Such revolting things. So low to the ground. So *nothing* to look at. To be a rat would be the worst imaginable fate. He had done this one a kindness. If his device worked, this rat would no longer be lord of the greasy crevice. It would rule the sky.

He saw no reason to give the rat more time to heal. He took it from his cage, opened the window, and flung it into the late autumn air. It arched into the golden sky, spreading its legs and tail. This was its instinct, and that motion was enough to open the wings. It caught an updraft, and the rat soared out and over the courtyard.

For a moment anyway.

The foolish thing scrabbled its limbs and then the wings separated from its body and both plummeted to the stones below. The wings bounced. The rat did not.

"Well, that's that," Albrecht said.

"I'm sorry," Jutta said.

"Sorry? Why on earth?"

"I'm sorry that the wings failed."

"Hardly. They were a smashing success." He thumped her on the back. "Come. I feel like celebrating."

Albrecht stored his hunting gear in the room next to his workshop. He eyed Jutta and handed her leather armor, a pair of knives, and his old sword.

"What is this for?"

"For you to wear." She sometimes needed a great deal of instruction.

"But . . . why would I need this? When you said you felt like celebrating, I thought you had a stein or two of ale in mind."

"Don't tell me you're saying nay."

"Nay? I wouldn't—"

He cackled. "Always the horse. *Nay.*"

Jutta blinked slowly, and Albrecht could tell his little joke vexed her. She was so sensitive. "Ah, yes, Your Majesty. I'm not putting my foot down on the armor and weapons. I am afraid, well, I don't understand what you mean them for. I was . . . curious."

"There's going to be a wedding," he said.

"You're still soaring right past me," Jutta said.

"I have decided that the kingdom is in need of a celebration and there is none so grand as a wedding."

"I don't doubt you, and yet—"

"And yet?" Jutta was trying his patience.

"And yet why are we dressed as if for a hunt?"

She really was so slow of wit. It was a good thing she was loyal, or he'd have to stuff and mount her. "We are dressed as if for a hunt because we are *going on a hunt*," he said slowly. "You and I are hunting for my bride."

Her neck stiffened and her head gave a little tremble, as though her horse aspect was about to emerge. But she kept herself intact. She dressed and hung the weapons around her, and he did the same. He went to the cabinet where he stored his fingers and thought about which would best serve. The poison finger. To catch a bride meant he'd have to be in close range, and what would be more useful than something that could inject enough poison to paralyze a bear in half a minute?

"Be prepared to spend the night in the woods," he said.

Jutta nodded. Albrecht supposed it would be no hardship for someone with an animal aspect to sleep anywhere. He didn't even mind that she'd be out of her cage. There was nothing she could do to him as a horse. After getting provisions from the kitchen, they stopped by the stables so he could get his mount.

"You're fine on foot, I take it."

Jutta nodded again. "These boots are as good as hooves. I'll keep up."

He was sure that was true. Jutta was getting older, but she remained powerful. She hadn't gone soft the way so many women do, not that he minded a bit of softness in women. But her work at the forge had hardened her hands and muscles and turned her skin into something like a hide. Even in her human form, she seemed half animal.

He wondered, looking at her, what that felt like. He'd never envied her this aspect—he'd hate to be prey. But he wanted to be able to shift. He hungered for it. His own experiments with flight had already taken so much effort, and he had not achieved the success he craved. But that would come. He was certain.

A groom saddled the mount. Albrecht swung a leg over his stallion's back, and then they were off at a trot, he in the lead and Jutta running lightly behind. He knew where he'd find Greta, or thereabouts, in the little cottage he'd seen her enter. He hadn't checked his trap since. There hadn't been time, and if he'd caught anything in the interim, it didn't matter, whether it was animal or human. He supposed it might be considered a waste, but a king had to be above such considerations.

His plan had crystallized slowly. He'd been drawn to Greta since the moment he laid eyes on her. There was her hair, as light as his. Her face, pale and symmetrical, like a well-made vessel. She'd been young, yes, but so was he, and he knew the purpose of attraction. It was to inspire procreation, something a man could not yet do on his own.

As the years passed, his desire increased. He loved watching her at work, her hair always in a neat braid down the center of her back. He knew she wanted him too. He could see it in the way her hand tightened around the knife handle whenever he entered. The way her cheeks pinkened as she looked up at him and then down again at whatever poor animal she was reducing to parts. Would she have stayed if she'd known she could have him? If she could be queen?

He had to admit he'd originally not thought of putting a crown on her head. The attraction was more urgent than that, and his interest in the benefit to her was less. But in the time that he'd been on the throne, he'd realized it was the perfect plan. There was the satisfaction it would give him. There was the joy it would give a kingdom starved for such things. And it would carry on a tradition started by his father, one in which a woman of common blood was elevated to royalty. His people would love him for this even more than they already did. She would be grateful and would repent abandoning him.

There was the chance, of course, that she'd bear a were. Her brother was one, his sister too. But he'd know what to do if and when the time came. He'd find a way to use it to his advantage.

Once he and Jutta had entered the forest, Albrecht slowed. The music would cover much of the noise he was making, but he didn't want anyone to know he was coming. He stopped and dismounted. Daylight was waning. Just threads, really, dropping through the partly bare tree branches. They'd move right before dawn.

XXXII

Ursula didn't sleep well. That had become normal: nights when she was awakened in her tent by noises, by scents. She'd burst from sleep, heart quivering. She'd lie still, trying to determine whether what had made her stir was real or imagined. The rupture had happened so many times—and it was always nothing—that she'd come to think of these events as night ghosts.

This time, a troubling sound ripped her awake. She dismissed it and tried to force herself back to sleep. Just before the heaviness claimed her, she heard something, the scuff of a boot against leaves and then an unnatural stillness. She held her breath. The sound could have been someone from the camp needing to empty their bladder. But if it had been, why the conspicuous silence afterward?

Ah, well; she was awake now. If she was going to catch someone watering a tree, so be it.

She poked her nose through the flap. Another scuff—this one followed by the soft whicker of a horse. She smelled her brother. She shifted to her bear form, knocking over her tent as she did. Mist curled around her paws as she turned toward the scent. She stepped onto the frosted ground, making no attempt to muffle her movements. She *wanted* the whole camp awake. She chased the scent.

Albrecht stood alone outside the cottage. His golden hair shone in the moonlight. He might have brought other men with him, but she couldn't smell any. Still, she knew to be wary. He slipped inside the door and she moved closer, her head low, every sense on alert.

What did he want? Greta and the werechildren were inside, along with their supplies. It made sense he would want the supplies. Then he could starve them out. Even he wouldn't do more than that, though. To kill refugees? Children? That was beneath him. He'd left them in their cages on the night of his attack, after all. She could not imagine he'd ever harm the little ones.

If she followed him inside, Albrecht might turn violent, and she couldn't risk that. Not near the children. Her best bet was to catch him when he left the cottage.

A noise behind her. The snap of a rope, the sound of scuffling, a low growl. *Sabine*. Ursula turned. She couldn't see the bear anywhere. Ursula followed the noise up, up, up—and there Sabine was, suspended high between two trees, caught in a trap. Ursula pondered her next move. She could either stop Albrecht or help Sabine. She couldn't do both. A rationale struck. If she rescued Sabine, then Sabine could help her.

Ursula reached the snare. The rope smelled of Albrecht's hands. The control she'd developed over the years as a princess vanished. When she was like this, it was hard to remember that she even had a human aspect, one that would weigh decisions at all. When she was fully her bear self, there was only the moment she was in, and only the thing she wanted then. She wanted Sabine. Nothing else mattered.

The ropes were out of reach and Sabine dangled overhead, upside down and struggling. Ursula followed the rope down the side of the tree. Enraged, she gnawed the rope around the tree. It was hard going because the rope was lashed so tightly around the trunk. Splinters pierced her tongue and gums and still the rope held. Where was Hans? Where was Esme? Did she have to do everything herself?

Frustrated, she switched to claws. This was better. She took great gouges out of the bark. The rope frayed, and then it snapped.

Sabine crashed to the ground with a *whuff*. When she could breathe again, she moaned. She was still wrapped in the net, so Ursula raked at it until it dropped away. Sabine lay on her back, gasping.

Ursula took her human form. "Sabine, what hurts?"

The black bear gave a low huff. She tried to roll over, but Ursula held her in place. Sabine snarled—a protest.

Ursula let go. "Can you shift? Why aren't you shifting—has he done something to you?"

Hans ran up, looking half asleep. Ursula grabbed his wrist. "Albrecht is here. Go after him."

He shifted and bounded off, having picked up Albrecht's trail. Sabine swatted Ursula away and limped after Hans. Ursula turned to follow as well, but they were too late. Albrecht had emerged with Greta over his shoulder, and he was vanishing into the woods. Hans swerved after them, a streak of gray.

Sabine wobbled and then stumbled. When Ursula reached her, Sabine was in her human form. Her right arm was broken, swollen with a most unnatural curve. She was sweating too. Ursula fell to her knees, putting a hand on Sabine's forehead.

"What are you doing?"

"You're hurt. Let me help."

"You should have let me chew my way out. Now your brother has Greta. Follow him. I'll be fine."

"But—"

Ursula stopped protesting when she saw Sabine's expression. Chastened, she took her bear form again and crashed through the camp. Burning with exertion and with shame, she ran, nose to the ground. The scent trail stretched in front of her, star-bright in her mind. She ran harder, confident she was faster. She could make this right.

Up ahead, a wounded horse screamed. Albrecht would now be on foot. She had him. She smelled the blood, steaming and rich with iron. Heart's blood. A mortal wound. Hans must have opened one of the poor animal's arteries.

She weaved through trees, pulled by the scent and the thrill of the chase. The sun had cracked the sky, swinging a low blade of light across the frosted ground. Ursula lifted her head. There was the fallen horse, dead, his neck torn open, hot blood sending curls of mist upward.

Ahead, Albrecht held a knife to Greta's neck. Jutta, in her horse form, stood behind them. Hans snarled, approaching slowly.

Albrecht snarled back. "Come closer and she dies."

He lifted Greta onto Jutta's back, keeping his blade close. He mounted the horse himself, sneered, and then shot away. Hans gave chase, raking Jutta's flank. Jutta screamed but kept running. Albrecht turned in the saddle, he pulled an arrow from his quiver, and aimed his bow.

Ursula flinched. The bow twanged. Hans howled and veered into the underbrush. Albrecht galloped ahead. Again a choice. She chose the wolf; she needed warriors more than maidens. The scent of his blood led her to a tree whose roots were drenched. She sniffed the soil around them, following the trail. The blood drops fell closer together now, and the line of them meandered, as though the boy was slowing to a stagger. The trail ended.

She found him deep inside a bush, curled into a quivering heap. She tore the shrub out by its roots and threw it aside. She'd have to carry him in her human form, because he was in no shape to hold on to her back.

By the time she reached the cottage with him, he'd shifted, a sign his injury was severe, possibly mortal. She laid him down outside. The door was open and revealed the damage her brother had done to the place she loved so much . . . broken chairs, broken porridge bowls. She hated him, truly hated him, something she'd never thought possible.

"Sabine! I need you!"

Sabine, her broken arm in a sling, rushed to her side, handed her clothing, and felt Hans's forehead.

"The arrow must come out," she said. "Then we stitch the wound and try to get him to shift back. He'll stand a better chance of healing as a wolf." She pressed a hand against the wound.

Ursula dressed in haste. "What if he can't?"

"There are ways. Some of us have been forced to do so many times."

Ursula wanted to ask what Sabine meant. It wasn't the time. She turned to one of the little weregoats, a girl who followed Sabine everywhere. "Bring me a needle and thread."

As Sabine ran the needle through a flame, Ursula dug a knee into the soil for leverage and pulled the arrow from Hans's chest. With the arrow came more blood. She pressed the wound to stop the flow as Sabine threaded the needle, as deftly as if her arm had not been broken.

As Ursula drew the needle through the torn flesh, Hans clutched Sabine's hand. Ursula felt a pang of jealousy. She turned back to the wound and finished her work.

His torn skin had been neatly mended, but the sight sickened her. Every one of them was so fragile. None of them could fend off an arrow, none could fend off a blade. She and her people would have to draw blood first. It was the only way they would survive.

"Can you shift?" Sabine asked.

Hans shook his head.

"You have to try," Sabine said.

He closed his eyes.

"Ursula, I can't help him, not like this." Sabine held up her broken arm.

"What do I have to do?"

"Make him feel as though he's fighting for his life."

Sabine was matter-of-fact about it, but there was bitter experience beneath her words. There were things about her Ursula hadn't known, differences between them she could not comprehend. No one would have dared force Ursula to change, though Albrecht certainly tried to goad her into it.

She welcomed her rage and became her bear self, shaking off her torn clothing and nipping his thigh, not hard enough to wound, but hard enough to hurt. He snarled. She bit his other leg. Hans's limbs sprouted hair. His jaw lengthened. His back curved and stretched into a tail and then he was the gray wolf, his wound hidden beneath fur.

As Ursula shifted back, Sabine said, "Bring water."

The little weregoat brought a bowl, and Sabine tipped it into his open mouth. Most ran out, but his tongue moved. Sabine fed him a trickle of water, his eyelids fluttering and tail twitching.

"Where's Greta?" Sabine wiped sweat, blood, and dust from her forehead. "Don't tell me Albrecht got away."

Ursula lowered her head.

"Is he going to kill her?"

Ursula swallowed. "I suspect my brother wants her alive or he would have killed her straightaway."

Albrecht's arrow lay next to Ursula, an angry thing sticky with blood. She scraped it clean with a thumbnail and traced the *A* that Jutta had engraved on it. Such vanity.

Sabine stroked Hans's head, scratching him gently behind the ears. He was breathing evenly now. "What will he do with her?"

"I don't know," she said.

Ursula could imagine Albrecht doing all sorts of things with Greta, none of them pleasant, none she wanted to say aloud. She didn't want Sabine to have to hear them. Nor did she want to speak them into existence, to acknowledge her brother's cruelty. She felt responsible. If she hadn't been born first, none of this would have happened. Had she not wanted to be queen . . . But she could not let herself complete that thought.

Sabine put a hand on her back. It was a gesture meant to console, but it was not one Ursula felt worthy to receive. Her job was to protect. She'd failed. Her job was to comfort. She didn't know how.

"We should tell Cappella," Sabine said.

Ursula was taken aback. Then she understood. She'd seen them wandering off together but hadn't made the connection. She felt shame that Sabine understood her people better than she did.

She looked out over the camp. A fire was going, and pots hung over it. No one lacked clothing or shoes, and there was even a neatly folded pile of additional garments, should anyone have need. Her people deserved better than what she had to offer.

She mulled what Sabine had said earlier about being forced to shift. She'd suffered in many ways that Ursula had never realized. A feeling that had been an undercurrent for weeks, as persistent in her as music was to the forest. The kingdom had been much worse for weres than Ursula had thought.

Her failure to understand this meant she was not ready to lead. And she'd done a bad job of things so far, with this being the worst day since the war itself. She was ignorant. If Hans died, it would be her fault. Sabine had been right not to want her. She'd been right about everything.

Ursula wasn't particularly close to the fire, but she suddenly felt unbearably hot.

"I'll be back in a few minutes. I'm going to the stream. Watch over him. I'll tell Cappella what happened on my way back."

Ursula knew what she wanted. To have Greta back among her people. For Hans to be well. She wanted revenge. A better life for her people. For all of them. She knew what they needed, and she would deliver it to them. It felt impossible, far more than she was equipped to bring about. But that was what it meant to be queen.

She hoped taking a swim in her bear form would provide her the clarity she needed—and that it would help her let go of her attachment to Sabine. Ursula wasn't worthy of her. She'd never felt so alone.

The storyteller is alone, and the weather has turned. He doesn't mind the cold wind off the sea as much as he minds the solitude. It is like this sometimes. If no one stops for him, then he becomes invisible, as if the people have collectively given themselves permission to look away.

People are like sheep, he thinks. There is either a crowd of them or there is no one, and when no one is there, stories suffocate, and the man fails to earn what he needs to eat.

He winds the key on the monkey's back. His mechanical friend opens its mouth and shrieks.

That stops them. Nothing like a cry of pain to capture the attention of people who suddenly remember they are not suffering.

"I hear your footsteps," the storyteller says, quietly so that they must come closer. "Tell me, are any among you wearing red shoes?"

No one speaks. No one ever does. Red shoes are rare, even though the stuff that makes the color—iron—is everywhere. Blood reeks of it. Weapons are made of it.

"Not a one among you wears red shoes," the storyteller says. "And I shall tell you why that is wise.

"Once upon a time, there was a beautiful girl. She knew her beauty set her above all the rest, and she became consumed by vanity. She wanted shoes that set her further apart.

"Red shoes. Red, the color of blood, of lips, of flowers asking for bees to dip deep into their throats."

He pauses. The audience is breathing, curling their toes, imagining blood and combat and lips and the stings of bees—all things that set human hearts to race, things that churn the red river inside all living bodies.

This is what he wants people to feel when they listen to him: to be carried on a river of blood to the sea where he's set up his nets. People are fish to him. They are something to catch.

"Whenever the girl wore the shoes, she thought of nothing but her own beauty. Beauty is a fine thing for a girl to have, but when it is all that she thinks of, she becomes useless."

"Useless," the audience whispers. They sound like the tide coming in.

The storyteller tugs the line. "A boy asked her to dance with him, but she would not keep step. She would not follow his lead. Instead the shoes, given life by the vanity inside her, danced to their own tune. They took their own steps. And they danced the girl away from the boy."

He lets his words crescendo. He is making music now, writing a song on the air.

"She could not stop dancing. *She could not stop!* Many people tried to help, but they could not touch her feet without slicing their hands. Her dancing even caused injury to the king. *The king!*

"The girl, consumed with her own vanity, danced herself out of the kingdom. She danced into a place of trees and wild animals. She danced until her skin turned dry as bark. Until her bones were branches. She danced herself to death. The only thing that remained were her shoes."

He has reeled them in from the sea of blood, red-drenched fish, gasping for breath. He winds the monkey again. The mouth opens. Shrieks. Coins fall in.

He will eat well tonight. He does not feel so alone.

PART
FIVE

XXXIII

Albrecht had not forgotten his first ride out of the woods on the back of a were. He'd been a boy in pain, humiliated by his fall. Once again, he was astride a were. But this time he was bringing home a queen. He felt neither pain nor humiliation. In his father's stories, this would be a moment of triumph for what was good and right.

When they arrived at the stable, Albrecht left Jutta behind. A groom could tend her wounds. Greta was surly and silent. Her bare feet were dirty, her soles rough. There hadn't been time for her to get shoes, of course. But he wouldn't have let her put them on anyway. Shoes only make it easier for a girl to run.

He wrapped a rope around her and tugged to remind her who was the hunter and who was the quarry.

Then he lifted her chin. "You might express some gratitude that you're still alive."

"Or I might not." She pulled away.

This was far more spark than she'd ever displayed in the kitchen. He loved it. She was worthy. His people would be elated at the prospect of a beautiful new queen and—shortly thereafter—an heir. If any resistance or doubt remained alive among them, this would crush it, bloodlessly.

"Did you know," he said, "that this finger is filled with a poison? I can use it to take away your pain. I can also use it to kill you."

"Why would you kill me after going to all this trouble to steal me?"

He laughed. She was right, of course. Beautiful, fiery, and smart. His plan had been brilliant. As they made their way to the tower, Albrecht couldn't resist pointing out his inventions. "If you wind the duck's key, its beak opens, and you can feed it morsels. It's very lifelike; it even defecates afterward. I was just a boy when I made it. Here we have iron ravens that can fling stones the size of plums. Their accuracy isn't perfect, but they are certainly terrifying, which is enough for me."

Greta said nothing. He thought she perhaps might resent being tied up, especially because the servants kept staring as they passed. He'd have to speak with them about this rudeness.

"If you promise to behave, I'll untie you," he said.

She gazed straight ahead.

"I cannot read your mind," he said.

"I'm quite sure you can guess what I'm thinking."

He paused in front of a clockwork man made of steel. It didn't do everything he'd hoped, but it had one amusing trick. "That one will kick you if you touch it. Would you like to see?"

Her eyes widened and she shook her head.

"You won't always find it so difficult to be good," he said. "I am certain."

He led her by the rope into his workroom. The forge had not been lit in days, so it was not sweltering. He'd also emptied the rat cages, flinging rat after rat out the window, so she wouldn't be able to see his progress there. Several of his best stuffed specimens were on display, though. A boar, an eagle, and a collection he thought she would like best: a family of ducklings, some of which he'd fitted with tiny shoes. He might make a wedding gift of those.

He watched her take in the room. Noticed the way her gaze rested on his cabinet of mechanical devices. It filled him with pride.

He picked up a small one. "This one crushes thumbs. Your brother didn't like it very much."

He held up a metal mask shaped like a rat. "Would you like to see how this works?"

She didn't answer. Still, the line of her jaw was pleasing when it was set like that. Strong and shapely. He smoothed a strand of hair that had come loose from her spectacular braid, tucking the end behind her ear. It was a perfect ear, small, full of detail, lit pink by the sun at the edges. If only he were able to build something so fine.

He felt an urge to bite her. He didn't. But he desperately wanted to make her cry out, to make her beautiful face twist in pain. To remind her that she was alive. That they were alive, together.

"Please, sit." He guided her into the chair in the middle of the room, removed the rope that bound her, and strapped her right wrist to the armrest before she realized what he was doing. She stood, struggling, and that made it easy for him to secure her left ankle too. He considered fastening all four straps, but she wouldn't be going anywhere. There was no need for such effort.

As she strained against the straps, he pressed the mask to her face, tightening the bands against the back of her head. He stuffed a spiked ball through the mouth hole and sealed a little door over it.

"I know that it's difficult for you to breathe," he said. "But there is a point to that. The point is for you to keep still."

She blinked through the eye slits. Her deep blue eyes were like gems.

"This is called a scold's bridle," he said. "It's designed to keep a nasty woman quiet. If you try to say anything, your tongue will be sliced open. But perhaps you've already discovered that."

She gagged. Blood dripped down her chin.

"Careful now," he told her. "If you vomit, it will be unpleasant for us both."

He went to his desk, knowing she could still see him. He lifted the metal box that had taken his finger.

"This device kills rats," Albrecht said. "When it's working properly, the head comes clean off." He showed her his hand. "Other things too."

Then he set down the trap, unlocked a cabinet, and removed a small box.

"I was dismayed at first to lose my finger, as you might imagine. But I've since come to realize I can design a much better finger than nature can. And that is my ambition. To be a great king by doing what men do best. We build."

He pulled the wrinkled remains of his finger from the box. Then he returned to Greta, holding it close to her face. It had gone soft and smelled of the alcohol he'd soaked it in. "Look at this. Pathetic, is it not?"

Behind the mask, her eyes grew shiny. He set the severed finger on her lap. Her left hand, still free, batted it away. Then he took both of her hands in his.

"Would you like me to remove the mask?"

Greta nodded, a tiny gesture.

To show her that he was a merciful man, he removed it. And then he wiped the blood from her chin.

"You will be good," he said. "You will do as I ask. All will be well."

She swallowed. Blood, he imagined. But also pride and all manner of other things that would only cause them problems. She had learned her first lesson. She had earned a prize. He took her to her chamber, which was across the hall from his.

And then he locked her inside.

⟞⟝

The kitchen staff grew quiet when Albrecht entered. It had been this way since he was a boy. But, unless he was imagining it, they were quieter than usual.

He cleared his throat. "I will be requiring food. Prepare a tray."

"Of course," the cook said. "For one?"

He could never remember her name. In his head, he called her Haddock Face.

"For two." Word of Greta's return would have made it to the kitchen. Haddock Face was testing him, but not as slyly as she thought. Hands shaking, she arranged bread and meat and cheese while he watched. She filled a pitcher with cider.

"Will that do, Your Majesty?"

He examined the arrangement. None of the usual delights was present. He supposed burning the farms had led to some scarcity. A shame but it had to be done. Ursula and her talk of treaties made it clear she would never agree to the reunification of the kingdom.

He grunted and brought the tray to the place his parents took their morning meal when his mother was still alive. He unlocked Greta's door and brought her in. She stepped away from him, moving near the window.

"It is a very fine view," he said. "A fine view and a far drop."

His heart quailed at the thought of falling. It always did. What a stupid thing, beating hearts. He hated having one. If he could have swapped in a reliable clockwork mechanism to keep himself alive, an iron heart, he would have in a moment. "We should eat. You are hungry, I am sure."

Greta looked at him impassively, crossed her arms, and then returned her gaze to the kingdom below.

"You'll do as I say," he said. His heart was still pounding, and her disobedience filled him with a rush of desire, not to have her, but to show her who was in control.

"I did, and you locked me into a room."

"Your room," he said.

"If I am locked into a room, what does it matter whether it's mine?"

"You left me once before. You will not do it again. You *will* do as I say." He wanted to punish her.

She narrowed her eyes. "I do not wish to."

"You do not *wish* to." As if she were in a position to make wishes. He grabbed her arm. "Do I look like some sort of wish-granting hobgoblin?"

"Do not ask me what you look like," she said. "You will not like my answer."

He laughed. Now she was being ridiculous. He knew full well the measure of his beauty as a man. He was the fairest in the land. Even a missing finger could not diminish his appeal.

"You'll wish a long time before encountering a better man than I. Come with me or I'll bring you myself, the way I carried you to the kingdom."

She looked at his hand on her arm. "I go nowhere with you willingly."

"You say that now," he said. "You will not say it always."

She pulled away again. Strands of hair had escaped her braid, and he wanted to touch them, to sink his fingers in deep and then tug. Spun gold itself was no more beautiful. He brought her close. She trembled. So much for the bravado she was showing. She reminded him of a snow-white dove.

He led her from the window, a firm hand on her elbow. He brought her before a little metal maiden standing on a lily pad. He twisted the maiden's arm and the pond filled with water. He twisted her other arm and a toad rose from the deep, opened its mouth, and revealed a cake of soap.

"You will wash before you eat. I cannot abide uncleanliness."

He could tell the device impressed her. She submerged her hands tentatively. Her fingers were long and graceful, like his. Yes, they had been roughened by the labors of life, but that was something that could be overcome. Something he was saving her from.

She dried her hands on the towel he offered, and then he brought her to the table, his hand tight enough around her arm to mark her flesh.

"Sit."

She hesitated. He held her gaze and saw her expression shift the moment she decided to obey.

He poured her cider. "Your gown will be blue with gold threads. It was my mother's."

"My gown?"

He caught a glimpse of her injured tongue. The scar it left behind would match his own. "For the wedding."

She blanched. "What wedding?"

"Ours. The people need one," he said. "Something to celebrate after the sorrow of war. That you are one of the vanquished will be seen as proof that I am just and merciful. The prince you will bear will be even more welcome news." He gestured at the table. "Eat. I've already been so kind as to pour you a drink."

She turned away.

"I'll not ask twice. Would you like me to fetch the bridle? A scold's bridle for the bride?"

She turned back. "I do not wish to marry you. Please."

"Eat." He smeared butter on a slice of bread and took a bite.

"You would take a bride who does not want you?"

"My concern is not what she wants. My concern, as always, is my kingdom."

There was a long silence between them. Better that than a complaint.

"If I marry you," she said, speaking gingerly, "you will spare my brother and the rest of the survivors. You will leave them alone."

"You are in no position to bargain *if* we marry. It is *when* we marry." And it was true. She had nothing to offer, no leverage to use. Her life was his.

"I will marry you only *if* you declare a truce. If you allow weres to live in peace. There are children in the woods. They should not be harmed."

"Why do you care about the fate of frissers? You aren't one yourself. They are an abomination. As for your brother, well, I have long made exceptions for him."

"Those are my conditions," she said.

Albrecht recognized his error. Ursula never would have asked the opinion of someone who had nothing to bargain with. She would simply remind her opponent who held the better hand of cards. With this, Greta had left *him* in the position of refusing her offer. Well then. That meant she was clever, another credit to him and the choice he'd made.

"Fine," he said.

She looked satisfied. That was *her* error. *Fine* meant nothing. The word did not signify the agreement she thought it did. He would honor her understanding of it for as long as it cost him nothing. After that? They would be married. Bound. There would be nothing she could do about it. Then he would do what he wanted when he wished.

She accepted a slice of bread. A small one, the heel. She ate it in tiny bites without a scraping of butter, as if the less she ate, the less his ownership of her would be. Everyone was hungry for something, though, and he already knew her weak spot: the frissers, her brother especially.

"We marry tomorrow night," he said.

She eyed him warily. "What if my brother comes for me? Will you ensure his safety?"

He smiled. She didn't realize he'd shot her brother. He had no plans to tell her.

"Of course. If your brother does, you will send him away yourself. If you do not, he will die. Either way, your choice is to marry me and bring about peace. Refuse, and his death is on your hands."

He put meat on her plate. "You should eat more." Animals that did not eat well did not breed well.

"I've had enough." She pushed the plate away.

"You need to nourish your body to keep it healthy." He laid his hand on the table, his poison-filled not-finger pointed at her.

She slipped the last of her bread in her mouth and chewed. Seeing pain on her face, he smiled.

"You should rest after this. You didn't get a good night's sleep."

Her expression—just a flash. She wanted to blame him for her rude awakening, but she did not. This was progress. She was trainable.

"Where will I sleep? With the maids, as before?"

"No," he said. "In your chamber. The one with the lock on the door."

She blinked. She had very fine eyes. She clasped her hands in her lap and kept her gaze there. He ate, slowly growing full, watching her all the while. Eventually she looked up and he felt himself harden.

"I would like to get a message to my brother. A message to leave me here, to stay away."

"Of course," Albrecht said. "Jutta will deliver it."

XXXIV

Hans had been stuck between sleep and wakefulness before, but this was different. He could control a dream, bend the narrative, turn a locked door into a thing made of cake he could eat, turn himself into a bird snapping up a trail of breadcrumbs. He had always been able to wake himself if he needed to.

This was nothing like that. He was drowning in a river of pain and he could not rise. Even when he felt the needle pierce his skin and mend it, one agonizing stitch at a time, he could do nothing more than squeeze Sabine's hand.

He could smell her and Ursula. Smell the fire. The blanket on top of him. The hands that had made it. The hands that had stolen it. The bodies it had covered and the sweat they had shed into it. It was a world woven of scents, and he was trapped in the darkness of it, shivering.

He could not smell his sister. Her scent had faded like smoke on the wind. He wanted to howl but couldn't. The wound in his chest was a pit, a fissure in the world after an earthquake, fathomless, hungry.

Was this punishment for killing the horse? It felt like it. Hans wanted the pain to stop, but he also wanted to suffer as he deserved. He was an animal, but he had never thought of himself as a beast. Not until now.

Then, when he thought he might die, a sound rang, high and sweet. The music found him where he was trapped, note after note, as steady as stitches, footsteps, a pulse. *Cappella.*

Hans focused on the sound. He forced himself to wake. He needed his consciousness the way lungs need air after a plunge into the deep. The music grew louder, but his eyelids were made of stone.

At last, he opened them. White sky stung through silhouetted branches and trees. Where was Cappella?

Across the clearing, softened through the green of long grass, a glint of metal. He blinked. Focused. She sat cross-legged at the base of a tree, her eyes closed, her fingers shaping breath into notes that had stitched his insides as surely as Ursula had repaired his flesh.

"He's awake." Sabine's voice, then her hand on his muzzle, turning his snout back toward hers. There was kindness in her eyes and also worry and sorrow.

He struggled and shifted into his human form.

"Shh, Hans. Stay still," she said. "Don't shift."

But he wouldn't. Couldn't. He pulled down the blanket. He sat, pushing away Sabine's hands. And then he was standing, wrapped only in the blanket, staggering across the clearing. His vision tunneled, and he felt people moving aside.

When he reached her, he fell to his knees and rested his head on her lap. The music stopped, and she put her hand on his back. It was exactly the right weight and size.

"Hans," she said.

She'd been crying. He pushed himself up, holding the blanket around his waist.

"I heard the music. Every note, even when I couldn't open my eyes."

"Where's Greta? Ursula won't tell us what happened."

And now he was hot, hot and shaking with rage. "Albrecht. Albrecht took her."

Hans spent most of the day in the cottage, resting in Greta's bed. He hated staying still. He wanted to go back to the kingdom. To fetch his sister. To tear out Albrecht's throat if he had to. He knew full well the dangers. None of it mattered.

If Cappella hadn't sat next to him, he would have gone mad, if not from the feeling of his muscle fibers healing, then with the memory of killing the horse. He'd done it without thinking as soon as he realized that Albrecht meant to abduct Greta. The animal reared up and he'd leapt, jaws wide. He'd struck the poor creature in its neck, and the feeling of his teeth tearing through the hide, the taste of sweat and dusty fur, the hot saltiness of blood exploding in his mouth . . . Killing in rage was like nothing he'd ever experienced.

He'd killed small animals from time to time for his family when they'd been hungry. Rabbits and such. That had been a different matter. There was a *need* for those deaths. His family needed to eat. With this horse, Hans intended only destruction. The hatred he felt for Albrecht, he'd turned on the horse, not because the horse had done anything to him but because it was in his way. And even then, he'd failed to save Greta. He was disgusted with himself.

Cappella put a hand on his forehead. "I know you have reason to be worried, but try to focus on healing."

Hans didn't reply. He'd torn out a living thing's throat. Torn it out and swallowed its windpipe. Soaked his muzzle in its blood. He couldn't stop thinking about the sounds it had made while dying. About the smell of its blood. About the thump of its body when it dropped. The horse was not a human, to be sure. But it had not loved its life any less.

The distance between life and death was short. The length of a fang, an arrow, a sword.

He'd never given much thought to Cappella's throat, but now he couldn't stop looking at hers, thinking of how he'd feel if someone had done the same to her. What if he got that angry again and acted on his wolfish instinct? Perhaps it was right that weres had been required to sleep in cages. That they'd been prevented from shifting outside the Row.

What if he hurt Cappella? What if someone else did? She was mortal. Breakable. She would someday die. He had seen it happen to his parents; it would happen to her too, and the sadness of knowing this overwhelmed him.

"I'm going to try to sleep." He closed his eyes, thinking she'd leave, but she didn't. He let himself become a wolf while she was still there.

When he awoke, she was gone, and night had fallen. Within weeks, the shortest, darkest days of the year would be upon them. Those had been his favorite when he was a little boy. He missed that time intensely, the hours spent indoors by the fire with his family, talking, mending things, making plans for spring.

He sat and took his human form again. His chest was still tender but much better than it had been. He forced himself out of bed and into his clothing and boots. He watched everyone through the window, sitting around the fire, faces grim in the orange light, gazing the longest at Cappella. The sight of her made his heart hurt all over again.

When he opened the door and walked outside, conversation stopped.

"Hans," Cappella said.

There was room to sit by her, and he took it.

Sabine had her arm splinted and strapped to her chest. "How are you feeling?"

"No worse than you," he said.

She smiled, but there was no happiness in it.

Ursula turned to him. "We were just discussing what King Albrecht might have planned for your sister."

"Planned?"

"We think he took her for a reason," Sabine said.

"What reason?"

"We hoped you'd know," Ursula said.

"*I* didn't share a womb with him." His heart stung again.

Cappella's fingers brushed his. He took her hand and she squeezed, as if to let him know she was on his side.

Ursula rubbed her hands together to warm them. "You *have* spent a great deal of time with him."

"Not as much as you." Hans knew he was being surly, but he didn't care. What was she going to do to him? Nothing. She needed him. He looked around the campfire. Everyone was staring at him, even the children.

Sabine exhaled. "This is what we think, Hans—that he took her to lure us in to rescue her. He plans to kill us on his own turf."

"Are you suggesting that we leave her there?"

"If it's a trap, we don't want to be snared by it," Ursula said.

"Fine. I know the castle well. I'll save her myself," he said.

"I can't allow it," Ursula said.

"She's my sister." He could not speak aloud his fear about what Albrecht would do with his devices, some of which Hans had built himself. The idea that Greta might suffer and bleed—that he would have had a hand in it—it was too much.

"I am your queen."

The fire popped, sending a spray of angry sparks into the darkness. No one spoke. Sabine looked angry, though Hans couldn't tell if it was with him or with Ursula.

"You are," he said. "And this is why your concern should be with my sister, who is also your subject and who has been taken"—he needed to steady his voice—"taken by your brother."

"But, Hans," Ursula said, "we don't even know if she's—"

"Don't say it," Sabine warned.

Ursula's expression changed. She held up a hand. "Shh." She'd heard something.

The hair on Hans's neck prickled. He felt the wolf coming on. That scent. He knew it: Jutta.

Ursula and Sabine leapt up just as Jutta emerged, limping, from the woods.

"Your brother sent me," Jutta said.

"Where's Greta?" Hans advanced until she pulled a knife from her belt and brandished it at him.

"Your sister is well." She stepped around him and stopped in front of Ursula.

"Your brother wants you to know that he and Greta will be married. This is a kindness he's showing you and your"—she looked at the survivors, her gaze stopping on the children—"your people."

"Greta wouldn't want that," Hans said. "She's never wanted that. Not with anyone. And Albrecht, especially—he can't do that to her."

"She has agreed," Jutta said. "And if I could give advice on the matter, Ursula, it would be to let her go. Let this go. Let your brother have this. Let his kingdom have this. You will be safer."

She turned to Hans. "Our future queen had a message for you in particular."

Hans knew what it would be before Jutta said it—that he wasn't to rescue her. It would be very like Greta to want to keep him safe. When Jutta said the words he feared, it was all he could do not to weep.

"Is that all?" Ursula said.

Jutta glanced at Sabine's feet. "Those are my boots."

"You left them behind when you shifted," Ursula said. "You forfeited them."

"And you always wanted them," Jutta said. "So why are they on her feet?"

"She needed them."

"Is that how it is?" Jutta said. "They're hers now. I hope that makes you happy."

And then she left, limping into the darkness.

XXXV

Nothing in Ursula's studies had prepared her for this. Her instruction in diplomacy and the art of war had always assumed that she'd be in her castle. That she'd have soldiers. That even in a time of siege there would be a certain amount of supplies laid in. Most of all, that her brother would be an ally.

She could scarcely think of him now without succumbing to a rage that only her bear form could accommodate. Albrecht had done this to her. There could be no more profound betrayal. She could scarcely believe this was her life now . . . campfires and desperation. Not quite three dozen people, many weres, many of them children, dependent on her for protection and survival. She was doing her best for them, but it wasn't enough.

And now he'd taken one of her people to be his wife. To produce an heir. To use as a human shield. Worse, Sabine and Hans were standing before Ursula telling her they intended to rescue Greta together—and that there was nothing she could do to stop them. She knew they were really challenging her to join them. Commanding their own queen. It was an impossible choice for so many reasons, not the least of which: If she went, she'd have to leave everyone else behind, and there was no guarantee that she'd return. She'd leave her people without their leader, which was like leaving a body without a head.

One of the weregoats balanced on a branch and spat pebbles on the heads of the fox brothers. Ursula ached. These were *children*. That Albrecht could have left them so vulnerable burned her veins. She wanted to wallow in rage, to bound through the forest until she was too exhausted to think. But she couldn't.

"I can't permit it," she said. "It's too dangerous. And you're wounded. Sabine has a broken arm."

"I'm healed enough," Hans insisted.

"As I am. Hans and I can do this," Sabine said. "Greta is counting on us."

"Greta told him not to come!"

Sabine curled her hands into fists. "She's Hans's sister. She's one of us. She should not have to sacrifice herself this way." Then she removed the boots that Ursula had given her and set them on the ground. "You always think you know better than anyone what we need. You don't. You never even ask."

"No, stop. *Please.*" Ursula handed the boots back to Sabine. "They're yours. And you're right. But we should plan. There's a right way—"

"You always have a right way to do things," Sabine said. "The way your instructors taught you. According to the traditions of the kingdom. The way your father would have wanted."

"That isn't fair," Ursula said. "You don't understand."

"I know what's right and I know what isn't. I know who I am and what I can accomplish. There's nothing else I need to understand. I'm going to do what's right. I'm going to do what I can." She put the boots back on, and Ursula felt a sliver better. Sabine wouldn't have done that had she truly given up on Ursula. And she had been right. Sabine *did* need the boots.

Cappella started a new song. The werechildren stopped scampering and listened intently, as if she'd bewitched them. That pipe. That golden pipe. Where had her aunt gotten the gold to make it?

Ursula remembered a story told during her childhood, one told so often everybody knew. Her mother had spun grass into gold, and a terrible person who was jealous had once tried to steal the twins, upsetting her mother so much she'd lost her ability to spin. Ursula's hackles rose. Something about the reality before her didn't square with the story she'd been told.

Esme had said that the king and queen believed she wished for something that was not hers. Ursula had thought it was gold. But what if that had been a lie? What if her mother had never been the one to spin the gold? What if it had been Esme all along? The whole story of the kingdom would unravel like so much rotting cloth.

Ursula had believed this story so deeply it felt like a memory of something she'd seen. But if it wasn't true, who could she trust if she couldn't even trust her own memories? She pressed her palms against her eyelids.

"Come, Ursula, let's go together," Sabine said.

She opened her eyes. Sabine. She could trust Sabine. "Who do I put in charge of the camp?"

"No one," she said. "People can look after one another. If there's to be a wedding, then the whole kingdom will be invited. There's no better time for us to slip in."

"What about Esme?" Ursula said. "She's a relation. She would have claim to power. She could watch over the camp, and she's a capable fighter."

Sabine looked pained. "If you think it necessary."

"I do. But another thing: People will notice me in the kingdom," Ursula said. "Everyone knows who I am. There will be no surprising Albrecht."

"Surely you know other ways into that castle," Sabine said. "Ways we won't be seen."

She did. Even so, Ursula *hated* the idea. She would have rather rushed in there as a bear by herself and taken her chances with the guards.

"My brother has no doubt laid traps."

"I have faith in us," Sabine said. "You should too."

Then, with her good arm, Sabine took Ursula's hand. There were no interlaced fingers. There was no softness to the touch. It felt like a bargain struck, an agreement between equals. And it was right, this bargain. But it hurt like fire.

XXXVI

Greta had been up all night. Her tongue throbbed. Surely once she was the king's wife, he wouldn't subject her to more torture. That was the trade-off she was counting on, being close enough to the danger that it could not harm her, like being in the eye of a storm. She was also counting on being able to protect others, her brother most of all.

The new day was blindingly beautiful, as if the world cared not that her life was forfeit. She'd probably never see Hans again, but if her bargain kept him alive, so be it. She was doing the right thing. She had to be.

Lotte and Susanna arrived to help ready Greta. She had known the maids for years. They'd worked in different parts of the castle, but they'd shared quarters, as all maids did. They'd been friendly, insofar as Greta was accessible. For the most part, she'd kept to herself and her thoughts.

They treated her differently now, and they kept looking at each other, as if they were having a private conversation through their gazes.

"You can talk to me the same way you always did," Greta said, taking care of her tongue.

Lotte lifted Greta's braid. "I've always wanted to touch it. It's so long and pretty."

"The prince—the king—he always stared at it," Susanna said. "All of us noticed. Do you think that's why he chose you?"

It was true that her hair was long. She'd never cut it. Her happiest memories were those in which her father braided her hair and her stepmother called it lovely as new butter. Greta wouldn't admit to being proud of it, though she knew she was. Was it such a bad thing for a girl to think something about herself was beautiful?

"I don't know if that is the case," Greta said. "I never—"

Lotte began undoing the braid. "Oh, it is. Everybody used to talk about it. We never thought he'd marry you, though. We thought it more likely that he'd—"

"Lotte! Don't say it."

"Toff, Susanna. You know he's plucked his share of flowers. And you started it—"

"I did no such thing. Look what you've done to Greta. She's crying."

Lotte blushed all the way down her neck. "I'm sorry. Please forgive me. And forgive Susanna for talking that way about your future husband. We know he'll always love you best. How could he not?" She took a comb to Greta's hair, gently scuffing out the tangles. Greta swallowed hard, trying to stop her tears.

"The bath will be ready soon," Susanna said. "Not that we're saying you need it."

Greta gave a bitter laugh. "Lotte just combed a branch out of my hair."

"Only a small one," Lotte said. "More of a twig."

"Cook pitched a fit when you left. Said you'd probably run off with a traveling merchant and left her all the birds to break down," Susanna said. "Where'd you go? Wait. No. I shouldn't have asked. It's just that—"

"It's all right." Greta didn't mind the question. She might have been curious too, were their positions reversed. She was struggling to say the word for where she'd been. It stuck in her throat like bread.

"Home," she said at last. "I was home."

"But isn't this your home, with the rest of us?" Lotte asked.

"It hasn't always been."

"Well, look at you now," Susanna said. "You're back with us and you will be the queen of all. It's like something out of a story. It's wonderful and we are so happy for you."

As they were helping Greta into the tub, Lotte gasped. "What happened to your feet?"

"I walked a bit without shoes," Greta said.

"We can fix that right up," Susanna said. "And you'll always have the softest slippers when you're queen. You'll never have to worry about sore feet again, that's for good and certain."

They gently scrubbed her with soap and then patted her dry with warm linens before rubbing scented oil into her skin. She dressed in a robe and they saw to her hair, combing in front of the fire until it was glossy and dry, chattering as they worked. She felt utterly alone, even more than if she'd been the only one in the room.

She would not cry again, though. She didn't want to give them anything to gossip about. What's more, she didn't want to look like a grieving bride. She didn't want to be pitied or mocked. No one need know the truth; it would be better for them to believe she'd entered into this marriage with a happy heart.

Once they'd finished with their combs, Susanna and Lotte set about braiding Greta's hair again, tucking in sprigs of tiny white berries as they went. The style was more complex than anything she'd worn before. They held it with pins that dug into her skin. She didn't mind the pain. It kept her from sinking into her sorrows.

Then the maids set about lacing Greta into her gown, which was the same insolent blue as the sky and decorated with a pattern woven in gold thread. The seams at the waist tapered in, while the sleeves flared like wings. It was lovely, the sort of thing Greta had dreamed of when she was a young girl hearing stories of kings and queens. It was the sort of thing she would have wished for, had she not known the price of wishes such as those.

They put matching shoes on her feet, slippers so delicate and lightweight they felt like nothing at all.

"This was Princess Ursula's room," Lotte said. "If you want to see your reflection, there's a tiny mirror inside the dressing table. She wasn't much for looking at herself."

"There's no need," Greta said.

"Don't be silly," Susanna said. "Of course there is."

"You look like a queen," Lotte said.

Greta felt like anything but.

⌒⌒⌒

"There you are," Albrecht said when Greta entered the room. She hadn't seen him at first. He was sitting in a chair facing the window. He stood and approached, taking her chin and moving it this way and that in the light, as if she were livestock at the market.

"You're looking well," he said. "Much better with the filth of the forest washed away."

"Thank you." She tried to smile but found she could not. Her lips felt not her own.

"My people will love you," he said. "Everyone loves a beautiful queen. Everyone loved my mother."

Greta didn't respond. She knew enough of him to know he meant no kindness. For Greta, beauty had turned out to be a trap. It had made Albrecht notice her and want her. She'd rather have been seen as ugly.

"I have a gift for you," he said.

She felt wary even as she suspected such a thing was traditional. Albrecht opened a metal box that had been lined with velvet. She braced herself for another monstrosity like the severed finger. Inside was a necklace of round white stones. He fastened it around her neck.

"This was my mother's," he said. "The stones hold the light from the day and give it back to you at night. You will never know the sorrows of darkness as long as you are my queen."

The necklace was heavy and felt cool against her skin. It was beautiful. She would have given anything not to have to wear it.

"And what do you have for me?" He sniffed her hair and sighed.

She stiffened.

"I know what you have to give." He looked down on her with his strange, pale eyes. "You may refuse me," he said. "We are not yet married."

She finally grasped his meaning. She hadn't expected this request until they'd exchanged vows. She'd dreaded it utterly. She wasn't ready. Her mouth went dry. She closed her eyes and took a deep breath.

Then she opened them and found her voice. "In that case, I refuse. Lotte and Susanna took care in dressing me. It would not do to diminish their efforts."

For a moment, he looked hurt. She'd forgotten that he had feelings like anyone else. She would try to remember this when she was his wife.

Then the skin around his lips turned white. "Are you not grateful that I rescued you from a life that was more suited to animals? Are you not grateful for these jewels?" He grabbed her wrist. His false finger bit into her skin.

"I asked for none of it."

"It's more than most have."

With his free hand, he reached for her hair, threading his fingers through the loops of her braids. He held tightly enough that she could not turn her head. Her heart went wild as if it were an animal inside her, transformed not by the light of the moon but by his shameless cruelty. If she could have uncaged it, she would've. Let her heart do its worst to him. But she couldn't. She couldn't even escape his grasping hand.

"Your hair is very nearly as fine as mine," he said.

He released her arm and lifted her dress and pushed her undergarments aside. He inserted his false finger into her most private area. She gasped. She wished she were made of something harder. Impenetrable. It hurt. It hurt.

"You are the only creature I've ever hunted who lived."

Her legs went weak. She wanted to vomit and to weep. His false finger was cold, and the rivets holding it together tore at her most delicate parts. Perhaps the worst part was the smile on his face. He couldn't even feel what he was doing to her. Not with that false finger of his. But he was smiling. He liked that he was hurting her. That power was his source of pleasure.

There was only one thing she could do: imagine she was no longer in her body. She was elsewhere. Floating above. Staying safe. Staying alive—for despite everything, she still wanted to, still needed to, for the sake of those she loved, for the hope of living in the woods again, hope she could not abandon after all.

At last he removed his finger. There was blood on it. Hers. He'd cut her, and he didn't even notice until he rearranged the bulge in his trousers.

"Ach, look what you've done to me." He pointed at the blood. "Clean it up."

He handed her a linen, and she wiped her blood away as well as she could. He was hard beneath her hand, and when she rubbed the blood out, he moaned. At first, she thought she was hurting him. Then she realized the opposite was true.

She let herself weep, let him think the blood on his clothes was the cause of her regret.

XXXVII

Hans heard footsteps on the damp leaves. He turned. Cappella, wrapped in her red cloak, was close enough to touch.

"Hans. Don't go. Please." The white streak in her hair made her look of worry seem more acute, more vulnerable. It was almost enough to get him to agree to whatever she wanted. But only almost.

"I promised always to take care of her. We promised each other."

"He nearly killed you. Greta wouldn't want to you to risk hurting yourself again. Or getting infected. You need rest. You lost so much blood."

"I feel fine, Pella." He still ached where the arrow had entered. But the weakness, the dizziness, the sense that his life was being pumped away . . . all of that had ended when he heard Cappella's music. Her song had healed him, even as he knew that was not possible, that it was his were nature that let his body knit the wound.

"But, Hans." She lifted her hand.

For a moment, he thought she might cup his cheek or run her hands through his hair. She didn't, though. He stood, unable to move. He'd killed a horse and chased Albrecht, but neither took as much courage as holding her hand. If he held it, how could he let it go? How could he leave?

"She needs me, Pella. And I'll be with Ursula and Sabine. We'll get her and bring her back here and all will be well."

"I'm afraid. I don't want you to go." She pulled him close.

"I wish I didn't have to." He touched his forehead to hers.

He could feel her breath on his lips as she spoke. "Am I a coward for staying?"

He swallowed the lump in his throat. "Greta would want you to look after the children. You know you're the only one they listen to."

"Hans," she said. She did not complete her thought.

And then Sabine was upon them. "It's time to go."

He peeled away from Cappella. Ursula paced at the edge of the clearing.

"Wait." Cappella took his hand. His heart flew into his mouth. "Please stay safe. Please come back." And then she kissed him, the softest touch, at the corner of his lips.

Unable to breathe for a moment, he touched the spot she'd kissed.

But he said nothing in return. He didn't want to make a liar of himself.

~ ~ ~

The weres set out through the woods, where they would stay for as long as they could before veering into the kingdom. At Ursula's instruction, they said little and carried nothing. They'd worn no cloaks that might snag the underbrush and make noise. They'd have to leave behind their clothing anyway, so less was better even as the air was cold enough to turn their breath to mist.

"My brother will be expecting us," she said.

"What does that mean?" Sabine asked.

Ursula spoke quietly. "Imagine the worst thing possible, and then expect something beyond that."

Hans's wound flared. He pressed it and it felt better, but only a bit. He wondered how much Ursula knew of Albrecht's devices.

"You mentioned traps," Sabine said. "How do we avoid them?"

"Don't touch anything made of metal."

They neared the border of the forest and kingdom. Ursula stopped and sniffed.

"What is it?" Sabine asked.

"I anticipated more guards."

"Albrecht knows that guards can't stop us," Sabine said.

Hans realized she was probably right, which meant the closer they got to the castle, the closer they came to Greta, the more dangerous things would be.

They reached the river that divided the two halves of the kingdom.

"It's time," Ursula said.

They stepped out of their clothes and became their animal selves. The river there was shallow and swift. Ursula plunged in first. Sabine followed, and Hans hoped he'd be as steady. Though he'd waded in it, he'd never crossed the river before. He'd had no need. And yet he was pleased to feel at home in the water. He liked the smell, of stone and silt and living things.

They emerged from the river not far from the castle, keeping low to the ground so they'd be hidden by grass. They were on the far side of the moat now. The drawbridge was down, and guests were streaming inside between two guards. Hans looked again, glad for the darkness of their wet fur. There was no better camouflage. He shifted his gaze to the guards. They were metal men. Had Albrecht figured out how to make them work? That was worrisome. Hans wanted to examine them, but Ursula waved him on.

They slipped down the hill and submerged themselves in the moat. Staying underwater the whole way, they swam across, taking deep breaths as their heads surfaced in the shadow of the castle.

Hans looked once more to the metal men. They'd be wound, of course.

Perhaps something would set them off. A touch? If he could get them opened, he could destroy them. Undo his past work. Instead Ursula led them behind one of the castle's crenellations.

She took her human form and fished out a key from a gap in the stone. The door unlocked with a soft click. She shifted again, and they stepped into a dark hallway. Hans's eyes adjusted to the light. He knew where they were—not too far from the tower.

Greta was nearby. He could smell her. He felt the urge to hurry. Ursula stopped abruptly. Someone was approaching. Ursula looked left and right and chose an open doorway on the right. Sabine followed.

When Hans realized what room they were entering, he yipped a warning. But it was too late. There was a rush of air. Gasps. Two heavy thuds. He froze. This was the room Albrecht had put a trapdoor into.

He peered over the edge and saw Sabine and Ursula down in a hole perhaps twenty feet deep. Sabine crouched over Ursula, who was not moving. But she was in her bear form, which meant she lived.

Hans had no idea how to reach them. If he went down himself, he might not make it out. There was nothing he could lower, and he did not dare call their names, lest they all be caught. Once he had his sister, he'd return for the bears.

He turned and went in search of Greta. The air was thick with scents. So many people. Food. Candles, torches, and lamps. But hers was the scent he knew best, and he filled his nose with it. There was her hair, her skin, her blood. That last scent made him pick up his pace, passing the door to the tower, running on quiet feet. He knew exactly where she was—the banquet hall.

That meant the wedding was happening. He hoped he wasn't too late.

XXXVIII

Greta watched the gathering crowd through a carved screen. The banquet room fluttered with golden banners. Wedding guests gathered, their smiles gleeful, no doubt at the prospect of the food and drink that would follow, as these had been hungry times.

Soldiers stood at the edges of the room, weapons ready. She knew who that steel was for. She hoped Jutta had delivered the message. Even more, she hoped Hans had listened. *Was* anyone coming? If Albrecht thought it possible, then it must be.

She felt torn between hope and despair—despair that she had to marry Albrecht, but a flicker of hope that perhaps, somehow, she might escape. She knew she shouldn't wish for that. But Albrecht had just shown her how he would treat her as his wife. It was worse than she'd feared.

Wearing his golden finger, now pitted with her blood, Albrecht stood next to Jutta, who wore two swords and had knives in each of her heavy leather boots. In the bright light of the banquet hall, the cloth of Albrecht's suit looked miraculous. Liquid. Alive. It drank the light of every torch, of every candle, of the sunbeams that washed through the windows. It was blinding and beautiful and unstained.

"It's time," Susanna said. "Out you go."

Greta stepped into the hall. She hoped no one could tell that she'd been weeping, that no one could tell every step gave her pain where Albrecht had violated her, insisting she remember that which she wanted desperately to forget. She walked in time with the faint strains of song from the forest. The music felt like a mercy. The more intently she listened, the more she felt like herself. This was going to be all right. She would survive.

She saw no sign of Hans. She felt relief. Also disappointment, but her relief was greater. She reached Albrecht's side, and Jutta looked at her with pity. A bit late for *that*.

Albrecht flung his arms wide to welcome his guests.

"This is the day," he said, "that this broken kingdom can be healed. I do so by taking this common-born woman as my wife."

Greta could not force herself to smile, but she did manage to keep her tears at bay.

"It is our great good fortune that I have made this choice. As my mother was the jewel of my father's kingdom, my bride is the same.

"This suit I wear . . . it was my father's. I am proud to carry on the tradition, as will my sons. As long as there are men in our line, we will wear this suit of gold, which has no equal."

In the brilliant light of the banquet hall, Albrecht's clothing shimmered. But as he stepped back to her side, Greta could see something wrong with it. Where her blood had touched the cloth, the threads were like fish in a stream, wriggling and then vanishing into the deep. His clothing was unraveling. Greta's stomach folded in on itself.

Albrecht was unaware of what was happening. He carried on with his speech, the words of which Greta could not absorb. She had attention for nothing but his suit. As the threads glistened and vanished, the weave of his clothing loosened, leaving bare skin visible in patches. Then the fabric sloughed into clots, and Albrecht looked down and stopped speaking.

No one made a sound.

The moment stretched and strained, as though time itself had been woven of the same fragile cloth. Albrecht grabbed a handful of his clothing and tugged. What remained dissolved into a powdery residue. The sword that had once hung from a golden belt at his waist clattered to the ground.

He cleared his throat. No words came out.

Slippers and boots scraped the stone floor as some guests angled to improve their views. The only thing Albrecht could do was pretend that it was intentional. That he meant to stand before his people wearing nothing but the skin he was born in. That to appear before them naked was a sign of the ultimate power.

A vein bulged in his forehead and Greta realized that to save herself, she would first have to save him. She felt the way she had the first time she'd lifted the wet guts from the belly of a dead animal. Steeling herself, she blocked the view of the guests. He grabbed her shoulders and spun her toward him, his face practically touching hers.

"Have you done this to humiliate me?"

"Of course not," Greta whispered.

"You lie."

"It was the blood," she said. "Blood does that to the gold your mother made. You knew this. You have known this since the day you cut me for the first time."

"Your blood," he said. "You did this to me."

"You did this to yourself."

She slipped out of his grip and faced the crowd, now desperately hoping to spot allies. She didn't. If she ran, she'd be stopped. Jutta, the guards, Albrecht: Anyone could overpower her. That was the way of violence. Strength won, whether it was right or not.

She could tell the crowd the truth—that he had assaulted her and that her blood had made the gold disintegrate. But who would believe her word? Who would believe that she hadn't wanted him?

She could also tell the truth about the conflict between kingdoms. That Ursula had never been a threat. That she'd never said her queendom would be a place for weres only. But what good was truth to people hungry for lies?

As Albrecht stood, naked and enraged, laughter broke out. It spread from one person to the next until the great hall was full of the overwhelming sight of people laughing, mouths open. The sound was overwhelming.

He picked up his sword and held the sharp edge to Greta's throat. It touched the stones of her necklace. She held her breath.

The laughter stopped.

For an awful moment, the banquet room was silent. She expected to die, to have her throat slit, for her blood to drench her feet. She braced herself. Then something burst through the door in the back of the room. A gray frenzy, snarling and leaping, pushing off the shoulders of men as he raced toward her. Hans. Hans had come. She wished he hadn't, but now that he was here, she wanted nothing more than to flee with him. To go beyond the woods to whatever lands lay elsewhere. There had to be someplace better than this.

Albrecht pushed the blade into her neck deep enough to cut. She froze. Jutta shrugged off her cloak, kicked away her boots, and stepped out of her clothing. Then she was a horse, rearing and whinnying, her hooves crashing against the stone floor. She careened toward Hans, who held his spot, his lips curled into a wet snarl. As Jutta tried to stamp on his skull, he evaded her, but her hooves were too fast and the space too small for him to fight back.

The wedding guests backed away, and the guards approached Hans from behind, weapons drawn. He stood no chance.

He'd tried to save her, but she was going to need to save him.

"Spare him," she said. "Spare him and I will do everything you ask of me always. I will give you sons. I will spin your gold. Whatever you want is yours." She could hardly feel her body, as if it had already numbed itself in anticipation of the suffering to come. Albrecht was going to split her open like a log for the fire. But that felt like nothing compared to watching her brother die. Without him, she was alone in the world.

Albrecht lowered his blade. He put on Jutta's white tunic and leather trousers and grabbed Greta's braid. She submitted. She would always submit for the sake of Hans.

"Let my brother go," she said as he pulled her toward a door at the north end of the hall. "Please."

Albrecht whistled through his teeth and Jutta returned.

"Take care of the wolf," he said. "I'll come when I can."

Albrecht dragged Greta by her hair out the door, into the corridor, and up into the tower, where his chambers awaited.

XXXIX

"Ursula."

Sabine's voice. Woozy, Ursula shifted back to her human form. Where were they? It took Ursula a few seconds to get her bearings. They'd come into the castle, turned into her mother's needlework room, and then the floor had given way. Ursula rolled over. She couldn't see Sabine, but she could smell her, feel her presence. "Are you hurt? Your arm—"

"I landed on my feet," Sabine said. "It took me a moment to rouse you. You scared me."

"My skull is harder than all that." They clasped hands, and Sabine pulled Ursula upright.

"The opening is too high up, and it's too far away from the walls," Sabine said. "Even if we could climb them."

Ursula burned with anger. This was too much. She wanted to be free of the burdens of responsibility. She wanted to feel the way she had when she was a girl running through the woods, becoming a bear, roaring because it was a wonderful thing to be alive. She'd lost everything she'd ever cared about.

"Sabine, I don't know what to do."

"So you're saying your instructors never prepared you for when you're at the bottom of a pit of your brother's making?"

"Curiously, they did not." She felt Sabine move closer and for a moment, her heart fluttered.

"There has to be another way out," Sabine said.

"Maybe Hans will come back."

"We can't wait for that. We certainly can't count on it. He's alone against the kingdom. We either free ourselves or we fail."

"But—"

"Start looking," Sabine said.

Holding her hands out, Ursula made her way to the wall. The foundations the old castle lay beneath this one. A number of the old rooms had been turned into the dungeon. This one must have been left out. She thought about the layout of the castle above. The dungeon stairs weren't much farther down the corridor, which meant they just needed to get through the wall. Then they could escape up the dungeon stairs.

"We need to get through this wall," Ursula said. "But it's solid stone."

"It's not," Sabine said. "I smell the presence of rats. If they've made it through, the wall can be breached. We need only to find out where and make the opening large enough for us."

It wouldn't be easy, but Sabine was right.

"You're brilliant." Ursula hadn't meant to say it out loud.

"I know," Sabine said.

"But what about your arm?" There was no way Sabine could help. She hadn't fully healed.

"I provided the brains," Sabine said. "And a considerable amount of nose. The rest is up to you."

Ursula put her hands to the wall, running her fingertips over the stones, searching for a seam wide enough to use. She ran her nose along the stones, trying to find the weakness the rats had discovered.

"Do you hear that?" Sabine said.

There were shouts overhead. It sounded like fighting. "Hans," Ursula said. "It has to be."

She caught a whiff of rat. Her fingers slid into a crack between two stones. She let herself shift—not all the way, just enough that her hands were armed with powerful claws. She'd never tried being between bear and human. She'd always aimed for the extremes. But she found this was a useful state. She was strong and also dexterous. She pulled at the crack. Her forearms strained. Her hands shook. She thought the stone might snap off her claws, which would be disastrous should she need to fight.

She let go. She panted, her fingertips aching, sweat trickling down her back.

"Don't stop," Sabine said. "We cannot fail."

"I don't think I can do this," she said.

"You must." Sabine moved close. She put her good arm around Ursula's waist. "I can pull you. We can do this together."

Ursula put her hands to the stone again. Found the gap. Everything she wanted depended on her success. Her life and Sabine's depended on it. She gave a mighty tug. Sabine pulled too. The stone broke. Ursula pulled off another chunk. Another. And another. And then the stone was gone, and enough around it. Sabine had not yet let go. Even in the darkness, Ursula closed her eyes. If this was the last time Sabine held her, she wanted to seal it in memory.

The smell of dungeon washed over her. Death, despair, rats, rot.

"Let's go," Sabine said.

Ursula stepped into the stinking dungeon. "We need a plan."

"I'll find Greta. Hans will be going after Albrecht, and he'll need some-one with two good arms."

"Brilliant," Ursula said again.

"I know. I'm right behind you. I'll see you at home."

Ursula didn't answer, even as the word *home* rang her heart like a bell. She'd already become the bear.

XL

Albrecht didn't release Greta until they were in his workshop.

She fell to her knees. "You didn't need to drag me. I would have come willingly. I told you I'd do anything you asked."

"I remember when you said you'd *never* come willingly. It wasn't so long ago." He stroked his gold finger before popping it off and setting it in its box. He replaced it with the poison-filled one.

"In the end, it doesn't matter," he told her. "Whether you are willing, whether you are not. Whether you want your brother to live, whether you want the rest of the weres to live. Whether you think, *Oh, he wouldn't harm children.* It doesn't matter. I have power over you, and I will use that power. I will use it to unify this kingdom, and I will eradicate every threat to that."

He stepped on her braid and watched her struggle. To struggle was to suffer, and she deserved to suffer profoundly. She'd embarrassed him. She'd made his people laugh. They'd laughed at him. Even now, the sound echoed. He was not to be laughed at. Not ever.

Nor did it matter that she'd offered herself to him. That was to save the traitorous wolf. As such, the offer was an insult. She should have *wanted* to be his wife. What woman would not want him? It wounded him, just as it had wounded him that his father had betrayed mankind and given half the kingdom to Ursula.

Greta was crying now. She'd lost one of her slippers on the way, and Albrecht thought it possible he had dislocated her shoulder as he hurried her along. One arm did hang rather low. He should have taken more care. When he caused damage, he liked for it to be by design.

He moved his foot and dragged her to the chair in the center of the room. When she saw it, she shrieked. He pushed her in it, strapped her there, and watched her take in his collection of tools and devices. She had no idea what he planned. That much was obvious.

"What are you doing?" Greta started to cry, and he licked the tears from her face, tasting the salt of her. She turned her head, trying to escape his tongue.

He unfastened one of her wrists, took her elbow in hand, and shoved her shoulder back into its socket. She gasped.

"There," he said, fastening the strap again.

"Please," she said. "I am your wife."

"Wife? That was no wedding."

"Please."

"Begging for me now?"

"I'm trying to do right by you," she said.

She wept and strained against the bindings. The hide had been tanned and hardened in the same fashion as armor. She'd need knives to get through it. Once he was done with her, she'd never be able to get away from him again. He wouldn't need restraints.

Taking his time, Albrecht opened the cabinet that held his best tools. He studied the collection before removing a blade he kept so sharp it practically made his eyes bleed to look at it. And then he turned back to Greta.

"I meant you no harm," she whispered. "I didn't mean for your clothing to unravel."

"What you *meant* doesn't matter, does it?"

He removed the catch from his poison finger. Its wet tip glistened, and he rammed it into her arm.

She gasped.

"That's the feeling of liquid mercy," he said. "It's a paralytic. The dose I gave is temporary, but useful for what I am about to do. You won't feel it. Well, for the most part."

Her pupils dilated, turning her blue eyes black.

He ran his thumb tenderly along the blade. It bit at his skin, but he was careful not to draw any of his own blood. He knew the weapon's appetites and moods.

"There's a trick to it," he said, as much to the blade as to Greta.

She looked bewildered even as her head lolled to the side.

He dropped to his knees and lifted her foot. It was small. Bare skin, neatly pared toenails. The maids had done a fine job preparing it.

"Cut deep, cut quick, and don't stop moving."

Greta whimpered. He could tell she was trying to speak and couldn't. He looked up at her and smiled.

Then, as he'd promised, the tip of his blade scored a red ring around her ankle. She cried out. Interesting. Perhaps he should have given her more liquid mercy. Or perhaps less.

"Once that is done, you slip the skin down and off. Like this." He peeled it from her ankle and snapped it toward her feet. "It's just like with rabbits."

It was a wet thing, her flesh, heavy with blood. He set it on the stone floor. Greta's breaths now were short, panting. Her eyes were wild. He saw the fight in them. But all the fight in her heart would be useless in a body that could not move.

Candles flickered. On the wall, their shadows mingled and made an entirely new beast.

He picked up her other foot. Quick. Deep. The wet snap.

"You have red shoes," he told Greta. "Red shoes to dance in on our wedding day."

And then he left to find the wolf.

XLI

Hans sat on the ground inside the smithy. His head pounded. Jutta crouched before him in her human form.

He tried to recall what had happened. Jutta had kicked him. He'd seen her sharp, dun-colored hoof coming at him, and it felt like slow motion until the moment of impact. And then the world was spinning fast. All around, so many angry humans. And then there was a hand on his ruff, huge and unyielding. And then the clank of a metal collar being fastened tight around his wolf neck, and Jutta's face close to his. "Do everything I tell you to do," she'd said, "and your sister will be fine. Just listen to me and I'll keep you both safe."

Once they reached the smithy, she'd pulled Hans's chain tight and hooked it to the wall. And then she'd dressed herself.

He hurt all over. His head, his chest, where his wound had started bleeding again. He kept his wolf ears pricked, not that it would matter. He was good and trapped. The chain was short enough that he couldn't even lie down. He could stand or he could sit.

He didn't know whether he should believe Jutta. But she hadn't killed him yet and she certainly could have. Still, he didn't trust her. For all he knew, she was saving him for Albrecht's benefit. She'd always done every-thing Albrecht wanted.

So what did Albrecht want now? To make Greta happy by keeping Hans alive? To hold Hans hostage so that he could make Greta do whatever he desired? Was Albrecht going to cut him open, as he'd once said he would?

That seemed the most likely. Albrecht had already shot him in front of Greta, so it seemed unthinkable he'd prize her happiness now. What's more, Albrecht had always wanted to understand what made a were shift. Hans knew this, and he'd rather die than suffer that. He looked at Jutta with pleading eyes.

Then he took his human form. Perhaps she had some conscience left. "Please, Jutta. Please."

She scraped blood and hair from her fingernails, looking anywhere but at his face.

As Hans slumped against the smithy wall, the scent of Albrecht returned like a nightmare, and worse, it came mixed with his sister's blood.

Hans became the wolf again.

"Thank you, Jutta," Albrecht said, entering the smithy. "I've been looking everywhere for my very, very bad dog."

Jutta wiped her hands on her tunic. "Are you all right? That's a lot of blood."

"It isn't mine," Albrecht said.

It was Greta's. And there was so much of it. A growl rose in him, one he could feel from his claws to his skull.

"Should we start with him?" Albrecht asked Jutta.

"Start?"

He made an exasperated sound. "We've talked about this."

"But do we even need the metal men? You and I know the truth. There is no frisser army in the forest. There are a few dozen people, many of whom are children. It would be better to let him return to the woods, perhaps without his tail. Let him serve as a warning to anyone who would challenge you. If you kill him, they might seek revenge."

Albrecht laughed. "It seems to me a corpse would speak more eloquently."

Jutta said nothing, but Hans could smell her fear, bitter and earthy. No doubt, she could smell his too.

She relented. "I see the wisdom in your words."

Albrecht grabbed Hans's muzzle, turning it from side to side. "How do you do it, boy? Is there something inside you I can put inside my clockwork men? Let's find out, shall we? A sharp knife, a table by the window—"

He did not finish his sentence. Behind him, a roar. Paws beating stones. And then Ursula was on top of Albrecht, his shoulders pinned. Hans had never fully appreciated the size of her paws; they were nearly twice as large as Sabine's, which had always made his own feel small.

The great brown bear opened her mouth and roared again, loud enough to tear the sky. Albrecht struggled and Jutta became her mare self, stamping and whinnying.

Ursula raked a paw across her brother's face. He screamed and rolled over, pressing his hands to it. There was so much blood that Hans had to look away. Ursula rose to her hind legs, her head knocking the ceiling of the smithy. Jutta skittered back, and her tail knocked a metal key with a glass eyeball onto the ground.

Ursula rushed her, and Jutta jumped sideways, crashing into a table cluttered with tools.

Then Ursula batted the key toward Hans. He took his human form, snatched it, and unlocked the collar around his neck. Shedding the weight of his chains, he took his wolf form once more.

"My face! My face!" Albrecht's screams rang the metal in the workshop. Ursula returned to him, pacing. The tips of her claws were red with his blood, and Hans expected at any moment for her to finish her brother off. He was crying, keening, holding his face.

Hans could see the rage in her, rippling down her neck and back. He'd felt that himself just before he tore the windpipe out of Albrecht's horse. He braced himself.

The killing moment did not come. Instead she looked at Hans, and he knew what she was saying with her eyes. *He is my brother.*

She turned to the castle. He followed. Even if Jutta came after them, she'd be hard-pressed to catch up. Fast as she was, bears and wolves were faster.

More likely, she'd tend to the king's injuries. Ursula had cut him to the bone, flaying his cheeks, nose, and lips. If there was any chance for peace between brother and sister, it surely had vanished. He was surprised that she hadn't killed him. But he was relieved for her. However cruel Albrecht was, he was her brother. Some part of her must have loved him still. He understood. He would love his sister, always.

And now he and Ursula would save her.

As they entered the courtyard, the music of the forest changed. It grew louder, angrier, more desperate. Hans's heart rolled. Something had happened. Something terrible. He ran faster through the night.

The air around them hissed and clattered. Ursula stood on her hind legs, batting away arrows raining down on them. She looked over her shoulder at him.

Back to the woods.

He did not wish to go. But he knew that they had no choice.

XLII

Greta couldn't see her feet. But she'd seen the knife. She'd felt its tip. Heard the awful tearing of her skin from the sinew and bone beneath. There was no mistaking the smell of blood or the feeling of it being pumped out of her body in great gushes. Already, the room around was darker than when she'd entered it, and she knew it was not for any lack of light. She wanted to struggle, but she could no more move her body than a tree could walk.

Candles made from the fat of animals flickered. She was used to their scent. She'd used a blade on so many animals, and now the blade had been turned on her. It had always seemed sad that a thin layer of skin, something easily slit by a blade, was all that kept a body intact. Souls should be housed in sturdier stuff. Oh, to have been more like one of the trees she loved so much. Their skins were so thick it took an ax to kill one.

To kill.

To be killed.

Albrecht.

He'd left the room after pinning the skin from her feet to a board.

It was so dark now, and the dark felt good and safe. Her body was heavy, as in the last minutes before she lost herself to sleep. Music found her. She couldn't tell where it was coming from. She didn't have the strength to sing along. But it was beautiful, beautiful music. It was a song with a story to tell. A secret. Something about . . . ah.

Listen. Just listen.

Hans. She wished him safety. She wished him love. Sabine. Sabine and Ursula. What would happen to them? To all the people? The werechildren? What world would they inherit?

Breathe.

Her feet hurt. She was standing on the point in the universe where every road of pain met. Like lighting spearing the sky over and over again. Crash.

Crash.

That noise. Albrecht was back. Touching her wrists.

No.

Too weak to struggle. The darkness was beautiful. A blanket.

"Greta."

Not Albrecht. Not Hans. Sabine. Greta tried to work her mouth.

"Shh. Shhh." Sabine's fingers on the straps. Greta's arms thumped at her sides. Then her ankles freed. *Don't cry, Sabine. Don't cry.*

Did she say it out loud? Greta could no longer distinguish the noise from inside her body and outside. Maybe that's what happened when your insides were set loose by a blade. There was no outside. There was no inside. There was you and the world and all you could feel of it. Eyes closed. Everything else open.

What was happening now? Something to her feet. Heat. Comfort. And then pain again. She wasn't in the chair anymore. She was wrapped around someone's shoulders. Sabine's. Greta was a cloak. A cloak made of flesh and blood. Well, less blood than before. The thought made her laugh. Or think of laughing. One or the other.

Either way, she had laughed, she understood, for the last time.

So many things for the last time.

So many lasts.

She did not know.

She never knew.

I did my best, she thought. *And now I want to go home, home to the woods where I was born. The woods where I belong.*

She listened. She yearned.

Music. There it was.

She hoped the song would carry her all the way.

XLIII

Cappella paced the forest near the clearing all night, waiting for Hans to return. When the music of the trees turned frantic, their branches crackling and moaning even in the absence of wind, she knew something had gone terribly wrong.

A short while later, Sabine burst out of the darkness, naked, in her human form, with Greta over her shoulders. There was no Hans. There was no Ursula. Cappella went numb.

Sabine set Greta down and collapsed. "Get help. Greta's been hurt."

The bottom of Greta's dress was wet. Even in the darkness, Cappella knew what liquid drenched it. The scent, the heaviness. Blood. Greta's skin, always pale, was white.

"Mother! Mother!"

Cappella unwrapped Greta's feet. Bone and sinew glistened in moonlight. She'd never seen anything so horrible.

Esme arrived, out of breath.

"What happened?"

"Albrecht," Sabine said.

"What should we do?" Cappella said.

"Tend to Sabine," Esme told her. "I'll see to Greta."

Sabine waved her off. "I'm fine. Just exhausted. Where's Ursula?"

"Not back." Cappella handed Sabine her cloak.

Esme lifted Greta's right leg. She held the skinless foot. Cappella expected her to wrap something around it. Leaves. Bandages. But she didn't. Instead her mother closed her eyes and rooted her free hand deep in the soil. Her body trembled and her lips moved. She thought she heard her mother whisper, "Flesh."

Overhead, branches shrieked. Greta whimpered. Esme pleaded, plunging her arm deeper into the ground. As far as Cappella could see, nothing was happening. Esme cursed and lifted the other foot so that she had one in each of her bloody hands. Cappella took hold of a leg, trying to help her mother, whose eyes were closed, her face twisted with effort, sending tears in haphazard trails down her skin.

Cappella was bloody too. On her hands. On her tunic. On the pipe in her apron. She could feel it sizzling. Could feel it coming apart. But there was nothing she could do.

Her mother begged. "Please," she said. "Please. I have nothing to give this time, but I am begging you."

As Esme spoke, a change came over Greta's feet. Skin, coated with fur, grew over the wounds. Cappella wondered if Greta had a hidden were nature. But the fur lasted only a few seconds before it turned to shreds.

"Gold, then," Esme cried out. "Give me gold!"

Her hands shook and a skin of gold coated Greta's feet. But this too dissolved. Greta's feet had soaked everything. Her gown, Esme, Cappella, even the soil. The air reeked.

Greta, her teeth chattering, whispered, "Hans."

"Shh," Sabine said. "Save your strength."

Greta would not be silent. "Let . . ."

Cappella put a hand on Greta's cheek, leaving a bloody handprint. "It's all right. Hush."

Greta took a rattling breath. "Me . . ."

Then one more word. "Go . . ." So faint, the rustle of a single leaf scraped by wind.

"Never," Esme said.

"P-please."

Esme cried out. Now it wasn't just Greta shaking. It was all of them and the earth below. The world around was a blur of sound and color. Dirt flew. The forest screamed. Cappella curled into a ball and held on.

And then the earth split in two.

Out of the gap, a tree rose.

A tree whose roots were the bloodied feet of a girl who had committed no crime. The roots born in blood grew swift and deep, as though they'd been hooked to the beating heart of the land.

From those fathomless roots spread a trunk so wide a dozen women holding hands could never hope to embrace it. The tree was tall. Not as tall as Albrecht's tower, but tall enough that it sheltered the ground beneath its branches, branches that reached for the heavens like many pairs of upraised arms.

The noise was raucous. Like a storm, but instead of the percussion of thunder and rain, there came a sound like the moaning of strings, and another of a half dozen tuning forks struck. The rising tree knocked Cappella aside. In her terrified egg position, she tumbled through the skeletons of fallen leaves and newborn soil.

Then the earth stopped heaving.

Cappella looked up. The branches were blacker than the sky itself.

Starlight found its way through, though, and the edges looked as if they burned with silver flames.

The forest had stopped singing. It was as though it was holding its breath. Greta's dress was in ribbons and a few scattered gems from the necklace she'd been wearing lay on the forest floor, glowing softly in the moonlight. But Greta wasn't there.

Cappella could not speak. Not even a whisper. She could not bring herself to move. She looked at the tree and wondered where Greta had gone. She couldn't see Sabine or her mother, though she could hear them on the far side of the massive tree, gasping and weeping. The absence of music ached.

After a while, the forest's song started again, along with a crackling that sounded like fire but gave no heat and made no smoke. It wasn't fire, it turned out, but the trees themselves, their trunks oozing a bloodred liquid that hardened swiftly, drinking in starlight till it gleamed.

Cappella was lying like that, her face wet with tears, the ruins of her pipe in her hand, when Hans and Ursula found her.

O nce there was a king..."

The storyteller's voice casts a spell that conjures silence: held breaths, the not-sound that precedes the storm of coins. He loves having this power. He loves it as much as people love to hear his tales of beauty and betrayal.

"He was a golden king, handsome to gaze upon. A brave leader. But wickedness is drawn to beauty, and this king was no exception.

"The king was promised a suit of gold. He paid for it. He paid more dearly than he could imagine. He did not get what he'd paid for, because the one who made the suit was nothing but a swindler."

The silence breaks. A voice pipes up. A child's. "What happened next?"

These are the words that always break the spell. They're hungry words. *What happened next?* This is how the storyteller knows he's become the king of the listening crowd.

He pauses, just a moment. "He punished her. The king consulted his grimoire. He transformed her into a tree that grew poisonous fruit. Whoever ate from it died, and the people became so angry that they chopped her down and burned her."

"Serves her right," the little voice says.

The storyteller turns toward the child. He no longer has eyes to see the one who owns the voice. But he sees the child with his heart. The storyteller sees him, and he smiles.

His white teeth, they are beautiful.

PART
SIX

XLIV

After Ursula left, Jutta carried Albrecht to her worktable. She swept everything off it: tools, bits of metal, weapons half-made. The smithy had no door and was open to the elements. Stinging air blew in, and Albrecht's face throbbed.

"Am I going to die?" he asked. The words came out garbled, wet.

"Not if I can help it," Jutta said. "But it's no small amount of blood."

He knew this. The shirt he wore stuck to his shoulders and chest.

There, in the smithy, standing in a puddle of Albrecht's blood, Jutta repaired his ribboned face. She'd always tended his wounds, but his boyhood injuries had been nothing like these. By the time she'd stitched his flesh, he had little left in the way of a nose and lips.

He wanted to ask how he looked, but he couldn't. It would take a while before he could speak again. And he was glad, at first, not to have his mirror anymore. He was glad he didn't have to see what his sister had done to him.

In the weeks that followed, his skin itched and burned as it rewove itself. In his pain, he sketched himself a new face and he planned his revenge. He knew how he looked well enough to re-create his nose. His lips. From his experience building articulated masks, he designed a lightweight one that would move with his jaw as he spoke. He instructed Jutta to make it with the last of his mother's gold, mixed with steel so that it would be strong and immune to the effects of blood. There would be more of that for sure.

After he finished designing his mask, he sketched more plans. He closed his mind to everything but his metal men. The pair he'd put at the entrance to the castle certainly hadn't kept his sister away. He needed a were. He needed to cut one open. To see if they contained the key. He considered dissecting Jutta, but she was more useful to him alive than dead.

If he could master these metal men, if he could create life that would not die, then he would be the most powerful king who'd ever lived. He would dispense with the need for women to give birth to subjects and soldiers. He could make his own. Use them to expand his kingdom. Metal men who would never be hungry. Never question him. Never turn against him. Never die. They would be unstoppable.

His fevered thoughts kept him from sleeping. They replaced his appetite. They warmed him, drove him, consumed him. They were not thoughts he wished to share, even with Jutta. But he knew they were right. Revolutionary, even. The future of man was metal. And he would be the one to bring it about. It would not be easy. But nothing worth doing was.

The more he worked on his metal men, the more he understood the nature of the challenge before him. He would not only have to get their limbs moving, he'd have to keep them moving. And he'd have to design ways for them to move in the formations that soldiering required. It was overwhelming. He wanted to quit, but that would mean that Ursula had won. That his father, who'd always doubted him, had won.

Hans's idea about the wings kept returning to Albrecht. Wings could keep the soldiers wound. But perhaps Albrecht's approach had been wrong.

Perhaps he'd been so accustomed to trying to make metal come alive that he'd overlooked a crucial first step. One that in retrospect seemed obvious.

Albrecht had already given himself a metal face. He'd given himself a metal finger. What was stopping him from giving himself metal skin everywhere? What was stopping him from giving himself wings?

He could turn himself into a flying soldier, the first flying soldier. He could do the same for other men in his kingdom. No man could shoot one down with an arrow. Not even a bear could pluck one from the sky. Albrecht would have what he'd always wanted. He would be a man. But he would have a second aspect. He would be everything the frissers were but better, because he could not be killed and because he'd made it himself, with the force of his hands and his mind. He'd be the golden gryphon.

Albrecht had made wings before, but never with this ferocity. As his face slowly healed, he built, he thought, he studied, shooting bird after bird with his smallest arrows so he could understand how their wings worked. How they were attached. Unfolded. Moved. Glided on updrafts.

He worked wrist deep in blood, his remaining fingers tracing every muscle and tendon. He split their tiny bones to understand how they could be so light. Days darkened into nights and Albrecht did nothing but the work, dreaming of the mysteries of the inner workings of birds, his fevered sleep gauzed in shades of red and white and pink.

He sketched plans for Jutta, who pounded out samples that he hung from wood beams spanning the room. Before long, his workshop was full of well-oiled wings, beating the air with a steady *tick-tick-tick.*

"My king," Jutta said one day. "Albrecht. Your people are hungry. The harvest was poor."

"Of course it was," he snapped. "The crops were burned."

Her voice was low. "They need to be fed. You need to be fed."

"There are things more important than food."

And then he dismissed her. He couldn't do *everything* for his subjects, so he was focusing on the most important thing. He heard whispers that he'd gone mad, but they didn't understand. It was not madness. It was the work of becoming a god.

Weeks passed and he did not succeed. He'd tried again and again with the rats. He'd failed. The wings always ripped off. Again, he thought of using frissers for his experiments. The rats were so small and the frissers so much bigger. But it wasn't just that. The rats had also been full grown. Perhaps a mature body was less adaptable by its very nature. It could not accept wings. A frisser child could.

Eventually his face healed enough to wear his golden mask. From that moment, he never took it off in the company of others excepting Jutta. He couldn't stand the staring of his servants, the maids especially. They'd once looked on him with hunger. Now he saw pity, disgust.

He realized that life was better with the mask on. It wasn't just that the mask hid his ruined face. When he wore it, people could not read his expressions. If he'd known how powerful that would make him feel . . . how invincible . . . he would have worn one all the time. He regretted learning this so late.

His face was a humiliation. He constructed a story about it, trusting Jutta to spread it by whispers: that Greta had cursed him, had given him a golden touch as a wedding gift, that he touched his face inadvertently and turned it to gold as well, and that the only way he'd managed not to turn everything else on him into gold was by killing her on their wedding night.

It didn't matter that people had seen him without the golden face after the wedding. By the time the tale had been repeated often enough, it had become true.

And it had always been true at its core. Greta had been a curse, and she was responsible for the fact of his lost face. All in all, he felt lucky. He had his ears and eyes. This meant he could still hunt. He also had his tongue and teeth, which meant he could still rule. Ursula might have had the claws, but it had been Greta who'd taken his beauty; he had taken everything else from her. In the end, he'd won. And that had always been all that ever mattered, all that ever would matter.

And he would win the ultimate battle against his sister once he had the little frissers to experiment on.

But even that was more complicated than he wished. He'd sent a group of soldiers into the woods to search for Greta's body. He knew that's where it had been taken; the trail of blood wasn't exactly subtle. The soldiers hadn't returned.

He assumed Ursula had killed them, but he could not be certain because their bodies had not been found, only their gear, scattered at the edge of the woods. They hadn't deserted. Deserters would never leave behind their weapons, boots, and armor. But why wouldn't Ursula have taken it? She must not have known it was there.

This meant someone else—something else—might have killed his men.

Since he was a boy with a broken leg, he'd told tales about a beast in the woods. He'd told them so often he believed them. Had his story become truth after all? Had he manifested a beast? The trees had changed since his wedding night. They were red now, a sickening color. And their music had changed too. It was louder. Angrier.

The beast had so far spared Ursula and her people. He'd seen the smoke rising from their camp. Perhaps it had a soft spot for animals. A bond from beast to beast.

"Jutta!" he said. "I need you!"

She came.

He explained his plans with respect to the werechildren. He disclosed what had happened to the group of soldiers, along with his theory.

"The woods have different rules for weres. You can go in safely, where real human beings can't. You are the only one who can bring me those children."

Something flickered across her face. "But . . . children?"

He waved away her concern. "Children who will turn into adults, who are and always will be the enemy of the kingdom," he said. "It's best to deal with them when they're small. Think of how much easier it is to uproot a sapling than a mature tree."

She looked out the window.

"Don't tell me you've lost your nerve," he said. "That you think *children* will get the best of you."

"It's not that at all."

He didn't like the edge to her voice. He removed his mask. "I've lost my face. I've lost my glory. I've lost my future. I want theirs in return."

Jutta looked away from his face and into the ravenous forge, and from her expression, he could tell that she'd do as he commanded. "Do not engage with my sister or any of the other grown frissers. Just the children. Put a cage in a wagon and leave it at the edge of the woods. Capture them. Bring them to me."

"It will be done," she said.

It will be done. There was no enthusiasm in her tone. He wanted her to feel what he felt.

"Imagine the soldiers we could build, Jutta. With the weres' capacity for transformation, enhanced by weaponry of my design and your manufacture. There is nothing we could not defend ourselves against. No force in the world could defeat us."

"How many children do you need?" Jutta asked.

"As many as you can catch."

She left, and Albrecht turned to a task he'd been putting off: the repair of his mirror. The frame would no longer serve. This was a pity given that Jutta had crafted it for him with his mother's gold. But he'd kept the shattered bits. Using a pot of glue he'd made from the boiled hides and bones of dead animals, he attached the pieces one by one to the wall. The smell was foul, but the substance was exactly right. Something rendered from a broken body in order to render something that had been broken whole once more.

It was a fine way to pass the time.

Just as he'd found a rhythm to hunting—inhale, point, shoot, drop—he slipped into a rhythm with each shard glued to the wall. Sort. Find. Place. Attach.

He could have put the pieces on the wall any which way. What did it matter if the edges matched? But he liked to be precise. He liked it when all the pieces came together. He'd done this with the kingdom. Put it back together. Restored its greatness. And now he would do it for his mirror, which had always been a faithful companion, reminding him that he was beautiful to look at. Strong. Worthy of his power and privilege. The mirror would not show him the face he'd grown up seeing, it was true. But perhaps what he saw in it would not displease him so very much.

Slowly the glass returned to its original shape. It was arduous, and his face grew warm behind his mask. But at last Albrecht stood before it. This was the moment he'd been waiting for, and he could feel his body recognize it. His blood felt thin and swift, and his skin prickled with anticipation. He removed his mask, feeling relief at the cool air on his skin.

He stepped closer. The wall behind the mirror hadn't been perfectly smooth, and as a result, the pieces of glass looked mottled, like the skin of a snake, with some bits catching more light than others.

He looked grotesque.

As broken as the mirror on the wall. He traced his scars with his golden finger. He looked at himself until his scars were no longer surprising to him, no longer alarming. They were simply the new landscape of his face. It might not yet be familiar territory, but neither did it seem strange anymore. This was the cost of power, a price he was willing to pay for his people. He did not hate his face.

He felt a strange fondness for his mirror, telling him the truth like this. They were even more like brothers now than they'd ever been. Both shattered. Both put back together. If they'd been distorted by circumstance, well, it only made them more fearsome to those who did not understand.

After he'd had his fill of his reflection, he put the mask back on and pulled the tapestry in front of the glass. He would look at himself again, but he did not wish to be caught by surprise.

XLV

Weeks later, in the coldest part of winter, Jutta had finished the cage for the little weres. She left the castle before dawn, her leather armor and favorite boots oiled so they wouldn't creak. She normally loved the sound of her equine feet—a heartbeat against the earth. But silence was her ally now.

She left the cart and the cage at the edge of the woods, along with a pair of single-natured horses she'd hooked to it, expecting a heavy load. She walked quietly enough that she could hear her own pulse. She loved this part of being outside. What was the world but a web of beating hearts, hers and those of others?

She slipped through the white mist that hugged the ground. It was darker in the woods, and the red branches stained the air. But her eyes adjusted, even as her skin tingled. This was where foes lived. Animals with strong jaws and sharp teeth. Animals as fleet of foot as she. The woods had always scared her. They scared her more now.

She pitied the trees. They were coated in something sickening and red, and there was nothing they could do about it. They had no hands. They could not move. They couldn't help one another.

She passed the spot where Hans had clawed her, where her own blood had seeped into the earth. Already the forest had erased evidence of that. Even if the trees stood still, life itself moved swiftly in the woods.

Jutta loved Albrecht. She always had. She could still remember him as a boy, the softness of his limbs, the downiness of his hair, the dimpled knuckles of his perfect little hands. Even as she loved him, she did not wish to hunt the children for him. This was too far, too much, too cruel.

She could not harm a child. She knew this now. She would warn the children. Warn Ursula. She would take whatever consequences came. She was afraid of what might happen. But she was more afraid of what might happen if she did as Albrecht commanded.

On the path ahead, something round and white caught her eye. She knelt and picked it up. A hole had been drilled through its center. She rolled it around her palm. She'd seen something like it before on the queen. No one else in the kingdom could afford such a thing. Greta had worn a necklace of those very gems on her wedding day. Jutta knew, deep in her bones, that this was where Greta had been taken.

Jutta walked on, keeping an eye out for more gemstones. They might just lead her to Greta, or at least to her remains. They should be burned. Returned to the soil. To do less was inhumane, and no matter what Albrecht thought of Jutta—that she was not fully human—she was. She was human. She was not lesser. If anything, her animal aspect made her *more*. This was something Jutta had never considered. It stopped her in her tracks. That being a were was something she could take pride in.

The deeper into the woods she went, the louder the music grew. She didn't even need to walk quietly now. No one could hear a thing above the din.

Her keen eyes zeroed in on a broken branch. She moved closer. Then she spied another stone, and another still, as though they'd been laid out in a trail. This must have been the way Greta fled, although she could not imagine how it had been possible, given the red shoes King Albrecht had bestowed. She must have had help. Not from Ursula. Not from Hans. From the other one—the werebear with her boots.

Deep in the forest, the trees had become enormous. Jutta was a large woman, every bit as big as Ursula, but many of these trunks were wider than she was tall. Bare branches scraped against one another, making mournful notes. She stopped to listen. A few yards ahead rose the biggest tree she'd ever glimpsed. This one made the rest, even the giants, look like saplings. The earth around it was disturbed, a handful of white stones scattered among the roots.

Jutta recognized where she was. Near the edge of the campsite, and not too far from the cottage. She'd been here earlier. How had she missed this tree? She moved closer, intending to look for Ursula from its shadow.

The music was unbearably loud now. Her skin hummed. Her teeth ached. She pulled a dagger from her boot just in case. She spotted another gem and scooped it up. This one had something brownish on it. She scraped it. Blood, long dried now.

She looked again at the tree and its strange, glistening bark. She slid her knife into it, aiming to carve away a specimen. The substance was too hard, too sticky. It took all her strength to free her knife.

Jutta wanted to flee. Every instinct in her told her to run. But where? If she returned without the children, Albrecht would conduct his experiment on her. She did not wish to harm children, but neither did she wish to be sliced open herself.

Her best option, her only option, was to throw herself at Ursula's feet and ask for mercy. She knew she shouldn't count on it. Jutta had always favored Albrecht. But perhaps if she warned Ursula what Albrecht planned to do . . . perhaps that would be enough to regain Ursula's favor. Maybe that would earn her safety. A place among the refugees.

She peered from behind the tree. People sat around fires. Children, most in their were form, played on logs. Ursula was nowhere to be seen. In the cottage, perhaps? That would be like her, to choose the sturdiest structure for her own. Something enormous cracked behind Jutta. She turned to face it and was swept up in a storm of branches.

Jutta lashed out. She felt herself rise. She kicked, but her legs were useless off the ground. Higher and higher she traveled, swinging her limbs, accomplishing nothing. She became her horse self, to use her great strength to defeat the ravenous branches. Her clothing split and dropped. Somewhere below, her knife hit the forest floor. So did her boots.

The music grew louder. She would have covered her ears if she'd been able to. Her eardrums were splitting. They felt wet and heavy. But her legs were pinned now, and she could do nothing.

She fought and whinnied, clacking her teeth against each other, her eyes wide, her skin coated with sweat. She felt . . . not herself. She was dizzy. And then nauseated. She could no longer move. It felt as though something heavy was pressing her skull. Her face. This was not good. Trees. A strange danger. She had always considered them a source of wood and nothing more. Wrong. She had been wrong. A flicker of thought, nothing she would have been able to put to words, but it was this: Had she remained true to her horse aspect, had she listened to her fear, would she have survived?

Her long tongue shriveled, and the world went dark as her eyeballs were consumed. She was no longer aware of what was happening when her skin was flayed and when her tendons and muscles turned to powder. Her sense of hearing was the last to leave.

The music became everything.

XLVI

Ursula had been following Jutta. She'd sneaked into the kingdom to dig potatoes in the farm district while everyone else huddled inside the cottage for warmth. It was freezing out, and soon the sun would set, turning the sky black and the air bitter.

She'd crept behind her quarry, glad for the noise of the forest to hide her footsteps, glad there was no wind to carry her scent. She had no desire to kill Jutta, but she would in an instant if the old mare threatened her people.

Every so often, Jutta crouched to pick something up. She seemed to be following a trail of sorts. Shortly after Jutta stopped and hid behind the enormous tree that had grown where Greta died, she flew into the air, bound tightly in branches. Then the tree devoured her. The speed took Ursula's breath away. One moment, it had been Jutta in the tree. The next, there was only a heap of something on the frozen soil. Clothing, a knife, and a certain pair of boots. Everything else was gone.

Jutta. Ursula had never *not* known her. Blacksmith. Servant. Her brother's confessor and collaborator. She'd been a mystery too, happy to betray her kind when Albrecht made his attack. Even so, no one deserved to die like that. The extent of the tree's nature was becoming clear. Where Jutta's knife had pierced its bark, it oozed something warm and red.

She put her palm to the trunk and whispered, "I'm sorry."

The tree responded with music that sounded like weeping. This, Ursula knew, was a place of terrible suffering, suffering she was powerless to fix. Sabine still had not told her how Greta had died. She wondered if she ever would. Either way, the tree had something to do with it. It felt like a gravestone. A memorial. A crypt.

She got down on one knee and collected Jutta's things. Her clothing. The knife. Her armor. Ursula was glad to have such fine gear. She was gladdest, though, to have one more pair of boots.

She put them on straightaway. They were finely made. Still warm. A perfect fit. She'd always known they would be.

⚬

Ursula had almost convinced herself that she'd stopped wanting Sabine. It didn't hurt so much now. She felt as frozen as the soil. A thaw was as unimaginable as spring felt in the hardest-biting days of winter.

Spring would come again to the world, but Sabine was lost to her. Their kiss had been real. It had happened. She'd felt invincible afterward. Her blood was churning and wild, the sort of force that could carve canyons if given enough time. Now that had no place to go except her dreams, and even they had no loyalty to her. Over and over, they brought visions of Sabine. Waking up was brutal. It was remembering everything she'd lost all over again.

The night that Albrecht murdered Greta, Ursula found Sabine sobbing and covered in blood. She thought Sabine had been bleeding. That she might die. That whole night, she'd held Sabine. As much as she wanted to hear the story of what had happened, she didn't press Sabine. She understood the essential part—that Greta was gone. That something had changed in the woods. When they woke up, still intertwined, Sabine pushed herself away.

They had not spoken since.

The day after Jutta died, Ursula was chopping wood with Hans. She swung the ax and cleaved a log. The wood itself was nearly as red as the bark. "Hans."

He grunted at her. Not exactly the way a subject should treat a queen, but he wasn't the only one. Nobody treated her like a queen anymore. People even called her Ursula. Sabine had started it. The rest of the camp followed her lead. Sometimes Ursula wondered what the world would be if queens were chosen and not born. Who would people choose? Probably not her. People rarely knew what was good for them. This was one of the first lessons Ursula had been taught. One of the reasons it was important to have a queen who knew how to make the right decisions.

Hans hadn't stopped moving since that awful night. He filled his hours with activity and spoke to no one but Cappella, and even with her, he rarely said more than a word or two at a time. Ursula wanted him to know that Jutta was dead. It might help.

"Do you recognize the boots I'm wearing?"

He turned to look. She saw the moment he remembered them. "Where did you get those?"

"She's dead."

"Dead, how? Did you hunt her?" Hans threw logs on the pile. They'd have to clean that up later, but she understood his rage.

"I did not hunt her. The tree . . ." It felt so strange to say out loud. "The tree that grew after your sister passed . . . Jutta was standing by it, and then the tree swept her up. It ate her."

She pulled the pearls from her pocket. "I found these on the ground. Jutta had been following a trail of them. They were my mother's. My brother must have given them to your sister. They must have dropped as Sabine carried her. They're quite valuable, as I understand it. They're yours now."

"Valuable? What am I supposed to do with these? Buy myself new boots?" He looked gutted. Ursula wanted to tell him it was all right to weep. She swung the ax instead, reducing a red log into halves and then quarters.

Hans kicked at the frozen ground. "Why did Jutta come here?"

"To find us again, I suppose. Perhaps to deliver another message from Albrecht."

"She's lucky the tree found her first," Hans said.

If Jutta had come into the woods looking for them, more men would follow as soon as Albrecht missed her. They had to be ready to fight.

"Hans." Ursula lowered the ax. He was once again looking at Cappella, who was singing softly to the werechildren who sat around her. Ursula was glad the girl had found a way to make herself useful.

"I wanted to kill Jutta myself," he said, his voice anguished. "She lied to me. She told me if I went with her, that my sister would be safe."

"You don't mean that. Not about killing." He was still a boy. Granted, not much younger than she, but she was queen, and it was her obligation to kill, by herself if need be, or through the armies and guards she commanded. To wield power was sometimes a matter of death. It was inescapable. She'd been raised to accept that.

"Weres are killers, are we not?"

"No," she said. "We can if we *must*. But that is not our nature."

He made a noise of disgust. "Then why did we sleep in cages every night? Why was that the law, even for a princess?"

The question stopped Ursula short. She'd slept in a cage because she was told to. Because she believed she needed to. It was a golden cage, softened by pillows. But it was a cage, nonetheless. She'd even missed it her first few nights sleeping in the woods.

"Because," she said. "Because . . ."

But she did not finish her sentence. She couldn't think of a reason for it other than she always had locked herself inside one.

Hans tidied the pile of wood, stealing glances at Cappella. The girl had overheard the whole exchange. It felt like a violation to be listened to, and the melody the girl was singing now made Ursula feel morose. She didn't need that; it was the very thing she was trying *not* to feel.

"Tell her to be silent," Ursula said. "Before long, soldiers will come. We have to be ready. And her music will call them like bees to blossoms."

Hans looked as though he wanted to make a remark, but he did as she commanded. Cappella stopped, ran a hand through her pied hair, and looked at Ursula. It made Ursula uncomfortable, as though Cappella saw things Ursula didn't know about herself. Making matters worse, the children groaned when she stopped singing. Ursula wasn't really one for children, but nobody liked disappointing them. She regretted her order, but she could hardly reverse it now. It would make her look weak, and they needed her to look strong.

That was how a leader looked. Certainty was everything. If she was ever going to reclaim the kingdom, she'd have to play the part.

She went back to swinging the ax until every last bloodred log had been reduced to a fraction of its former self. Split like her kingdom, split like her heart, with nothing left to do but burn.

Ursula found Sabine inside the cottage, kneading dough for bread. This was what she did now that her broken arm was healed. Baked bread using potatoes she dried and ground every evening, late into the night. Grinding, kneading, punching. Weeks of silence put a growing wall between them.

Ursula missed the old Sabine. The one who was merry and easy to be with. The one who helped her find the strength she needed to break through the dungeon wall. This version of Sabine seemed much more like one of Albrecht's windup devices, moving mechanically, without any spark of life behind her eyes. What Sabine needed was a good fight to let that energy out.

This silence had to end.

"Sabine." Ursula used her most commanding voice because she was too afraid to show any softness.

Sabine looked up, her hands deep in light brown dough. Ursula's heart caught.

"Let's get out of here."

There was no joy in Sabine's face. No enthusiasm. If she came along it would be out of duty.

Sabine opened the window. "Nicola."

The little weregoat who often joined Sabine in the kitchen trotted in.

"Wash your hands," Sabine said. "I'll need you to finish this bread for me."

━━━

Ursula brought Sabine to the place they'd first met. "Do you remember this?"

Sabine smelled of yeast and rising bread, things that reminded Ursula of potential. She rolled her eyes. "You used to wear much prettier shoes."

Ursula looked at Sabine's boots. "You're not one to talk."

"They look better on me," Sabine said. "I'm tired of this. Tired of potatoes. Of not having enough food for the children. I overheard them talking to one another about honey cakes and what they'd give for one. It made me want to cry."

Ursula took a deep breath. "There is honey in the woods. There are bees—"

"That's not the point. This is no sort of life. Of sitting here and waiting for men we've never harmed to attack us."

"What do you think we should do?" Ursula hated even asking. She was supposed to have the answers. "Should we attack first? Albrecht is wounded. Only in the face, so it's nothing vital, but—"

Sabine burst out laughing. "Only in the face. Didn't you tell me he was the vainest person you'd ever met?"

"Yes, but I meant—"

"I know what you meant. Let me laugh at your evil brother's stupid face." Then her face grew serious. "Did you know that's the first time you've asked me what I thought we should do? This is your weakness, Ursula. Your conceit. You haven't once asked any of us what we want. You haven't asked any one of us for our opinions and ideas. You've taken control. You've trained us to fight. But all you want is for things to be as they were before, except with you in charge."

"That isn't true," Ursula said. "I'm going to make everything better."

"You don't make things better by keeping the system of power the same," Sabine said.

"I'm not the system of power. I'm a person. I'm the one responsible for ruling. I never asked for it. I'm doing my best." Even as she said the words, she felt the hollowness of them. She might not have asked for it, but she'd wanted it. And it was true she hadn't asked her people what they wanted. What did that matter? She knew what they needed, which was more important.

Sabine turned away. "I don't want to argue with you."

"What do you want, then? Tell me and I'll give it to you. I'll give you anything."

"Ursula." Sabine's voice was quiet. "We've been having this fight since the day we met."

"It wasn't a fight," Ursula said. "It was a good day. The best day. You're not remembering it right. Don't rewrite the past. Don't erase our history."

Sabine's expression became wistful, and Ursula understood she was suffering too.

"I do remember one part," Sabine said. "I remember what an incredibly slow runner you were."

"What?" Ursula wanted to protest. That hadn't been the case. But Sabine had already shed her clothes and taken her bear form. Ursula understood. She undressed herself, reveling in the moment it took her to become a bear. Sabine was giving her a gift. She'd take it.

Ursula shot off, but Sabine was the swifter one now. Try as she might, Ursula could not keep up. They ran, turning the woods into a blur, Ursula's senses gorging themselves until they reached another clearing, where Sabine stopped. Turned. Reared up. Waited.

Ursula crashed into her. On her hind legs, she was taller than Sabine, but Sabine held her own. They stood, paws on each other's shoulders. They snarled, and there was heat and spit and the rich musk of bear fur. It might have looked like a fight, this exchange. But it was a game, a game where they'd make up the rules as they went, both playing to win.

Ursula had no words as a bear, but she didn't need them. Unlike human silence, this form was bliss. She'd never been happier than when she wrestled wordlessly with Sabine. Because it made them stronger. Because they belonged to each other. Because every time they did, they grew closer. And even if they could not have each other, that fact would never change. They were equals. Two halves of a whole. A pair.

Ursula tried her hardest to knock Sabine off her feet. She knew she wouldn't be able to. That was one of the things she loved best about her: her steadfastness. It wasn't true that Ursula could only rely on herself. She could be sure of Sabine too. It didn't mean she could have her, but that certainty was everything. Their paws slipped and they were grappling, and either one could have cut the other with teeth, with claws. But they didn't. Because that's what love was: being close enough to hurt, and careful enough not to.

XLVII

Albrecht knew that Jutta was lost. When she hadn't returned the morning after he'd sent her, he was alarmed. In the weeks since, he'd grown morose. The best-case scenario was that Ursula had taken her prisoner.

He pulled back the tapestry covering his mirror. He was looking pale and soft. He felt strong enough to look for Jutta, though, if only to see the look of surprise on his sister's face when he arrived at her camp, weapons in hand.

He covered the mirror. *Think.* He had to think. Whatever was happening in the woods, whatever had turned the trees red, was dangerous. He never would have admitted it, but Albrecht was afraid. It was only a matter of time before his people learned the truth of the forest. Any one of them venturing into the woods for food, it seemed, would not come out. There would be a panic. He would be blamed.

He didn't understand what had happened. He couldn't explain it. What had changed? His sister had gone into the woods and somehow, her presence had poisoned it. It was probably all the frissers. Hans. That black bear. So many unnatural beings in one place—it was no wonder even nature was rebelling.

It made it all the more urgent that he get his hands on the frisser children. If he could not walk into the forest, he was going to need to lure them out. He closed his eyes and stroked his scars.

There were risks. But what were his strengths? *The wings.* He could attach them to his own back with a harness. He could soar over the woods, safely out of reach. He could see exactly what was going on below, and he could drop things for the children to find, things that would lead them to where he'd have a cart waiting.

It was simple, really. He laughed out loud at the ease and clarity of it. He'd spent his whole life building devices that he knew would be useful. And sure enough, without even knowing why, he'd made exactly what he needed, and it was ready when he needed it. It almost felt like destiny.

He put his palm to the window. It was cold and it hummed with music from the woods. He tapped the glass with his golden not-finger. Someday he would like to raze that forest. Burn it down. Silence the noise. But that would have to wait until he'd emptied it of frissers.

The self-winding wings Hans had imagined for him hung from the ceiling, their spread twice his height. Albrecht stood beneath them, admiring their intricacy and beauty. He saw exactly how he could attach the harness. He'd have to modify some of his leather armor, but that's what knives were for.

Other complications would arise, he knew. But he would knock them down, one by one, until none remained.

The question remained: Would they work?

This was a mild way of facing the possibility that failure meant death. He'd tried a few times to take off from the ground weeks earlier with Jutta, tying the wings on with ropes. He'd never flown more than a few feet. He would have liked to blame the harness, but he knew the truth. He wasn't strong enough to take off.

He'd have to do what the birds did when they were learning how to fly—leap from a height. If baby birds could do that, then he could too. Even so, the thought sickened him.

He still remembered falling out of the tree, the awful pain of breaking his leg. The idea of shattering his entire body made him dizzy and numb.

He forced himself instead to imagine succeeding. He envisioned himself carving a path through air over the forest, studying it from above. That hope pushed him onward. But he didn't want to take too many chances. Best, he thought, to let a rat try it first.

It hadn't worked to stitch the wings to their flesh; every rat he'd sent out the window had plummeted to a swift death. But if he made a leather harness like the one that he intended to make for himself, and if the harness worked for the rat, then there was no reason it should not work for him.

All day long, he sliced leather using his bladed fingertip. He wove the tiny strips until they were the perfect size for the smallest rat in his menagerie.

The creature protested at being forced to wear it.

"You should be thanking me," he said. "This might be the thing that keeps you alive."

The rat bit him, and Albrecht flicked its nose, drawing blood.

"You," Albrecht said, "have an ugly little face. And I should know. But I like your fighting spirit."

He worked the straps through the slots beneath the wings and wound the mechanism. He loved the sound of this, the way the pitch rose the tighter it got. It sent a thrill up his spine every time.

The landscape below had been sugared with snow. The trees had no leaves, and their redness made them stand out like veins against the whitened earth.

It wasn't snowing at the moment, but the sky was cushioned with clouds. Albrecht would have a wonderful, shadowless view of his flying rat as it ventured forth.

He unlatched the window and winced at the frigid blast. His bladed notfinger rang with cold. That certainly would be a drawback of being made of metal. The rat was warm but would not be for long. In a swift motion, he pitched the creature into the winter-white air.

There was a long moment where nothing happened. The rat arced outward. His limbs and tail flared. He dropped. Albrecht's heart sank.

But then the wings flapped. The rat's descent ended. Its path straightened. And off it went, becoming smaller and smaller as it approached the woods. Albrecht watched it until he could see it no longer.

When the mechanism ran out, the rat would fall. It would fall, and it would die. He would not.

There was a knock on his door. He pulled the window closed.

"Enter!"

A maid appeared with food. He'd forgotten that he was not wearing his mask; he didn't like the feeling of perspiring behind it as he worked. But her expression reminded him.

"No pastries?" he asked. "Nothing sweet?"

She looked away.

"Set it down." He pointed to the worktable. He could always tell when someone was too disturbed by his injuries to look directly upon them.

"I will need cakes," he said.

"More than one?

"Many more."

"But, Your Majesty—"

He held up a hand. "I don't want to hear anything except that I will have them by nightfall. They are necessary for the security of this kingdom."

He put his bladed not-finger under her chin and lifted it until she was looking into his eyes. Tears welled up and she blinked. He supposed the blade might be sharp. Or it might just be his face, terrifying her. Either way, he liked the feeling. When her breath came in little hitches, he lowered his finger. There was a bead of blood on her chin. A thing of beauty, red as rubies—no, red as the woods below.

Bloodred. Beautiful.

"Yes, Your Majesty."

The blood fell, a perfect drop that broke against the stones when it landed, spiky at its edges, like a crown.

The maid brought the cakes that night. Dozens tucked into a basket. They smelled warm and sweet. He broke one open and inhaled through his ruined nostrils. He devoured it, and the sweetness suffused him.

Then he covered the basket. He would need the remainder in the morning.

XLVIII

Cappella found a spot away from the others. She needed to do something painful, something private. Something she'd put off for too long.

Shivering in the cold, she dug a shallow hole the length of her arm. It was hard going in the frozen soil. She used her hands, and when she was done, her fingertips burned and bled, but she welcomed the pain. It hurt less than everything else.

She took one last look at her pipe. Where Greta's blood had touched it, the gold had dissolved, and she was left with something that looked like tattered lace. When she'd tried to play it, she found that it was useless.

Weeks passed. None of her repairs had worked. She needed to let it go, and at last, she felt ready.

She covered it with soil and crouched, arms wrapped around her knees. The pipe was a thing, not a living being. Nothing like Greta. Her loss was nothing like what Hans had suffered. And yet she grieved its loss. Deeply, and it shamed her.

Greta's death had not just broken her pipe; it had broken something between her and Hans. This too was irreparable. She could not bring Greta back. She didn't know how to help Hans.

She blew on her fingertips to warm them, but they stayed numb.

One evening while they were inside their tree, her mother had tried to help.

"What we saw," Esme said, "was terrible. What was done to her should not have been done to any living thing. What she suffered should not have happened."

"But it did." Cappella took no care to keep the anger from her voice. "I hate Albrecht for doing this."

"*Hate* is a strong word, my darling."

Cappella fumed. Her mother had always cautioned her against hate. She wasn't to hate eating mushrooms. She wasn't to hate going to bed when she wasn't tired. She wasn't to hate the endless rain of spring. What was the use of having a word if it was too strong to use? When did *hate* apply, if not to someone who could do something so cruel?

She exploded in anger. "Look at Hans. Look at how sad he is. He's alone in the world now. She was his last family."

In the dim hollow, Cappella could see anguish in her mother's face. Was it anguish over Greta? Or because Cappella had said the word *hate*? She didn't care. Let her mother suffer too.

"I hate him. I don't care that he is my family, that he is our family. I hate him."

Her mother reached for her hand and held it. "Where will that hate get you?"

Cappella pulled away. "Why does it have to get me anywhere? Why can't I just feel it?"

Her mother said nothing for a long, long time. "I hated my sister," she said. "I hated her after what she did to me."

The thought of her mother hating anyone struck Cappella as shocking. "What did she do to you?"

"I've let all of that go," Esme said. "It doesn't mean I have forgotten it, but I released it as something that can still make me suffer. I stewed about it for years. How it was unjust. How what she'd said about me, what she was willing to *believe* about me, was untrue. How nothing I could say to her would change her mind. How she'd made a choice. I hated her even as I missed her. All it did was make me lonely."

"But what did she do and why won't you tell me? How am I supposed to know anything if you keep the truth from me?" Cappella hurt all over. She'd cried so much her face felt raw, but she didn't know how to stop.

"Don't make me speak the words aloud, Cappella. Don't make me feel that pain again."

The anger that had felt like a bubble inside her burst. Her mother was lying to her even now. She hadn't gotten over it. It still made her suffer. She'd just learned to live with it. Esme was lying to herself too, something that struck Cappella as impossibly sad. She'd thought that adulthood meant you could face the truth. She'd thought it was characterized by unflinching honesty. But it wasn't. Not for everyone. Not for her mother.

"How long did it take you to feel better?"

Her mother put a finger on her lips and squinted. "I've never thought about it." Then her lips curved into a gentle smile. "But I was angry until you came along, and then I had no time for anything else."

Cappella snuffled and wiped her nose. "I hope you're not suggesting I have a baby, because that would be disgusting."

Her mother burst into a deep belly laugh that lasted a good long time. For a moment, Cappella's grief subsided, but as soon as she became aware of its absence, it returned.

"I don't know how to help Hans," she said. "I don't know what to say to him. I'm afraid to say the wrong thing."

"Just be with him," her mother said. "Play music for him."

"I have to tell you something, Mama." Cappella hadn't called her that since she was little. "My pipe. My pipe was ruined."

"The blood," her mother said. "There was so much of it. That was always the problem with the gold."

As soon as her mother mentioned gold, a piece of the puzzle fell into place. Her mother was the gold spinner. She'd seen her do it. How could she not have known this this? The queen had never been the one to make gold; it had been her mother all along. This had been the source of the rupture between them. Her mother must also have left the gold coins for Hans and Greta. That was another thing her gold spinning had done—sent her wolf to the kingdom.

"I can make you a new one, you know," Esme said. "Exactly like the old one."

And there it was. The truth. Cappella had figured it out, but she was relieved her mother had told her anyway. Cappella wanted a new pipe. She missed the weight of hers in her hand. Missed how it felt to breathe music into the world. She missed the way she could say things to people, make them feel things, even make them *do* things sometimes with her music. She'd helped heal Hans. She was certain of it. Whenever she played, people would come to her. She made substance from nothing more than breath. What was that but a binding sort of magic? It wasn't like her mother's, but it was magic all the same.

She refused her mother's offer.

She didn't want her mother to make anything else for her. She loved her, flaws and all. But she no longer wanted to depend on her. It was time for Cappella to find out who she was, apart from being Esme's daughter. There was only one way to do that.

There was much Cappella didn't know. She didn't even know who her father was. She'd never felt the absence before, but she felt it acutely now— not for a person, but for what it told her about herself, about who she might become. In the absence of the truth, she realized something. That her identity was her own to forge, with her own hands, her own heart, her own unquenchable desire.

I am a musician. It was a fact. It was a promise.

She had to make her pipe herself. And she would. But it would not be made of gold.

The next day, she found Hans sitting alone on the riverbank, looking out at the kingdom. She joined him. He didn't acknowledge her, but he moved his hand closer to hers. She closed the gap, weaving her fingers through his. The air turned their breath white.

"Don't you want to be close to the fire? With the others?"

Hans shook his head. "I don't get cold."

It wasn't true. He might have been warmer in general because he was a were, but his fingers were icy. It didn't matter, though. She knew what he was really saying—that he wanted solitude. She almost left him there. But he hadn't let go of her hand, and she took that as a sign. A bit of hope.

"Is it all right if I stay?" she asked.

He nodded.

As they sat, their hands laced, they didn't talk about Greta. They didn't talk about Albrecht.

"You haven't played any music in a long time," Hans said finally. "I've missed it."

"My pipe." She chose her words carefully. "It was broken. I'll need a new one."

"How does a golden pipe break?" He leaned away from her, and she hated the cold that bloomed between them.

"It was an accident." She didn't want to tell him about all the blood.

"Can something be made from the old one?"

"I tried for weeks. I want a different sort of pipe this time around. I want one made of wood."

"I've no idea where you're going to find any of that," he said.

"Hans—" she started. Then she looked at his face. He was joking. *He'd made a joke.* She wanted to weep from joy. To tell a joke in the midst of heartbreak was to hope. To hope was to believe in change. In better days.

"Will you help me?" she asked.

"What I know about making musical instruments could fit on the back of one of Ursula's fleas."

"I'm telling Ursula you said she has fleas."

"You wouldn't!" He grabbed her wrists as if to hold her in place. They were both laughing.

"Oh, I most definitely would. Unless you help me make a new pipe."

"Then I don't see that I have any choice in the matter." He hung his head in mock shame, and she was so happy to see it that she flung her arms around his neck. His face was warm, and his skin smelled of woodsmoke.

"Pella," he said. He was crying. "I could have saved her, and I didn't, and Sabine won't even tell me how she died, which means it was awful."

She realized that he didn't know that she'd seen Greta die too. She didn't want to tell him what she'd witnessed. It was too terrible to know. But then it struck her that was exactly what her mother had done to her. Nothing good had come of concealing painful truths. It was not the kind of person she wanted to be. Cappella put her face on his shoulder, and he had his on hers, and she wept with him as she told him what had happened to his sister.

"It's not your fault," she said afterward. "You did everything you could."

"I feel ashamed."

"You have nothing to be ashamed of," she said.

"I'm ashamed to be alive."

"Don't say that, Hans. Don't say it."

"But it's true."

"Her death is not your fault. Albrecht did this. No one else."

"What right have I to be happy, though? We'd promised we'd always take care of each other. I failed her." He pulled away.

She chose her words with care. She spoke slowly, teeth chattering. "It's the right of every living thing to feel joy at being alive. We don't feel this all the time, maybe. That's not possible. Not when there are people like Albrecht in this world. But if we didn't feel the good things, at least some of the time, then what is the point of living?"

He didn't answer. She didn't mind. She knew he was thinking.

"And the thing is, Hans—" She swallowed. It was so hard to speak her whole heart. "The thing is, I need you. I know I don't have any right to you. I'm not your flesh and blood. I'm just your friend. But when you say you are ashamed to have survived, when you say you don't want to feel happiness, it kills me."

"Cappella." He put his hands on her cheeks. "I've no parents. I've no sister. You are everything I have left."

He brought his lips to hers and kissed her gently, briefly.

Cappella didn't feel the cold anymore. She needed more of him.

"You're everything I've ever wanted," she said.

His gray eyes had never looked so dark, so intense. But she understood. He was as hungry for her as she was for him. He kissed her again, and it was not gentle. He kissed her with force, with desperation, and she found that she could not get enough of it. Could not get close enough to him. She needed him the way a flame needs wood and air. There was no fire without that. Kissing him like this, she felt consumed by the heat. But she was not becoming ash; she was being transformed. Made new. She'd never felt so profoundly alive.

"Well," he said afterward.

She couldn't find any words. Her lips felt tender, as though she'd need to learn all over again how to work them.

"Shall we make you a new pipe?" he asked.

She made the most serious face she could. "But where will we find the wood?"

He looked back at her and shrugged. "Your guess is as good as mine."

She was about to suggest they try to find a tree when something whizzed overhead.

She thought at first it was a bird, but only owls wintered in the woods.

"What was that?" she asked.

Hans's expression was pure horror. His skin was gray, and she thought he might faint.

"Albrecht," he said.

She didn't know what he meant.

"That was a rat. One of his rats."

"But—"

"The wings. That's what we were working on. He's done it. He's made a rat fly."

Cries came from the camp.

Hans grabbed her hand. They took off running.

XLIX

At the sound of the children's screams, Ursula became the bear. She crashed through the underbrush until she was practically on top of them, looking frantically to the left and right for whatever had terrified them so.

"It was flying," Nicola said. "It had metal wings."

Ursula took her human form. "What was?"

"That." Sebastian pointed to the ground. The twitching hind legs of a rat poked out of the snow.

Ursula lifted the rat by its tail, freeing the rest of its body and a pair of feather-light metal wings lashed on with leather strips. The rat's body had been broken irreparably. She hated for children to see this.

She carried the rat back to where she'd left her clothing. She examined the wings on its back. A winding mechanism of some sort lay between them. She didn't dare touch it, lest she harm the rat further. Even through the harness, she could feel its frantic heartbeat. The poor, poor creature. She turned it over again. Its eyes were wide and rolling, and blood oozed from its ears. She snapped its neck to end its suffering. Shivering, she dressed.

By then, Hans and Cappella were upon her.

"That's one of Albrecht's devices," he said.

"I suspected as much. But I don't understand how a rat with wings figures into his metal-man schemes."

"The wings will keep a metal man wound. They'll keep it going."

"Then why did the rat crash?" Ursula asked.

"I don't know," Hans said. "But it means he's getting closer."

"That he has succeeded with a rat is no proof he knows how to do this for anything larger," Ursula said, as much to convince herself as Hans and Cappella. "Meanwhile, we should burn this poor creature."

"Why would he send it?" Cappella asked. "Does it mean anything?"

"At the very least, it means he's still thinking about us," Ursula said.

"We need to patrol," Hans said.

"That's for me to decide," Ursula said. She immediately regretted her words and her tone. She knew she'd embarrassed him, and in front of Cappella. This was exactly the sort of thing Sabine was talking about when she'd said Ursula never considered anyone else's opinion but her own. "Hans, you're right, of course. I thank you."

❧

Dinner was quiet. People huddled around fires, eating soup and thin slices of potato bread because the wheat stores had been exhausted. The children's noses were red and running, and there was none of the usual laughter that tended to erupt during mealtime.

Afterward, Ursula turned to Sabine. "Walk with me."

Once they were away from the rest, Ursula said, "What do you think he meant by sending the rat?"

"Whatever it was, it didn't exactly strike terror in my heart," Sabine said. "I pitied it."

"He was testing his concept, I think. Seeing if he could make a metal soldier fly."

"If he can't make a rat fly, he's not going to make anything larger fly, let alone some sort of undying metal soldier. But even if he did, we could knock it out of the sky with a rock. We could sink it in the river."

Ursula felt a rush of love for Sabine. An immortal soldier would give most people nightmares. Here Sabine was already figuring out how to end one.

"What if he succeeds?"

"We can talk about ifs forever," Sabine said. "If Albrecht attacks. If he sends more flying rats. If he somehow manages to make a flying man. But it doesn't change what we must do."

"I know, fight back. But we cannot fight—"

"That wasn't what I was going to say," Sabine said. She put a hand on Ursula's forearm, and they stopped walking.

"All my life I've been at the mercy of the king. Your father," Sabine said. "I was taken from my parents. I had to live where he said. I had to sleep in a cage. I had to make my way in the world by turning myself into an amusement for others. I don't want to do this anymore. I think we should leave."

"But this is my land," Ursula said. "Our land. This is our home."

"He'll attack us. We'll attack back. The only end of that cycle is death," Sabine said. "I don't want any part of it. I want to live. I love the woods too. But I want to make a home someplace else." Light from the near-full moon bounced off the snow and illuminated Sabine's expression. She wanted Ursula to understand. To see things her way. But Ursula couldn't. She'd learned diplomacy. She'd learned combat. When one failed, you used the other. Running away was never an option. What was life if she didn't have a kingdom? What kind of leader was she if she gave up her home?

"What if we stole his metal men?"

"Ursula," Sabine said. "We have no army. We have farmers. Elderly people. Children."

"I should have killed my brother when I had the chance."

"And then, what, did you plan to stroll back into the castle and take over?"

"The people in the kingdom are miserable," Ursula said. "They're as hungry as we are. I've seen them when I've made runs for supplies. I even left some of the potatoes where they'd be found. They'd welcome me."

"Perhaps they would," Sabine said. "Or perhaps they would view you as the monster Albrecht's told them you are."

"What would you have me do?" Ursula asked.

"Better than this," Sabine said. "I just got out of a cage. I have little desire to go back inside one."

"But there will be no cages!" Ursula couldn't help but yell.

"Maybe none that you can see," Sabine shot back.

They stood facing each other, breathing clouds of mist into the night.

Ursula had never been so dispirited. The two of them might as well have been speaking different languages. If Ursula didn't understand Sabine, the reverse was true as well.

"We'll figure it out," Sabine said.

Ursula didn't think so. She'd gone over everything she'd ever been taught about diplomacy, which had failed. About fighting, which looked hopeless. She knew Sabine was trying to tell her something, trying to get her to think in new ways, and it felt impossible.

And in any case, this was Ursula's work to do, and she had failed. The next attack Albrecht made might end them.

"Are you coming?" Sabine asked.

Ursula shook her head. "I'll be on patrol. Don't wait up."

L

Albrecht had his plan. There was much to do and little time in which to do it, but the pressure exhilarated him. He was going to lure the children out of the forest himself, but first, he needed to distract his sister.

He instructed his guard to make a raid on Ursula's camp that night. He did not tell them of his concerns—that there was something waiting in the forest that could kill them. He didn't need to. Everyone knew the men sent earlier had not returned. Everyone knew the blacksmith had disappeared too. In all likelihood, he was sending his men to their death, and they knew it. But kings must do what kings must do.

Once the men were off, he pounded downstairs to the kitchen and clapped his hand on the baker's shoulder. "You! I have a task!" He had some cakes already, but the plan had two phases. He would need cakes for each. He described what he wanted this time.

At first, she'd pleaded that they hadn't enough flour and spices for such a project. "The shortages of flour are dire."

"Use everything you have."

She opened her mouth to protest. He touched his pitted, golden not-finger to her lips, and she closed her mouth without another peep. By the time the sun had reached its peak in the winter-white sky, she done exactly as he asked. Enormous slabs of gingerbread lay before him on a long table in the back of the kitchen. He touched one. Warm. Sturdy. Perfect.

He did not regret using all their supplies. What he was doing was more important than filling the mouths of servants. They'd understand when the time came. They'd thank him.

He transported the gingerbread to the edge of the woods and found Jutta's cart. It took a bit of doing to unhitch the horses that had died while waiting for her to return. But he was strong, and he managed. Then he hitched his own steed, another pure white one that would blend with the snow, to Jutta's cart. The cage it held was intact, though coated in a skin of ice. That too would be useful. He pressed the slabs of warm cake against the cage. The icy bars melted and then refroze, holding it in place like a wall. One by one he pressed the slabs in place, leaving room for the door.

When he was finished, he ran his nose along the edge and inhaled. Delicious. He moved the cart to a new location closer to the cottage and the clearing (and away from the frozen horses), and then returned to the castle to watch the sunset from his tower. The world below was scabbed in snow; nothing new had fallen, so everything old had grown hard and withered in the freezing air. It looked like a world hungry for change.

He could be cold wearing the wings, cold enough that he did not wish to take his not-finger with him. He unstrapped it and laid it on a table. His hand felt naked without it, but it couldn't be helped. He lowered the wings from the ceiling. All he'd have to do was fasten himself into the harness and then release the chain to be ready. But he couldn't bring himself to do it. Not yet.

Cold pierced the window and gnawed at his leg, a permanent reminder of what it meant to fall. He'd hated heights since he'd tumbled from the tree. But if he did not master his hatred, he'd fail. He considered recruiting one of his guards for the job. Demanding he wear the wings and fly and do what was necessary to protect the kingdom.

But no. A guard might not be capable of flight and certainly would not have experience with the wings. He would risk their destruction, and they'd be difficult to replace now that he'd lost Jutta and Hans. And if the plan succeeded, Albrecht would have to share credit. This was dangerous, not only for him but for the kingdom. A kingdom needed a single hero. This was how unity worked. There could be only one.

When the last light of the sun disappeared and the full moon rose, it was time.

He'd rely on moonlight to cut through the darkness, showing him where to drop the little cakes he'd use as bait. He'd lure the children to the edge of the woods and trap them in the gingerbread cage. The moonlight was just enough to see by, and the darkness was just enough to hide him. It was perfect.

Albrecht stepped back into the harness. He fastened the straps, then unhooked the wings. They felt like nothing on his back, and yet when he slipped his wrists into the straps and moved them, he could feel the way they grabbed the air.

Even so, a sick sensation riddled his bones when he took a step toward the window.

He had to do this. Ursula could not win.

The first bright star pricked the velvet of night. He tucked the remaining honey cakes into a pouch at his waist. He opened the window as wide as it could go. Freezing air tightened his skin and made him gasp. The opening was too small, and passing through this window sideways would be harder than he'd first thought. But there was another way he could make it through. The window had smaller, fixed panes of glass on either side. All he had to do was tear a new mouth in the wall of the tower, just as Ursula had torn one in his face.

He rubbed lamp oil on his face to keep his skin warm and then donned his golden mask and gloves. He backed up, counted to three, and ran. The cold glass and frozen lead gave way more easily than he'd imagined.

There was a pop. A blast of air. He was through.

He could not breathe at first. He could scarcely feel the handholds on the wings through his thick leather gloves, but he trusted they were there. He beat the wings downward, flexing his chest and arm muscles. The wings caught a current. He'd stopped streaking toward the earth and was instead climbing, up, up, and out over the kingdom he ruled, the wind playing wild games with his hair. The forest was beneath him now, scribbled black lines over the gray-white snow. To be this far above, to see the world in miniature, felt as right as anything had ever felt.

He was a lion. The golden gryphon. The most powerful man in the history of his kingdom. The most powerful man in any kingdom. The most powerful man who'd ever lived.

Ahead, the cart. Below, the small orange fires of his sister and her pathetic people burned. He angled toward them, trusting they would not think to look up as he soared overhead. The next time he brought the wings down, he loosened the pouch that held the cakes. One by one they fell as he rushed forward, leaving behind a trail of sweet and fragrant things, the sort that hungry children can't resist.

When he crossed back into the kingdom, he slowed his wings. He descended as gracefully as if he'd been born to fly. And, indeed, he felt that he had been. That this moment was the fulcrum of his destiny. He touched the earth, stepped out of the wings, and unfolded them over the top of the cage. Then he climbed inside to wait.

LI

After they burned the body of the poor rat, Hans and Cappella hunted for a branch she could use to make a new pipe.

"What about this one?"

He handed her a branch. It was the right thickness, it was straight, and if they could cut it in half, they could hollow it out and then glue the halves together. He'd seen Albrecht make glue from the hides and hooves of animals, and they still had the frozen carcass of the horse he'd killed. The meat had been eaten, of course, and some of the bones turned to soup already. But the hooves and knees remained. They'd be perfect.

She hefted it in her palm. "It doesn't feel right."

"How is it supposed to feel?"

Cappella sighed. "I can't explain it, but I'll know it when I'm holding it."

That, he understood. He'd known the moment he saw Cappella that they'd been made for each other. The look he'd seen on her face was the feeling he felt in his chest: joy, surprise, delight. He wished for those days again, sometimes. He wished to be the cub sprinting alongside her in the woods, feeling nothing but his feet against the earth and the brightness of the air in his lungs. He'd never feel that way again, he knew. To grow up was to set aside the lightness of childhood.

He stood next to the enormous tree that marked the spot where Greta died. He put his hand on the trunk, thinking of her. Missing her. The air was bitterly cold and hard to breathe and it made his eyes water. He felt frozen in sadness. Though there was no wind to speak of, and no leaves to rustle overhead, the branches moved. They moved; there was a moan. Then something snapped, and on the ground in front of him lay a branch.

It was perfect. The same length as her old pipe, and the right thickness, and it was beautifully straight.

He held it up. "Look at this one!"

She came over, and she was so warm beside him, bundled in her red cloak. The frosty air had turned her cheeks and lips pink, and her misty breath had hung crystals on the strands of her straight black hair around her face.

She took the stick and gauged its weight, tilting her head and nodding. She examined an end. "Huh."

"What?" He hadn't looked at it closely; he'd been too excited to show her.

"It's hollow already."

He looked through it. "Does the wood feel frozen to you?"

She laughed. "Hans, *everything* is frozen." She tapped the stick. The sound it made wasn't like any wood he'd heard. It was almost like the sound a pot made when you flicked your fingers against it, like the sound she imagined a bone would make striking another bone.

Whatever had turned the bark red might have affected the wood itself. Made it harder. Stronger.

"Do you think it will work?"

"We'll have to carve holes and see." She crossed her arms around herself and shivered.

"Here." He wrapped his arms around her. "Let me warm you."

They hadn't been standing that way long before the sound of giggling erupted. Hans let her go and Cappella sighed.

"You littles are terrible. Every last one of you," she said. Nicola and the fox brothers were in the front. They were always the ringleaders. But all the children were there. The other goats, the raccoons. Cappella was mortified to have had an audience for such a private moment.

"Were you kissing?" Nicola asked.

"Whatever you were doing was worse than horse soup," Sebastian said.

"Nothing is worse than horse soup," Simon said.

"This was worse," Sebastian said.

"Was not," Simon said.

They started hitting each other. The other children laughed.

"Look what we found." Nicola held out a half-eaten honey cake.

"Where did you find that?" Cappella asked.

"Nicola!" Sebastian said. "Now they're going to want some, and then there won't be enough."

"We don't want any," Hans said. "But we do want to know where you found it. How do you know it's safe to eat?"

"It's safe," Nicola said. "We each had a bite, and nothing happened."

"We think Sabine made them and hid them for us to find," Simon said.

Hans supposed it was possible. "We should take this back to Sabine and Ursula, just to be sure."

"Look!" Sebastian said. "Here's another!" He was a few yards ahead. Nicola ran to join him.

Simon ran past them both. "And another!"

And then the children were off, following a trail of honey cakes. Hans's stomach growled at the thought of having one. They'd served them in the castle every Moon Festival. Enormous heaps of them scenting the air so thick he could practically taste them through his memories. He might never have missed a food so much.

"Should we follow them?" Cappella asked.

Hans nodded. Hand in hand, they raced after the children. Each time they found another cake, they'd squeal. The sound pierced him to the bone. Joy. He wasn't about to take this away from them.

When Hans and Cappella caught up to the little weres, they'd gone just past the edge of the woods. Where the trees stopped, the landscape opened to reveal an abandoned cart. It held a gingerbread house with a metal roof that reflected bits of moonlight, as sharp as teeth. The air smelled of honey, spice, flour. His mouth watered.

"Stop," Cappella yelled.

Moonlight lit the edges of her, glazing her black-and-white hair, her fierce hand clutching the perfect stick they'd found.

"Stop," she said again.

But the children saw the gingerbread. They smelled it. And that part of them that hungered for sweet, hungered for goodness and believed in it more than in evil, clambered into the wagon. They tore bites from it. They stuffed their mouths and marveled at this house built of everything they'd dreamed of these long and hungry months.

Hans understood. He knew what wanting tasted like. "Maybe we should let them."

Cappella inched closer. "It seems wrong. Why is that here? Where's the driver?"

"A traveling merchant? I don't know. Perhaps he's gone for a walk. Or has set up camp for the night. What harm could it be? There's no one around. We'll keep an eye on them. They're safe with us."

"All right," she said. "Let's let them have their fun."

They watched the children munch happily. No one came. It all seemed fine, like a bit of luck.

He turned to her. "We could have fun too."

She tipped her face up and looked at him. Her frozen hair sparkled, and her skin looked so bright and fresh. *Alive*, he thought. This was what it looked like to be alive.

When she closed her eyes, he kissed her. They pressed against each other, close enough that he could feel her heartbeat. He put his hands under her cloak, feeling the curve of her waist, the rise of her breasts. He could smell her hair, her skin, the forest all over her. She pressed closer still, and he worried that she might feel how much he wanted her. But he also wanted her to know.

He knew, in some primal part of him, that this moment, this feeling, meant something. Which meant that he too wanted to live. He kissed her over and over. Tugged at her lips with his teeth. Ran his tongue along hers. Wrapped his arms around her and felt her backside. He thought he'd memorized her already, but that had been with his eyes. Now he memorized her with everything else.

Greta's death had broken him. He still grieved. But in the midst of that, he could also feel joy. That thing he'd thought was lost forever wasn't.

"Cappella," he whispered.

She dropped the branch she'd been holding, and then her hands were all over him too. It felt so good he could barely stand it. But then, with a sigh, she pulled away.

"Hans. We have to watch the children."

She was right. They pressed their foreheads together, their breath misting around their faces. He loved her. Her loved her so much. He loved her beyond the bounds of his grief, and before this moment, he'd thought that was the biggest thing in the universe.

They turned to the gingerbread wagon. She covered her mouth with her hand.

One by one, the children were being pulled inside. Animal sounds rang out; they were scared enough to shift. Hans took his wolf form just as Albrecht slid out of the cart, his face covered in a golden mask.

Hans snarled, hoping Cappella would have the sense to run. Instead she stood by his side, as if preparing to fight. He snarled at her again. *Run. Please!*

Albrecht whipped the horse and the cart sped forward. Hans took off after it, his feet tearing at the icy snow. The cart drew closer and Hans leapt on board, his body crashing against the cage. The impact stunned him. As soon as he could, he stood.

Ahead was the castle. Behind him, Cappella and the forest. She screamed a pitch that sent the forest into a flurry of its own.

He held on and thought about what he'd have to do. He knew he'd face Albrecht, guards, and who knew who else, and he'd have to do it alone. *Think, Hans, think.* He tried, but nothing came to him.

~~~

He crouched as they rumbled over the bridge, catching a glimpse of Albrecht's metal monkeys. The air was ice, but clouds had gathered, dimming the white light of the moon. Snow was coming. Hans rattled the door of the cage. Inside, the children trembled, all in their animal forms, surrounded by a tumble of clothing. Nicola's bleat nearly made him weep. He had to free them. He could do that and toss them one by one out of the cart. If the children were taken inside the castle, they'd be lost.

He jammed a claw inside the lock, but it broke off below the quick, and still the door didn't come unlatched. He was breathing hard now. They'd passed through the merchants' district and were approaching the drawbridge. He could jump into the moat and run to the woods for reinforcements, but the children would all be in the castle by then, and even if he did have the werebears with him, he doubted their chances of saving the children— certainly not all of them.

The cart passed through the portcullis and stopped in the courtyard. He heard the thud of Albrecht's boots hitting stone. Hans held his breath, listening for footsteps. None came. He lifted his head. Too late, he turned. Albrecht had tricked him. He was perched on top of the metal roof, a roof that Hans now recognized as enormous wings.

Hans landed hard on the icy cobblestones, his paws skidding. He rolled on his back, looking for Albrecht. Hans flipped to his feet as Albrecht leapt on top of him. He collapsed, and then Albrecht clamped a collar around his neck. It was so tight that he gagged, and he knew the only way he could survive was to take his human form, a near impossibility when he was this roiled with fear.

Albrecht wrapped his thighs around Hans's ribs, and he held a chain attached to the collar in one hand and pressed Hans's face into the ground with the other. "Ha! Mine again, wolf. But this time I'll be nowhere near as kind."

Hans couldn't breathe. His nose scraped against the gritty ice. He wouldn't survive much longer without taking his human form. He imagined hands and feet. Bare shoulders. Small teeth and a tongue that could make words. He imagined becoming naked and defenseless in one last bid to live.

He felt the change coming. Felt the king struggling on top of him, pulling the chain. And then Hans did it. He shifted. He could breathe. Not well, because the king was still sitting on him. He was freezing, so cold he burned. But he was alive. The children were alive, and Albrecht didn't have Cappella. There was cause for hope.

Albrecht lifted him by the neck, and then Hans was standing, unclothed and shoeless in the courtyard. It was snowing now, and guards had come. His skin was gooseflesh.

"Take the children to the dungeon," he said. "Be careful that none should escape. There are already enough rats in the castle."

Holding the chain like a leash, Albrecht dragged Hans inside, through long corridors, and up the tower stairs and to a darkened room nearly as cold as outside. There was the click of a flint and then a lamp was lit. But Hans already knew where he was.

The window in Albrecht's workshop was no more. It was a jagged mouth of glass and splintered wood, and through it came curls of frosty air. The worktable stood in front of the gaping window. Hans smelled blood. Not fresh. Vestiges that made him want to vomit. It was Greta's.

"I suppose you think I intend to put you in the chair." Albrecht jerked the chain and Hans tripped.

Hans said nothing. He was on his knees now, terrified, trying to think of how he could fight off Albrecht. He'd submitted to torture before. He'd withstood pain to protect his sister. He knew what Albrecht wanted from him. He focused on his breathing, trying to keep calm and be ready for a chance to run.

"We won't be using the chair this time," Albrecht said. "I have something else in mind." He led him to the worktable. Leather restraints hung from each side.

"Up you go." Albrecht jerked the chain.

Hans looked out the window, his teeth chattering. It was too dark to see the woods, but they were there all the same. So was Cappella, his reason to fight.

"I said up." Albrecht jerked again, and Hans nearly shifted. He sat on the table, looking for something, anything that might help. Albrecht slipped on a finger.

"Do you like it?" he asked.

Hans ignored the question.

"It's my own design. It's full of poison."

"Let me go," Hans said.

"That's all you've got?" Albrecht asked.

Hans kicked him in the groin, and Albrecht bent in two. Hans leapt off the table, but Albrecht had not released the chain. He jerked it, and Hans hit the stone floor.

Albrecht stood over him. His poison finger shot forward. Hans felt the burn of metal in his skin, and then a strange warmth coursing through him. His tongue thickened and his vision turned hazy.

The forest went silent, as if it were holding its breath in anticipation of something deeply awful. In the silence, Hans could hear everything else. The sound of Albrecht's shoes on the stone. His ragged breathing through his mask. His own heart pounding.

Hans was numb. He couldn't move. Keeping his eyes open, staying conscious, took every bit of strength.

"Do you remember the rat experiments?" Albrecht asked. "Of course you do. I remember the way you used to tend the poor creature afterward. You thought I didn't know, but I did. You always were a soft one.

"You hurt me when you left me, Hans. Both you and your sister. Now that I have you back, I'm going to use you. It's what I should have done a long time ago. I'm going to cut you open. I'm going to watch you become the wolf. And then I'm going to understand what pain can really do. It's a teacher, Hans. The best one. And your pain is going to teach me everything I need to know to build my metal men. How to make them live."

Hans felt his body being lifted to the table. He could hear his limbs being arranged. Could hear the tightening of leather. Could smell the wood of the table. Could feel the sting of tears that he could not stop.

Albrecht pulled a chair in front of Hans and sat, leaning forward on his elbows, as if they were two old friends facing each other over a table laid with food, about to reminisce over something shared, something sweet.

"Everything I've wanted since I was a boy, I have. I am king. My people are safe. I am on the cusp of making clockwork men. My soldiers will end the insurgents who threaten us all, my sister among them. And they will raze the forest itself, which has become a monstrous thing all on its own. It can eat a man, Hans. Did you know that? Did you know that place you ran to, that place that you love so much, that place that you call home, is evil?"

The timbre of his voice changed as he spoke. Hans understood the content of what the king was saying. But the horror of it felt distant, muted. He had to make his own tongue bleed to hold on to consciousness.

"Once I've cut you open, once I've understood what animates you, the secret to your life, I'll move on to the children in the dungeon. They'll become my first soldiers.

"I knew you'd follow the cart," Albrecht said. "I'm so glad you did. It would have been so difficult to put you in the cage, and I would have hated to shoot something as useful as you twice."

Then Albrecht slipped on a different finger, this one equipped with a pair of blades. That was the last thing Hans remembered before the poison won.

LII

Cappella ran for the camp. She couldn't feel her hands or her feet. She'd gone numb with fear. She would rather have been killed herself than tell everyone the children were gone. She stumbled when she arrived. She'd winded herself and couldn't speak, and when someone came over to help her up with the gentlest of hands, Cappella burst into tears.

"The children," she said. "He has the children. Albrecht does."

People panicked. It was chaos: cries of grief, weres taking their animal form. Ursula loomed. "How did this happen?"

Cappella was so ashamed to tell her. She should have stopped them from getting onto the wagon. She knew it, even then. But she'd wanted to be with Hans, and she'd let that happen, and now he was gone, the children too.

She told Ursula everything. Ursula cursed and Cappella feared for a moment she'd be struck. Her mother stood between her and the angry were.

"This isn't Cappella's fault."

Ursula stepped back. "I know. This is my brother's doing. But—"

"We have to go get them," Sabine said. "You and I can do it together."

"This is my task," Ursula said. "My brother is my responsibility. I cannot ask anyone else to do what needs to be done—to slay the king."

Sabine's mouth opened. "Are you certain?"

Ursula nodded. "You stay here, Sabine. Guard the camp."

"I'm going with you," Sabine said.

The music of the forest now was terrible, terrifying. She couldn't remember a time it had been so loud or so dissonant for so long, and she understood what the trees were feeling and what they were saying. It was exactly what she felt and what she could not say, could never say, because there was too much shame. If she'd had a pipe, she would have played along with the forest. She knew that's what the trees were asking of her. But she didn't even have that, and she'd left the wood for her new pipe behind at the edge of the trees.

Then the forest went silent. The sudden absence of sound was eerie. There was a crunch of snow. Someone was coming. Many people. A soldier burst from the darkness, his sword high. A dozen more followed. Ursula and Sabine killed two before Cappella had a chance to scream. But they were outnumbered, and when a pair of men tied Sabine in ropes and held a knife to her throat, everybody froze.

The remaining weres were no match for Albrecht's men. They brought out ropes, enough to tie up everyone.

"Line up!" the first soldier yelled.

"Don't do it," Ursula said. "Run, everyone!"

Then came something like the crack of a whip. Branches shot forward. The trees snared the men. It happened in the space of a blink. Albrecht's men hung overhead, each one suspended in the bare branches. They writhed and cursed and reached for weapons.

As Ursula's people watched from below, Albrecht's men shriveled. Their screams ceased. Their corpses folded upon themselves like dry leaves. Their clothing and weapons dropped. Their flesh became dust.

No one watching said a word. Their horror was expressed in silence. In stillness.

The music started again, and the red branches glistened and crackled in the freezing night air.

Sabine spoke first. "Gather the weapons. The boots, the armor. We'll need it all."

Cappella helped, and soon all the supplies were heaped at the edge of the clearing. Ursula handed her mother a knife. Then she put a hand on Cappella's shoulder. "If more of Albrecht's men come, hide. The woods will take care of them."

Cappella nodded. She knew why Ursula was telling her this. She wouldn't be able to defend herself or anyone else. Hiding was her best way to survive. She was useless.

Worse than that. Her mother stood at her elbow, and Cappella felt a sudden burst of fresh rage. Part of the anger was at Albrecht, but part was for her mother, who'd kept her naive.

Her mother should have told her things. Everything. That way she could have made herself ready. Her mother had concealed things not to spare Cappella, but to spare herself the pain of truth.

Her rage made her want to hit Esme. To drive her elbow into the soft space below her ribs. Rather than do this thing she knew to be wrong, Cappella ran.

—————————

Her mother called behind her, but Cappella wouldn't stop. She needed to take action. She couldn't fight. She couldn't help Hans or Sabine or Ursula. Couldn't rescue any of the children or even protect the people who remained. She had one thing to do, one gift to give.

She needed to find the wood. Finish the pipe. Play the music. The forest wanted her to. It *needed* her to. It had given her the very piece of wood she required. She'd lost it, but she could find it again. She could finish the work. She had to.

Snow was falling when she reached the edge of the woods—landscape remade by fresh snow. Whiteness was everywhere she looked. Snow had gathered on their branches, changing their shapes, confusing her memories. Which ones had she stood beneath with Hans?

Before she'd closed her eyes and kissed him, she'd taken them in, knowing that she'd want to save the moment for her memories. Then she remembered. She ran to the spot and studied the ground. *There.* A lump in the snow. Her fingers closed around the branch. She sat on a snow-covered stone looking at this perfect stick. She had no knife. Ursula had given weapons to everyone she thought could use them well. She had not given one to Cappella.

"Cappella." It was her mother. She'd followed her, found her. She was winded, her breath coming in puffs of mist.

"Leave me alone," Cappella said.

"Come back with me."

Cappella knew she'd have to, if only for a knife she could use to carve her pipe. But she didn't want Esme to think she could just say something and have Cappella do it. Not anymore.

"I don't want to."

"Please," Esme said.

"You should have told me the truth about who you are. About who I am. About this world we live in."

"I've never lied to you," Esme said.

There was a difference between the truth and the absence of a lie. Cappella knew this now. "Who's my father, then?"

The question shocked Esme. She stood still, only her expression shifting, like water in a river. Her mother was thinking about what to say. About how much she could get away with not saying.

Cappella lashed out. "Even now, you're thinking of ways to conceal the truth. You might not be planning to lie. But I can see from your face that you are trying to craft an answer that will satisfy me, even as it is empty."

Esme exhaled. Her breath coated her hair with beads that were first silver and then stark white in the moonlight.

She spoke at last, her voice small, weary. "I don't know. Cappella, I do not know. I—" She fell to her knees. "There is something I will tell you. Something I should have told you years ago, but I was afraid it would make you feel less than mine. I was afraid you would not want me as a mother. All my life, I have been rejected, cast aside, and I could not bear that from you."

Then she told Cappella everything. About the lie her father told the Golden Lion. About the exchange she'd made with the woods. About the music that followed. About her sister and the king and what they'd accused her of doing. They'd said she'd wanted to steal Ursula and Albrecht because she had no womb. That part of it—that she was without one—was true, and it made everything else seem true as a result.

Her mother told her about her escape from the dungeon. How she'd tried to make a child and failed. And then about the day the woods had offered up Cappella, how that had felt like forgiveness, even redemption.

Cappella could feel the truth of it, the grief, the sorrow, the love that all truths contain. She dropped to the snow and embraced her mother. Her anger was melting, being transformed into something gentler even as it was complex. She ached for all her mother had suffered. She wished things had been different. The truth had given her answers and it had given her more questions. But one thing she was certain of. Esme was hers. Esme was her mother.

"A person doesn't need a womb to be a mother," Cappella said. "And a womb doesn't make someone a woman. Anyone who'd make such a claim is not only cruel but foolish."

And as for not having a father, well, perhaps Cappella had been fortunate there. Esme's own father had betrayed her and her sister. The king had betrayed the queen and his children. The lies of one father, the betrayal of another: These wrongs had set in motion many sorrows. It didn't mean that all fathers were like this. Hans's father had been good; he'd told her so.

Fatherhood shouldn't entitle a man to sacrifice his daughter for gold. Nothing entitled a man to reach for a woman who was not his wife. Nothing entitled a man to someone who did not want him. And nothing made it all right for the queen to sacrifice her sister rather than face the truth about her own life and its limits. Sisters should not betray each other for the sake of arrangements made by men for their own advantage.

There was something broken in the world between women and men, and perhaps that started with the idea of such distinctions in the first place. It was the same system that punished and caged weres like Hans. Why was it lesser to be a woman? Why was it a crime to be more than one thing? Why could people not be exactly who they chose to be in the world? Who was harmed when people lived their own truths?

Cappella wasn't lesser for being fatherless. It was who she was: the daughter of a woman, the child of the woods.

Cappella knew she couldn't fix the brokenness of the world. Not alone. But she could see it, and she could tell the truth about it. That was what the forest had done with its music. And that truth had been powerful. Combined with her mother's love and her mother's hunger, it had made her.

She picked up the piece of wood.

"I want to make a new pipe," she said. "But I haven't got a knife."

"I do."

"Mother," Cappella said.

Esme gave her the knife.

LIII

Ursula and Sabine raced into the kingdom. Snow spiraled down and their breath was visible as they ran side by side in human form. Everyone else had remained behind, protecting one another. Their plan was simple: to save Hans and the children. If Ursula could kill Albrecht in the meantime, she would.

It had been the work of moments to dismantle the guards on the bridge, human hands around metal throats. Albrecht wasn't a fool. Ursula knew metal men on the bridge meant he was saving the flesh-and-blood guards for Hans and the children.

It struck her as she entered the courtyard that she no longer thought of this castle as home. That her goal was no longer to get it back. She didn't want the kingdom anymore. She wanted the well-being of her people. Together they would figure out what that meant.

She and Sabine stood before an empty cart filled with the remains of gingerbread and honey cakes. She could smell the children on them. She could smell Hans. Could smell her brother.

"I'm ready if you are," Sabine said. "Do we do this as bears?"

"As bears," Ursula said. "As ourselves."

Sabine put a hand on her forearm. "Wait."

Something in Sabine's voice made Ursula's heart pound. Then Sabine tugged her close. She took Ursula's hand and ran it gently along the wound Ursula had once stitched. The scar gleamed in the moonlight, a reminder of pain. A reminder that bodies heal. Ursula could scarcely breathe. There was that look again, the intent one. This time, Sabine leaned toward her.

It was a wonderful thing to kiss the girl she loved. A girl who was a bear. A girl whose lips were keys that opened every good thing in Ursula. Sabine tasted of snow and tears. Her skin smelled like the woods. Ursula's body was a river in a rainstorm, rushing, churning, wild, rising against banks, powerful enough to rip trees from the soil and lift houses off their foundations, but gentle enough to change course when it needed to. That strength, that give. It was everything. Sabine was everything.

Sabine pulled away.

"I thought . . ." Ursula said.

"I know," Sabine said.

The look she gave Ursula said everything else—that this was a kiss given when there was no time for such things, a kiss given in case there would never again be such a time.

This was a kiss stolen from death.

Ursula burned with it.

The moon pulsed behind snow-filled clouds. Ursula had never felt so strong. Side by side, she and Sabine became their bear selves. Ursula was a large person, and she took up even more space as a bear. The more space she could take in the world, the better. That left less for her brother and anyone trying to hold her back. And to have Sabine beside her, strong, black, and beautiful: It was everything Ursula had ever wanted.

Ursula jerked her nose toward the kitchen door, the one used by everyone considered unimportant. That was how they'd enter this time. They traveled around a corner and encountered a single guard, human. From his expression, Ursula knew he wouldn't fight.

They burst into the kitchen, where bakers thumped and shaped a few paltry loaves. Ursula stopped to shake snowflakes from her fur. Her brother's bread ruined, she bounded into the main hall of the castle.

<hr />

As they raced through the corridors, Ursula skidded and crashed into people too slow or stunned to get out of the way. Her claws weren't meant for stone floors and woven rugs. They were meant for wide-open spaces and soil that yielded. She ran anyway, desperately seeking signs of Hans and the children.

Sabine ran beside her. Ursula was scared, but she was not alone. As long as she had Sabine, she would never be alone. She had always known this, but it was only now that she understood what it meant, that their bond was more important than anything else, including the queendom.

They came to something of a crossroads, and now they had a choice: to head up the tower or down into the dungeon. The smell of were came from both directions.

They decided with a glance. Ursula would follow the scent up the tower, where Albrecht was most likely to be. Sabine would go below in search of Hans and the children. As they parted, they touched noses, exactly as they had the day they met.

Life had been so different then. Ursula had slept in a cage without questioning it. She'd fought for her right to the throne, which she now knew was nothing but a larger cage with invisible bars. Ursula had never known freedom. She'd never had choices. She'd had only the story she'd told herself about her life, that if she was strong enough, that if she was willing to fight with words, fists, and claws, that if she could make herself like a man, then she would be worthy of ruling. Then her life would be good, and she could make life good for others.

She'd done all these things, and she'd still been deemed unworthy, first by her father, who split the kingdom, and then by her brother, who'd stolen it.

Even after that, she'd tried to lead. She'd tried without a queendom, without a castle, without guards or even always a roof over her head. She'd saved lives, yes. But they'd continued to survive not because of her but because of the labors of everyone. Survival wasn't a matter of strength or force, birthright or gender. It took courage and love for others—two things her brother would never have, two things she had in abundance. Survival did not require a queen. It took a community.

The staircase wasn't much wider than Ursula. Every so often as she ascended, she slammed against the stone walls. She felt no pain. Only the urge to climb and the desperate desire to find her brother and kill him. She caught a whiff of blood and roared. It was Hans's, and it was coming from the direction of Albrecht's chamber.

At the top, a guard blocked the way. He crouched, aiming his spear. She lowered her head and charged. The guard was quick. But Ursula was quicker, and she outweighed him by hundreds of pounds. He tried to jam his spear into her chest but ended up getting his wrist snapped in the process. His spear clattered down the steps, followed by the thud of his body.

The stairs opened onto a landing, with another guard before a thick door. He was huge, and all his vulnerable bits were covered in a thick, dark leather that gleamed in the torchlight. His eyes widened. But just as quickly they narrowed again.

He crouched and aimed his spear.

Ursula was tired. She'd run so far. So fast. Up such a staircase without so much as a pause. But she was close. She wasn't going to rest now. She reared up and swung her paw at him, slicing the leather of his breastplate.

This guard was quicker than the last. His spear found a soft spot and slipped between her ribs. It burned. She jerked away, and the spear snapped in two, its tip deep in her chest. She made an involuntary sound, part bellow, part yelp.

The guard reached for his sword. Ursula stood on her hind legs, so the spear didn't work its way in deeper. The guard's eyes narrowed again.

She struck. This time, he crashed against the closed door, stunned. Ursula knocked him down the stairs. The noise was awful: meat and bones against stone.

Ursula heaved herself up. The spear in her side felt like an extra rib, one that didn't fit and was made of fire. She bit at the broken end of the spear but couldn't pull it out. She might live yet. That she remained in her bear form gave her hope the spear had missed everything vital.

She threw her shoulder against the locked door. Every blow was agony, but it was nothing compared to the fear of what she'd lose if she failed. Again and again she battered the door, until the wood splintered and burst, and she was in Albrecht's enormous workshop.

Framed by the remains of his shattered window, Albrecht stood with his back to her. He held his hand by his face, the light glinting off a finger that split into twin blades. In front of him was a table. Beside him, one last metal man.

Faceup on the table, his hands and feet strapped in, was Hans.

Ursula charged.

LIV

Five holes. That's what Cappella's pipe needed, one for each of the senses. A good song could reach all of them, and this was what she wanted to do, to turn her breath and touch into something that felt as vivid as life itself. She wanted to write the truth of the world on the wind.

She put the tip of the knife to the branch and pressed. The wood was hard, but in a way that made it easier to cut a clean hole. She worked carefully until the first one was complete. She set down her knife and put her finger over it. She'd done it. A perfect hole placed exactly where she wanted it to be.

She started the next one. Snow fell as she worked. She fought the urge to rush. Getting it right was more important. As her mother watched, she made the third opening. Then the fourth. She finished the fifth hole and set down the knife.

She touched a finger to each one, ensuring they were uniform and smooth. Finding the tiniest imperfection in the fifth, she picked up the knife once more and scraped. The blade slipped, nicking her finger. She gasped, in part because of the pain and in part because she was afraid that she'd ruined the pipe.

But she hadn't. She'd bloodied it, but it was nothing that couldn't be wiped away. It would not be undone by bloodshed.

She looked at her mother, expecting a scolding about taking care with things that could cut. None came.

She wiped away the blood, took a deep breath, and put the pipe to her lips. She played a note, long and true.

"Come with me," her mother said. "I'm going to take you back to where this began."

This time, Cappella did.

She followed until her mother stopped, fell to her knees, and scraped away snow and grass. Even with her cloak, Cappella was freezing. What was this place? Between her mother's hands appeared the opening of a tunnel.

"What's down there?"

"A way in. One last secret."

Esme took her hand and pulled her forward through the darkness. Down they went, and the passage widened, even as the air felt damp and close. And then they were rising again, and a deep gray circle appeared—an opening. They moved toward it and then through it, and then they were aboveground near the castle. They entered the unguarded courtyard and stood at the base of the tower that loomed over the kingdom.

"I once made a bargain with the woods to save my sister," Esme said. "It didn't work. It made the world worse. But out of that same bargain came you, Cappella. You can undo what I have done. Play your pipe, my daughter. Play it like you've never played before."

Cappella looked at the instrument she'd made. It felt nothing like a weapon, and part of her feared that's what the moment called for. She hesitated.

"Please," her mother said. "Play your music to rally those who've been hurt by the king. Gather them all. I'll do the rest. I have to end what I set in motion many years ago with the lie I told to save my sister. I need to return to the beginning. It's the only way."

Cappella didn't know what her mother meant, although that was how some songs ended, with a variation of the beginning. Still, she was afraid, not of what her mother planned, but of what her own music might do. What if it did to men what the trees had done to Albrecht's soldiers? She didn't want that. That would never be her way.

"Please," her mother said again.

Cappella looked at the top of the tower, at the rectangle of golden light that gleamed through a broken window. Hans was in there. She knew it. She felt it.

"What should I play?"

"Only you can answer that." Esme put her hands to the stone and began to climb.

Cappella raised the pipe to her lips. She didn't know what she would play. But she was a musician. Songs were what she knew best. The answer would come to her. She had faith.

Her first notes were weak. Thin. Broken on their edges. She thought of Hans, and the sound improved. She felt less cold. She added more notes, stringing them like gems, one after the other, mixing sorrow with the sweetness. She played her memories of Hans, of the days when he was a cub and she was a girl and the forest spread before them as if it had no end.

She felt all the good things of her childhood rise through her: her mother's hand on her head, the smell of Hans's fur when it was wet, the taste of summer berries still warm from the bush, the sound of music all around her, and the sweet greenness of spring. She could feel it all again and she knew it for what it was: a spell that would last as long as a breath. That was how goodness felt. A brief burst of magic. Beautiful.

She started to feel something new: powerful.

As she played, the music of the forest grew louder. She could still hear her own song rising above it. But there was no mistaking that something in the forest had been awakened. The music it made sounded almost like words, like speech, like something that would force itself to be understood, whether listeners wanted to hear it or not.

As its music blended with hers, another noise began. This one sounded like something straining against the core of the earth itself. It was terrible, terrifying; it made her heart race. Still, she played.

Then came a great cracking sound, like thunder, but from the earth and not the sky. Then a low boom. And another, and another. As if something from the woods was on its way.

LV

Albrecht lifted his hand with the twin blades. He studied the blood on their tips and wondered if that glittering liquid was what made the boy on the table in front of him become a wolf. Or was it his heart? His liver or lungs? Something in his brain? What made a body live? What kept it alive?

He understood well what ended a life. But what created it—what made something live—was a mystery. He would tear this boy into pieces to understand the magic that made him. Because Albrecht was finally able to admit for himself that's what frissers were to him. Magic. It was unfair his sister had been graced with that magic but not he. He wanted it, and if he couldn't come by it by birthright, he would take it.

From below, he heard pipe music. It got under his skin in the worst way.

"Silence!" he yelled.

The musician kept playing. Enraged, Albrecht slid his finger into Hans's slit-open chest. Hans's eyes opened. He jerked. Perhaps the liquid mercy had worn off. No matter. The goal was to open up Hans and then watch him change into his wolf form, not to spare the boy pain. Albrecht tasted the blood. Warm. Rich in metal and salt. But it tasted no different from his own.

"Shift, boy." Albrecht leaned over him. Looked at the wolf's black-ringed eyes. He was losing his patience. So be it. If Hans died, Albrecht had spare children in the dungeon.

Hans moaned. His lips moved, as if he was trying to say something. "P-p-p" was the only sound that came out. He held his human form.

Albrecht dragged the tip of his knife across a fresh length of skin. "Send the wolf out to play," he said. "You'll feel better. I promise."

Someone banged the door.

He'd ordered no interruptions. "Guard! Stop that noise!"

The banging continued. The door would hold. He'd had it reinforced. But how was he supposed to work with such distractions? He yelled again, frustrated at Hans, frustrated with his men, enraged at the music that never, ever stopped.

Then came a cracking of wood. The door burst open. He turned, ready to make the intruder regret it. A great brown bear skidded into the room and stood on her hind legs. Her fur was wet, and it smelled of the woods.

"Hello, Ursula."

Albrecht brandished his not-finger. It wasn't the weapon he would have chosen, but it was sharp. It would do damage. His hand was quick, and if she came any closer, he'd strike.

"Let us end this quarrel," he said. "With your surrender or with your death. The choice is yours."

Ursula lowered herself to all fours. Standing, she was taller than he. On her paws, though, she was smaller. He eyed her claws. Easily the equal of his knife. But he was her better. He always had been. He would show her, once and for all, now.

Her lip curled. She growled. Albrecht stood his ground, waving his bladed finger. When her gaze shifted to the boy on the table, Albrecht lunged.

She dodged, quicker than he expected. But it cost her blood, enough that her paw slipped in it.

He stepped back, out of striking distance. Her black lips curled, and he could see blood on her teeth. Whatever injury she had was severe.

"Are you sure you don't want to run away, sister? Go back to the forest with the rest of the beasts? Something tells me you're dead if you don't. And maybe even if you do." He moved so that he was between her and Hans. Whatever happened, Hans could not get free.

"Your very life is bleeding out on this floor, inside a chamber you'd always expected would be yours," he said. "I'll tell you what. I'll put a marker on the spot where you die, so that everyone who walks into this room from now until the end of time steps on your memory."

She bellowed, spraying him with bloody spit. Then she stood on her hind legs. He looked at Hans to give her an opening. She took it, and his knife did what the guard's spear had not. With a thrust that was sweet, swift, and deep, Albrecht found the space between her ribs, one he'd become familiar with by working with the corpses of countless animals.

He'd put a hole in her heart. He'd done it. Ended her.

Blood gushed from her chest, and she began to shift back to her human form. She dropped to the stones, an ugly monster with huge, bladed paws, a hairy back, and a woman's face and breasts. It was a shame that things had had to happen this way. It was a shame she had to be born his sister and born first. She really was a magnificent beast.

He knelt beside her and waited for her to die.

Hans was weeping. Outside, the piper played. Albrecht, newly enraged at being distracted from this beautiful moment, cursed the sound and resolved to kill whoever was playing it. He stomped to the window, no longer afraid of heights.

"Piper," he said. "I'm coming for you."

LVI

The last time Sabine had left Ursula after a kiss, she'd meant it to be forever. She'd made a promise to herself not to betray her own soul. She could not love a queen. Would not.

Sometimes you have to break a promise to mend your heart.

While Ursula headed up the tower stairs, Sabine was returning to the dungeon. The place of rats and bones. The place her parents had died. And on this visit, she wasn't just passing through, as she had been the last time. She was saving the weres. She could smell them, the goats, the foxes, the raccoons.

Two guards stood at the top of the stairs. Sabine swatted them aside, thinking of her parents. No one had come for them. No one else would come for these children. No one else could. She mustn't fail.

The dungeon stairs were old and steep, remnants of a former castle that had long ago fallen. In some ways, it reminded her of the woods. When trees fell, new ones grew on top of them, sometimes even wrapping their roots around the downed logs. Then the fallen trees rotted away, leaving nothing but a grasping fist of roots, circling empty air. Ghost logs. The dungeon was full of ghosts too. She could feel them.

All this time, she'd thought the forest and the castle had nothing in common. That one was alive, and one was not. But they did have something in common. Both were haunted. As trees rise from the dust of their dead ancestors, men put castles on the bones of the old ones. Death comes for stone just as much as it comes for living tissue. Death would come for Ursula, and Sabine did not want this to happen before they'd had a life together. She did not want to be haunted by her own stubbornness. She wanted to find something in between stone and soil, a place where flesh and fur could thrive.

She raced down the stairs, desperate with love for Ursula, desperate to save the little weres. She met guards at the bottom too. Every movement was controlled and deliberate. Every blow landed with her full weight behind it.

In the space of a song, Sabine vanquished every guard. Every last one without shedding a single drop of her blood. She wished she could have saved her parents. She wished her they could have seen her now. But then again, amid the ghosts of the dungeon, perhaps they already had.

There was the matter of the key. She stood outside the cell that held the children. She could hear them crying, their bleats and squeals. She'd done her best to console them. But they were locked inside. She realized one of the guards must carry the key. So she shifted to her human form and returned to where she'd left them, broken on the stones.

The first guard she searched had nothing in his hands and no light in his eyes. She'd killed this man, far from her first. She'd had to kill in self-defense, many times. Any preciousness she might have felt about dealing out death was long gone. She would prefer not to kill. But she lived in a world that demanded it of her. She saw no reason to love her life any less than certain men hated it.

She rolled over the second guard and found the key at his waist. She pulled at it, and then his fingers closed around her wrists. She jerked her hand away and looked at him in the dim torchlight. He suffered. The pain he felt was written on his face in his own blood, and she felt a stab of pity. It was not fair, a bear against a man.

Then a sound rose from his throat. Rough, hostile. He spat on her face. "Damned frisser," he said.

She'd considered mercy. No longer. She wiped away his spittle and put her hand to his throat. Her fingers, slender, long, and exceptionally strong, did what needed to be done. In her swiftness, she did show mercy of a sort.

She took the key. She unlocked the door. The children surrounded her, all but Nicola in their animal form.

"I knew you'd come," Nicola said. "I kept telling them. I kept telling them that this was the bad part of the story and that it would have a happy ending, that the bear would come to us on a puff of smoke."

"That's right, Nicola. That's right," Sabine said. "Shall we go find Ursula?"

She didn't need an answer. She never would, when that was the question. After Nicola shifted, Sabine followed. They raced up the stairs, and as they did, Cappella's pipe called them. It called them, and it called the rats, a river of them, flowing upstairs.

LVII

Cappella breathed into her pipe as though she was giving life to something new. She breathed out music, and it met every song from every tree in the forest, thousands of strands weaving together. The sound was enormous.

Behind her, the ground shook. *Boom. Boom. Boom.* Like footsteps, but from no creature she could imagine. Her body jolted, but she stood her ground, playing on, her gaze fixed on her mother scaling the stone tower.

Esme was impossibly high, near the window now, clinging to the stones, trembling. It struck Cappella that her mother might fall. If she did, she would die. She held her breath involuntarily.

Her mother yelled, "Don't stop playing! Whatever happens, don't stop!"

The footsteps were closer now, close enough that bits of ice bounced around her feet. From behind came a crash, as though a mountain were tumbling down. She blew into her pipe and turned to look.

There was an enormous gap in the courtyard wall, and in the center of it, tossing stones aside, was a giant tree; no, it looked more like a massive woman with skin made of bark and long hair of whip-thin branches draped in leaves. This was no tree. It was no woman. It was both. Her footsteps shook the earth.

Esme shrieked. Cappella turned as Esme slipped from the wall. She spiraled down. The hand of the tree woman shot out. She caught Esme just before she hit the ground. Then there was a great cracking sound and a rush of wind, and the tree woman snatched Cappella too.

Cappella was so terrified she could scarcely breathe. The tree woman straightened herself. Cappella desperately wanted to curl up in a ball. She clutched her pipe in her fist and trembled.

"Play your pipe," her mother said. "Play it."

Cappella did. She summoned the strength of everyone who'd suffered at Albrecht's hands. She summoned their solidarity. She summoned their help and understanding.

The tree woman lifted Cappella and Esme up to the gaping tower window. Hans lay on a table, his hands and feet bound, his chest oozing blood. Behind him, Albrecht crouched next to Ursula, who was half in her human form, half in her bear form.

The shadow of the tree woman reached him. He turned to look, his face emotionless behind his golden mask. Emotionless except for his eyes. He left Ursula and stepped toward the window, yelling at Cappella, his bladed false finger dripping blood.

Behind him, something moved. Something Cappella thought at first were the stones on the floor. But they weren't. They were rats. Dozens, hundreds running toward Albrecht, running toward her music.

The rats clawed at Albrecht's clothing. They climbed his legs and wrapped around his arms and burrowed into his tunic. He swatted at them with his awful metal finger, cutting his own flesh. Still they hung on, and still Cappella played, her music urging the rats onward.

His mask fell off. It rattled on the ground, and his pale skin bloomed with bite marks on his hands, his neck, his face. The rats tore at his golden hair, tossing strands of it to the stones below.

Then a black bear burst in. Sabine, followed by the werechildren in their animal forms. Sabine dropped to her knees beside Ursula, turning into a human as she moved. Cappella played a blast of music just for them, a flash of love so intense her chest ached. She played about bonds that cannot be broken, neither by violence nor the ravages of time. Not even death itself. Cappella was certain of what her song could do, as long as she did not stop.

Albrecht, his arms swinging, staggered toward the jagged opening in the tower wall.

He was coming for Cappella. His eyes locked on to hers.

"You," he said.

Behind him, something moved. Nicola. She butted her tiny horns into the metal man. It fell and knocked Albrecht forward. He tumbled out the window. The tree woman's hand shot forward again.

She'd caught him.

Cappella looked down, still playing her pipe, and there he was, swinging hundreds of feet above the stone-covered earth, his hand wrapped around a branch.

"Please," he said.

Her mother crouched. She held out a hand. "Nephew."

He looked at her with wild and distrustful eyes.

"I have to tell you something," she said. "Your mother never spun grass into gold. That was me."

"So what?"

"It means that everything you've believed about yourself is a lie."

"What does a mother matter?" His face looked newly stricken, and Cappella knew he was saying things he did not believe. That he could not make himself believe. She played louder still.

347

"You were the one who wanted to take me. To eat me. You were jealous," he said. "I've heard the tale."

"Lies," Esme said. "I'm the reason you were born in the first place."

"Help me, then," he said.

"Take my hand."

He reached for it. She held on to him. "Now give me your other."

As he offered up his hand with the bladed finger, Esme grabbed his wrist.

"This is for my daughter," she said.

She twisted hard, and she drove the forked blades deep into his eyes. Then she dropped his other hand.

His arms pinwheeled. His legs kicked. He screamed through his fine white teeth.

Cappella looked at her mother, astonished.

"You can put down your pipe, daughter," she said. "Go and save your wolf."

Cappella climbed through the window.

"Hans!" she cried.

Red cloak flying behind her, she ran to him.

LVIII

Deep below the surface of the earth, a dead girl told herself a tale.

Once upon a time, there was a girl with a golden braid. She'd been born in the woods and forced to leave. She'd returned again, though she was not the same.

She thought she'd remain in the woods forever, rooted there by what she'd suffered. But then a song had called her, and she'd pulled herself up from the depths.

Her feet, which had once worn red shoes, were nearly as hard as stone. They were something no mere knife could cut. Not anymore. And they carried her back to the castle, one last time, to do what needed to be done.

She could have eaten the king and ended him. She could have done what Ursula had tried and failed to do. She could have done what Esme had been willing to do. She could have let him fall.

But she wanted something else for the man she'd almost married.

Her time with the trees had told her the thing he'd feared most since he was a boy. She let him live that fear, knowing that the last thing he'd ever see before he fell was a blade of his own construction flying toward his eyes.

And then she let him live through it. She chose to let him live like this, fallen, eyeless, mutilated, with nothing left but his voice and his memories. He'd suffer more that way, she thought.

She sometimes rued her decision to let him live, especially after she heard what he did with that beautiful voice. But here's the hard truth: A man without remorse cannot be redeemed.

Even so, she loved living in the forest where she'd been born, but this time as a tree herself, her roots intertwined with theirs, their music and hers rising through the soil and into the cupped hand of the sky that fed them. Every day she felt wonder. She felt joy. She was alive.

Was she the queen of the forest? Perhaps in size. But she was no more important than the greenest shoot. She was a part of something even bigger than herself, something she could feel, especially at night, when the trees were at their stillest.

━━⟋⟍⟋━━

The halves of the kingdom and the forest beside it had reunited once more.

They had reunited, but they were not the same. At the request of the werebear who once was a queen, the forest had spread its arms all the way around the kingdom. Ursula and Sabine lived in the woods together, for that's where and how they had always been happiest. Saddest too. But that is where one lives best—in the spaces formed and sanctified by joy and sorrow.

Ursula, who had been saved by the love of another bear, did not remain queen. She had no interest in it anymore. She also never drew blood again, although she taught many werechildren how to protect themselves should they need to.

Nor did Cappella become a queen, though she had a claim of sorts to the throne. She was not only the daughter of Esme, not exactly. She was also born of generosity and grief, a daughter without a father who became a woman who *was* enough. She'd always been enough, even if there was no part of her that ever could become a warrior.

Cappella did become a partner to a werewolf. A wolf who'd always loved her. Who'd given her a red cloak. And whose life she was able to save, not with a weapon of destruction, but with one of creation.

The werewolf who was a warrior, but not the monster he feared he'd become, also did not become king. He wanted only to spend time with his wife. To listen to her music. And to watch their children adore her, as children always had.

That left Esme. She had no more call to make gold, and indeed could not have done so, even if she'd wanted to. The pact she'd made with the woods, the gift of her womb for gold, had ended. She'd received Cappella. And Cappella had undone the sadness that golden wishes had wrought.

Esme was the last blood relative who could take the throne.

Even she did not.

She had learned something from the gifts given to her by the woods, who had no ruler but who lived together, shading the young from the harshest rays, sharing nourishment from beneath, lives and roots intertwined, creating and sustaining life, even beyond death.

Why shouldn't human beings do the same?

Night approaches. The death of another day. The eyeless storyteller pauses. This is his favorite part of the tale. He can feel the people hanging on his words.

"The piper played his pipe and led the children out of the kingdom," he says, his voice soft and lovely as a length of fur.

He pauses again, with what is left of his once-beautiful lips parted so that people will know there are a few words yet to come.

"The pied piper stole the children away. He stole them from their parents. The children were never seen again, and the grief of their kin lifted stone mountains all around the kingdom."

The crowd around him is utterly silent, but he knows they are still there. He can feel the air move with their breaths. The sniffles of the ones who've been brought to tears.

And now it's dark. The eyeless storyteller knows this because the air around him is cold. His leg hurts. Day or night, though, he now spends all his time in darkness. He spends much of it shivering in the cold.

But, oh, how he remembers the light.

He remembers it. And he remembers gold. And he remembers the long, pale hair of the one who should have been his wife, had she not been such a wretch and a liar. They would have had beautiful sons. Beautiful sons who would have ruled a beautiful kingdom. That was how things were supposed to be. That was how the story was supposed to have gone.

With his four-fingered hand, the eyeless man winds the monkey one last time for the people who mill about, hoping for another tale. Just a little more of something that feels like flesh and blood.

And he tells one, about a handsome prince with a beautiful voice who loved a girl with a long golden braid. She hung it out of the tower to lure him in. And she did. But once upon a time, because of her treachery, the king had fallen.

It had been a very long fall.

"And when the king landed, branches below had slashed his face and put out his eyes. He'd lost everything. His kingdom. The girl. His beauty. But he still had his voice."

The clockwork monkey extends its hand. The sharpest-eyed among them notices it has only four fingers, like the storyteller. The people fill its palm with coins. The monkey ingests them. And the storyteller hefts it, grabs his blanket, and walks away.

Over the soft churn of the pale gray sea and the rougher clink of coins, the storyteller hears the people whisper. He knows exactly what they are saying to one another, once, twice, three times. The things they are saying become their truth.

The rat who is listening, the rat who is me, knows otherwise. And now, dear reader, so do you.

ACKNOWLEDGMENTS

Once upon a time, there was a kid who loved fairy tales. She grew up but did not outgrow this love, even as they troubled her.

Strange things, these stories: full of talking bears and wolves and forests and blood and gold and kings and queens and, every so often, music.

Into the Bloodred Woods comes from the stories that both fed and poisoned me. And it came from my experiences in the world, both the rotten and the redemptive.

I'm not going to lie—this book took forever to write, and it exists in many wildly different forms. I came up with the idea in 2009, following a writing prompt that got me thinking about rats and girls and castles and the power of story to make us believe.

The idea for the book grew and changed as I came to better understand old stories and their intersection with life today, especially when storytellers with bad intentions rise to power.

I needed to grow in a lot of ways to write this book the way I wanted to. Fortunately I had an absolutely massive group of wonderful human beings help me along this path.

I'm grateful for my Scholastic family: my editor, Jody Corbett, who immediately understood the vision for this book and coaxed me forward with great patience and humor—through a ding-dang pandemic, of all things.

And to these wonderful humans: production editor Melissa Schirmer, designer Stephanie Yang, and cover artist Marcela Bolívar. The legendary David Levithan. The world-class marketing team of Erin Berger, Rachel Feld, Shannon Pender, and Zakiya Jamal. My beloved library marketing folks, Lizette Serrano, Emily Heddleson, and Danielle Yadao, as well as publicity wonders Taylan Salvati and Lauren Donovan. The sales team, without whom I would find no readers, and also the audio team, who bring the book to life in astounding ways: Paul Gagne, Melanie Gagne, Lori Benton, and John Pels.

Thanks also to my agent, Jennifer Laughran, who started taking care of me long before she represented me, because her heart is that capacious.

To my wonderful friends who read various versions of the book: wonderful Elana K. Arnold, Heidi Schulz, Jolie Stekly, Liz Garton Scanlon, Linda Urban, Michele Bacon, Lish McBride, Aileen Johnson, Jesse Klausmeier, Rebecca Kirshenbaum, Anna-Marie McLemore, Bridget Harrington, and Barry Goldblatt. I'm also grateful to Erin Nuttall, whose master's thesis, "The Power of a Storyteller: Creating Non-Violent Narratives for Strong Female Characters," gave me critical insight into my creative ambition at exactly the right time. To my colleagues at VCFA, especially Will Alexander, who nudged me further into the realm of the fantastic.

As always, my deepest gratitude goes to my family: my husband, Adam; our daughters, Lucy and Alice; and our cats and dogs. My life with you is beyond anything I could have imagined.

ABOUT THE AUTHOR

Martha Brockenbrough is the critically acclaimed author of the novels *The Game of Love and Death* and *Devine Intervention*, as well as numerous nonfiction titles, picture books, and chapter books. She teaches at Vermont College of Fine Arts and lives in Seattle, Washington, with her husband, their two daughters, two dogs, and two cats. You can visit her online at marthabrockenbrough.com.